# Lynelle by the Sea

Laurie Lico Albanese

# *Lynelle by the Sea*

A NOVEL

A DUTTON BOOK

DUTTON
Published by the Penguin Group
Penguin Putnam Inc., 375 Hudson Street, New York, New York 10014, U.S.A.
Penguin Books Ltd, 27 Wrights Lane, London W8 5TZ, England
Penguin Books Australia Ltd, Ringwood, Victoria, Australia
Penguin Books Canada Ltd, 10 Alcorn Avenue, Toronto, Ontario, Canada M4V 3B2
Penguin Books (N.Z.) Ltd, 182–190 Wairau Road, Auckland 10, New Zealand

Penguin Books Ltd, Registered Offices: Harmondsworth, Middlesex, England

First published by Dutton, a member of Penguin Putnam Inc.

First Printing, January, 2000
10  9  8  7  6  5  4  3  2  1

"Whatever Will Be, Will Be (Que Sera, Sera)" words and music by Jay Livingston and Ray Evans © 1955, 1984 Jay Livingston Music, Inc. (ASCAP) and Universal-Northern Music Company, a division of Universal Studios. Copyright Renewed. International Copyright Secured. All Rights Reserved.

 REGISTERED TRADEMARK—MARCA REGISTRADA

LIBRARY OF CONGRESS CATALOGING-IN-PUBLICATION DATA:
Albanese, Laurie Lico.
    Lynelle by the sea / Laurie Lico Albanese.
      p.   cm.
    ISBN 0-525-94536-9 (alk. paper)
    I. Title.
    PS3562.I324L9    2000
    813'.54—dc21                                    99-42638
                                                        CIP

Printed in the United States of America
Set in Goudy
Designed by Eve L. Kirch

PUBLISHER'S NOTE
This is a work of fiction. Names, characters, places, and incidents either are the products of the author's imagination or are used fictitiously, and any resemblance to actual persons, living or dead, business establishments, events, or locales is entirely coincidental.

This book is printed on acid-free paper.

*For Frank,*
*who taught me true love,*
*and saved me.*

# Lynelle
## by the Sea

# PROLOGUE

# Singing Island

SEEN from the air, Singing Island is a peninsula shaped like a musical note: four narrow miles of Florida marsh and a one-lane road fluting from the mainland into a round ball of beach and dunes that has slowly filled with eighty-four houses, one marina, two retirement communities, five cottage motels, and a sprawling, red-roofed luxury hotel. In 1963 a half-mile bridge was built to connect the full end of the peninsula to the mainland, providing a more direct route for snowbirds traveling from West Palm Beach Airport to their havens near the ocean. Palmetto Bridge is notable for its remarkable arc, built high to accommodate the masts of luxury sailboats passing into the great bay.

Most tourists and many winter inhabitants of Singing Island believe the musical shape of the peninsula accounts for its name, and occasionally they wonder aloud to one another why it is called an island when obviously it is part of the continent. Only a few men and women know the native legend for which the land was named.

Legend says that before the boats with white sails and the men with white faces arrived in the great bay, only the People came to the land, and the land was an island. To reach the island the People crossed a narrow strip of water in hollowed birch canoes. The water was green and sometimes yellow at high noon, fertile with pompano and other sweet fish the men caught with nets and stored in baskets weighted in the tide pools. The women dug for shellfish, gathering up the sharp razor clams to use for tools and adornment, storing oysters in nets floating in the still water pockets, and later tossing the empty shells into a refuse pile that grew as high and wide as many men. While the parents and older children worked, the young ones played on the far shore of the island. They chased birds along the shore, or divided into teams and played games using balls made from palm leaves.

One day a huge storm blew in from the ocean. The mothers saw the sky turn black and the palm trees bend like saw grass in the wind. They ran across the island just in time to see the ocean rise up and pull the children out to sea. The small ones' screams came up with the waves, each call its own note that was quickly drowned by the raging waters.

Some of the women tried to swim out to the children, but the storm dragged them under. One mother launched a canoe into the waves, but that, too, disappeared. Another did the same, and then another, until all the birch canoes were swallowed up. Soon there was nothing to see or hear but the dark storm churning the ocean, and the men and women wailing.

The People dug their feet into the sand and held a vigil that lasted as long as the storm. For two days the mothers of the dead, the aunts and grandmothers, wailed at the edge of the water. The men threw their fish back into the sea. They apologized to the sea spirits for making them angry.

On the third morning, the wind stopped and the waters calmed. The sky cleared, and the beach was returned. But it was changed. Where there was once a smooth, sandy slope, a river of broken seashells now rimmed the shore. Every time the tide washed out over the shells, the clear tinkling sound of a hundred small voices rang through the air.

The People, who were brokenhearted over the loss of so many young ones, saw this as a sign that the sea spirits were no longer angry with them. The proof came when they turned to go back to the mainland and discovered they were able to walk across a long neck of land *that had sprung up during the storm. On that strip of land, in a row of mourning, they fell to their knees and thanked the spirits for sending back what they could. They declared this place a holy ground and gave it up to the white men only after a bitter struggle.*

*Today, some visitors to Singing Island are haunted by the voices in the tides. Others hear wind chimes in the jingling shell shards, or a moan underneath the wind. Many hear nothing but the slap and tease of the water stroking the sand. But at certain moments, when they are facing the sea, they feel their chests fill with the breath of an unfinished song.*

# CHAPTER 1

## Lynelle

ELIZABETH, NEW JERSEY

How I came to steal that baby named Dylan isn't a long story unless you want it to be. To me it was as simple as picking him up out of the stroller, holding him close to my skin, walking like he belonged to me, and moving through the people who didn't even look twice, who barely stepped aside to let me pass with my bundle.

It's not a long story unless you don't know how it feels to have a baby grow in your belly, the way it makes you lazy, makes you lay on the couch with the sun heating up through the windowpane, the way it makes you long to lick the salt off something, yearn for something pickled, pucker for something sour, drool for something sweet. Teeth and nails sharpen so that tearing apart a chicken is easy, so that cracking the bones and sucking out their marrow is something you do without thinking, do with a new relish brought on by the life in your belly.

"Just what the heck are you doing, Lynelle?"

I was expecting my own child back then. My husband Hogan was sitting across the supper table from me, staring with this horrified look at the chicken bones piled like a little graveyard next to my plate. Something about Hogan and the way he can say "what the heck" in that back-home way made me ashamed. I grabbed a little blue napkin out of the wooden holder that Hogan had made me and I covered up those chewed bones, I laughed and stood to clear the table. Hogan likes that, likes bringing out the girl in me. He reached out a hand as I squeezed by him in our little tiny kitchen, and caught me real gentle on the bottom of my belly.

I stopped in front of him, saw that pink tongue peeping out from the front of his grin, and I let Hogan nuzzle his face against me, against the widening bowl of baby growing between my belly button and my thighs. I felt an overwhelming desire for him, a desire too strong for a woman in my condition, a desire so strong that it pushed right through those thoughts of not-in-my-condition and I had to take a deep breath to get over that light-headed feeling that Hogan can bring upon me with his dark hair curling down the back of his neck and his two front teeth just a tiny bit crooked, one chipped. It's that chip Hogan's tongue looks for, rests upon, worries against when he's working or thinking. It's the chip that I look at to know when something's on his mind.

"Lynelle, you sure do look good in this baby," Hogan said. He lifted up my red maternity blouse and pressed his mouth against my belly, and that was it. I let myself go except for whispering, "Hogan, go wash your hands for me, please, and take off them dirty work clothes."

I gave him a squeeze on the thigh to take the edge off my request, and moved away so he could stand up and get by me. The walk from our kitchen table to the sofa in our teeny living room is nothing more than a drop. I fell onto it, wriggled out of my maternity pants, and listened to the sound of Hogan splashing water in the bathroom, unzipping his green airport jumper.

We're from the South, Hogan and me. His family hails from Tennessee and Tallahassee, while I'm from the middle parts of Florida where black and tan rivers run through the swamplands and down into the citrus groves. I was born five years after they built Walt Disney World, but I've never been there. My mama passed when I was seven and me and Daddy had enough of a time just living. Daddy did okay raising me considering how much of it we spent alone in mobile homes between Ocala and Port Charlotte, but I know I have that look, a black kettle-edged look around my eyes that can turn inside out and take me away from anyone, any time. Hogan calls them my come-hither-go-away eyes.

I was working at a bank in Gainesville when me and Hogan met. We were both filling in for friends on a bowling team, and it was Hogan's smile, the way he lights up fast, that turned my head. Hogan knows the names of things, he knows airplanes and engines, rivers and wildflowers. He says, "Honeysuckle, wisteria, jack-in-the-pulpit, scarlet sage, larkspur, morning glory, Queen Anne's lace," and all the blood goes to my head. He says it with a rumble in his throat, like a mountain man come to sit down awhile and woo a woman with poetry. It's enough to make me not mind the smell of beer on his breath in the morning.

We live in New Jersey now on account of Hogan's job, which is working food and last-minute luggage on the runways at Newark Airport. We live so close to the airport that the planes pass over our apartment day and night, and before their roar blended in with the background noise of life, me and Hogan used to lay in bed and take turns making up stories about where the planes were going, or who was going on them.

"Coming in for a landing," Hogan said. He was buck naked, his front tail as tall as a proud young tree rooting up from a patch of shiny brown grass.

"Check your landing gear and make a slow descent, Captain," I said, for I was almost as protective of the baby in my belly as I was desirous of him to be moving inside me.

Later, much later, I feared it was too much sex that hurt my baby. Even though the doctor said it did no harm, I could cut off my arms now just thinking of how I pulled Hogan to me, how I moaned and rocked and then lay there afterward with all four of our palms pressed against my belly, feeling the baby moving herself back and forth even after we were still. Anyone who thinks a baby in the womb is just a lump of tissue has never felt that.

The year I was pregnant we spent Christmas up North, due to my condition. My daddy, who lives over in the Florida panhandle now with his third wife, Tina, called one day to ask if he could send us something for the baby.

"I should give y'all something special being this'll be my first grandbaby," he said.

I could picture him sitting in his folding chair on the porch outside their trailer house, portable phone in his hand, gray stubble on his face. By the way he talked I knew he was chewing the soggy end of an old cigar between his teeth.

"Daddy, that's real nice of you," I said. We already had a new bassinet filled with yellow and green outfits from the girls at work, so I told Daddy we needed a stroller and a car seat. Then I asked if he had any baby pictures of me and my mama together.

*Chaw, chaw.* That cigar went a full circle in his mouth. I listened hard and heard a truck starting up in his trailer park.

"Daddy?"

"We didn't take too many pictures, little girl."

All those years with only one small picture of me and her, from a distance. It had seemed enough, but I wanted more. I was straining to see Mama's face, and I couldn't do it on my own.

"I seem to recall some kind of pink box, with pictures and such," Daddy said at last. "Maybe your aunt Fay knows where it is."

I called Aunt Fay, my mama's big sister, who lives out in the Ozarks now and has a hot tub built on her back porch. Halfway between forty and fifty and she's still young at heart.

I asked Aunt Fay about the pink box and told her how my ankles were swelling and the baby was waking me at night with the kicking. Aunt Fay said she had no idea where that box might be, on account of having moved around a lot herself, but she promised to look for it.

"You be sure to keep them feet up," she said. "And don't reach for anything on a top shelf. You got that handsome husband of yours to do that."

In his spare time when he isn't working, teasing me, or loving me, my husband likes to carve things. Back home they call it whittling but what Hogan can do with a piece of wood and some glue is more like art than craft to me. Over the years he made me the napkin holder and napkin rings, cherrywood candlesticks, and even a set of little box turtles that nestle one on top of the other. Soon as I got pregnant he started turning out baby toys one-two-three, whistling air through that chip on his tooth and handing up a bone-shaped baby rattle with three rings carved right out from the branch itself, and then this tiny flat brown bear with the cutest little face (I told him, "This is really art, Ho, making a piece of wood into something so lovable").

For Christmas Hogan gave me a footstool he made out of oak, and come Christmas afternoon I was sitting on our old brown couch with my feet up on that stool, sort of reading a baby book but mostly looking at the way my calves blended into my swollen ankles.

Outside our third-floor window everything was cold and covered with snow, but I was hot enough to be wearing a sleeveless blue-jean jumper. I was having night sweats already, and strange dreams about flowers that sucked up and died. In one dream I was kneeling at my mama's grave sobbing because there wasn't a single green thing growing there.

It was strange the way my mama started coming back to me. She died before I really knew her, and the truth is that I'd grown used to her being gone, had smoothed over the lump of loss she once was. But that winter I'd be making the bed and suddenly see Mama's hands folding down the corner of a sheet, or I'd sit down to eat and recall the way she liked her corn on the cob hot and dripping with butter. It was a surprise and a comfort, even if I couldn't really see her face and the way she'd smile or look at me. But not the dreams. The dreams were the dark side of remembering.

"Listen, Hogan, this book says lots of pregnant ladies get bad dreams," I said.

Hogan was sitting at the kitchen table with a can of beer in one hand and a big atlas spread open in front of him. He was bundled up against the cold, having long since stopped complaining about how I kept turning down the heat and opening up the windows to let frosty snowflakes land on my hot arms.

"Denver," Hogan said to me. "I like Denver."

"You know I can't travel," I said, "and anyways I'm talking to you about something important here, about the dreams I've been having."

"Well, Lynnie, I am talking about the baby too," he said. "I like the name Denver, or maybe something in Hawaii."

I was speaking to Hogan in half profile, just the tip of his nose, the sides of his ears peeking out from under a John Deere cap. I leveled a stare at him, a stare that always shut up any rude customer at the bank. "Are you crazy, Hogan?"

He turned to smile at me, but I wasn't taken in by that grin or the tongue teasing between his teeth.

"The way I figure, I'd like to name this baby for one of the beautiful places in the world, maybe a place we been together," he said. On account of him working for the airport, we can fly places real cheap and have been on more than a dozen airplane trips together. "Remember Denver? The deepest green trees you ever seen, the bluest sky?"

"Hogan, I'm not naming my baby after some stupid city. You know I'm hoping to name this girl after my mama."

We'd already spoke of this at great length and I believed we'd settled upon Gracelyn, which was my mama's name, or maybe a shorter, more to-date version like Grace. But of course Hogan had pretended to agree while keeping ahold of his own idea, as always.

"Okay, Lynnie, I've got you a deal. If it's a girl, you can name it after your mama. But say it's a son, a chip off the old block kind of thing, then I want to pick his name."

His eyes lit up like they were looking out over a runway, or across a great big mountain sky, and in the end I just let him say what he wanted, knowing full well it was a girl in my belly and that I would name her for my mama.

My baby girl, Grace Denver Carter, was born on the seventh day of February at two-thirty in the afternoon. She was born with sky blue eyes two shades paler than Hogan's and filled with light as if she could already see something ordinary people could not. She was born on a Tuesday, and everyone knows that Monday's child is fair of face while Tuesday's child is full of grace. I agreed to Denver for a middle name, instead of my maiden name of Page, because of the light in her eyes.

Grace came easy into this world, with me wide awake and Hogan holding my hand, both of us shouting and looking down at the bloody bend of my legs. I had to push and grunt like a big old sow, but when her head crowned the rest of her slid out shiny and clean, pale pink skin clear as water, little white fingers with perfect half-moon nails. One of the nurses lifted her up onto my belly while her little body was still attached to me by the long purple cord.

"She's a miracle, Lynnie," Hogan whispered in my ear. He held his hand over her, his palm making a blanket that was bigger than her entire little behind.

After we ate a supper of soft hospital meat and mashed potatoes Hogan went home, leaving Grace and me alone. She was cleaned up, dressed in a white hospital gown with a pink cap on her head and little white mittens on her hands. She slept in a high plastic cradle right next to my bed, where I could lay on my side and take her in. I slept barely a wink from sunset to past five in the morning. All night long I just kept thinking *Welcome to the world, welcome to the world,* and all kinds of things kept coming into my head until I was actually talking to her out loud.

"I remember my own mama," I told her. "Everybody thinks I don't remember, but I do. I remember sitting on her bed with all her shiny jewelry spread between us and Mama's laugh ringing like a bell. I remember her dusting the house with the radio turned up loud, her cleaning and scaling a bunch of fish and then squeezing out lemons to clean the smell off her skin. I remember her singing lullabies to me, even if I can't remember what they were. I know she loved to sing, and I know she would've loved you, my baby Grace."

I talked and talked like I had been waiting for that girl all my life. There was a pad wedged between my legs, stiff and big as a pillow and filling with my trickling blood. The doctor had numbed me to stitch up the small tear Grace made coming out, but during the night the numbness went away and the pain began to come in slow like a bruise somebody was pressing against. I didn't mind. I felt alive that night, alive with both joy and pain spreading out from the center of me. I felt my life flashing through me, the scrape of tight brown shoes rubbing my heels raw the first day of school, the night I slept with my ear pressed against my bedroom door so I could listen in case Mama cried out from her sudden sickness, the way Hogan touched the sides of my face the very first time we kissed. The ache between my legs grew to a throbbing of pains and pleasures coming closer into one, a mixed-up river of Hogan loving me, Grace pushing out of me, my hipbones spreading and creaking open slowly like a rubbery wishbone stretched to the limit, my girl Grace fresh in the world as proof and payment for everything I lived through up to then. I felt strong as a backwoods witch just for having carried and birthed her, and even though I was beginning to feel tired as a bone I felt the wonder of myself was electric, and the strength I could give my girl was something fierce.

"You won't have to do any of it alone, baby Grace," I said to her, "no you won't because I'll be right there with you forever. I'm not going anywhere, I'm not dying on nobody."

She slept on and on, the stars twirling outside our window and her chest rising in tiny breaths.


Just before dawn Grace began to stir and an old black nurse came into my hospital room and told me to put her to my breast and let her suck. "Nothing coming yet, but the sucking will bring in your milk," she said. She picked Grace up and handed her to me in the bed.

"Go on now, baby," the nurse whispered. She looked like somebody's old granny, with her hair pinned up and wispy gray pieces falling alongside her wrinkled face. Until that minute I'd been planning to use formula, which most people say is so much easier, but that lady, looking at me like something wonderful was about to happen right in my own body, made me want to try.

I untied the top of my hospital gown and put Grace up to my bare skin. She opened her mouth wide, her nose sniffing and her face nuzzling against me. Her suckle felt just like the lick of a newborn puppy, soft and warm. No pain at all.

"She ain't sucking hard yet, but she will," said the nurse. "She will. You just keep on putting her there."

The rest of the day I did it every chance I had, picked her up, pushed the nipple into her mouth, jiggled her around until her tiny mouth closed down and her mewing soothed.

"Hogan, it don't even hurt," I said. He just watched with his face filled up, his hands and body still as I ever seen them.


It was Hogan, of course, who took us home from the hospital that night. Nothing was wrong with Grace then. She weighed just under seven pounds at birth, and the same on the day of her homecoming, thirty hours later. The nurses said it was normal for her to sleep so much. Count your blessings, they said, 'cause it won't last long.

Grace was dressed in a tiny pink knit dress with mother-of-pearl buttons, newly made by Hogan's ma and sent up to us by overnight mail. Just before our leaving the nurses took the hospital photo, which I was planning to have made into button pins for Hogan and me and his ma and pop. Grace scrunched up her eyes and balled her fists when the camera flashed. She let out a little cry, and her tongue came out between her lips.

"Lookit that, Hogan, she's already doing your thing with her tongue." I laughed.

Outside it was freezing cold, with new snow flurries coming down upon the mounds of snow already there. The nurses wheeled me out to the car in a wheelchair and put Grace into the car seat themselves. Hogan drove so slow you'd think he had a load of chicken eggs stacked on our car roof.


At home we found that my girlfriend Allison had come by and put a pot of spaghetti sauce on the stove and a bunch of white and pink carnations in a glass jar in the middle of the kitchen table. Me and Hogan sat down to rest and eat, but Grace had a different idea. She was opening and closing her mouth like a fish, pink and flushed, crying first in little guppy cries, then louder and louder. I stood up, walked, jiggled her, walked, sang, cooed. She cried so long it put a fear in me.

"Hogan, listen to her," I said.

"How can I help but listen?" He was walking alongside me, staring into her face.

"What should I do?"

"I don't know."

"Don't say you don't know, Hogan, 'cause we got to be together on this."

Walking, walking. Bouncing her on my shoulder, talking in a whisper.

"Maybe a bottle?"

"The nurse said I shouldn't give her anything, just let her suck on me."

"Just water? To fill her up?"

"Hogan, I'm telling you what she said, and she was just like somebody's granny."

"Well what, then?" Hogan gave a little chuckle, which I took to be the nasty kind.

"Hogan, don't you laugh at me."

"I ain't laughing at you, Lynnie, I'm laughing at us together, covering this same track in the rug here like we're going somewhere."

"Oh." I didn't see anything to laugh about.

Hogan put his arms on my shoulders. "Just relax, Lynnie. You're doing great. She's beautiful. Look at you. You're both beautiful."

I didn't feel beautiful. I felt worried and weary to the bone. A whole day and night without sleep.

"Why don't you lay down on the bed together and let her suck like that. Maybe it'll calm her."

Soon as I laid down on the bed and put Grace onto my nipple she stopped crying, drinking up the thin white liquid that was not quite milk but seemed to satisfy her just the same.

Hogan lay next to us and together we watched her smooth, sweet face going off into the safest dreamland in the world. Mama and Daddy holding her. Hogan rubbing my forehead. All of us touching skin. Quiet, at last.

"Lynnie, I forgot to tell you," Hogan whispered into the low blue light in the room. His voice was almost a dream.

"Hmmm?"

"When I called your daddy with the news, he said he remembered something."

"Yeah?"

"He said that when you were a baby your mama used to take you on long walks under the trees and you went crazy for the leaves with the sun coming through them. When the wind blew and the leaves danced he said you used to laugh and laugh and clap your hands and try to catch those pieces of shadow and light."

I remembered. I opened my eyes a bit to look out between my lashes and I could see those dancing shadows and almost, almost, in the corner of the room, I could see my mama clapping, too. Her hands, her long yellow dress, the shape of her hair. But not her face. I couldn't see her face.

Later that night I felt Hogan lift Grace off the bed. I was almost drugged asleep, but woke enough to remind him to put Grace on her side in the cradle. To be sure to put her on her side like they showed us in the hospital. I tried to sit up, but my head was too heavy.

"I'm doing it right, Lynnie," said Hogan. After he put her down he came over to me, tucked the blanket around my shoulders.

"She's just perfect," he said, but I had to see for myself. I sat up, crawled across the bedcovers. Didn't even have to get out of bed to see her because the cradle was that close in our tiny room.

She was perfect. Sleeping on her side under a white blanket. Little pink cap back on her head. Very, very still.

"Beautiful," I said. I kissed her on the cheek, and it was warm. I remember that it was warm.

I was asleep, deep-down seaweed-tangled sleep, dreaming nothing but the color green, when I heard Hogan shouting into the telephone. It was a struggle to come up. My hair was webbed across my face, my heart pounding from the effort and the fright coming up with me.

"Get up, Lynnie, we got to get the baby breathing."

Hogan towered over me, his feet on the mattress, holding my baby in his arms. The back of her head was a fuzzy ball fallen over to one side.

I jumped up and grabbed her out of his arms. Grace was gray, her eyes sunk far away and staring past me.

"What happened? What did you do?"

"I found her this way."

"Call 911."

"I did, I already did."

I put my fingers under her nostrils. Nothing. I plugged up her nose. She didn't move. She didn't blink.

"Oh, Jesus, where are you, where are you?"

I dropped down to the mattress with Grace flat out under me and pushed on her chest, put my whole mouth over her tiny petal lips and tried to blow breath back into her.

"Come on, let's get downstairs." Hogan tugged my arms from under me. We wrapped Grace up in our bed quilt and ran down the stairs in our nightclothes, out into the white, dead quiet street. The ambulance wailed from around the corner and I ran through the snow waving my arms.

It would be merciful if I couldn't remember but it is crisp and clear in my mind, the close air in that ambulance making it hard for me to breathe, the oxygen mask that covered Grace's whole face, her hands and fingers still by her sides, the bed quilt dropped on the floor, a girl not any older than me working slowly at my baby's chest with little red pads stuck onto blue wires.

"She needs the blanket, she'll be too cold," I said, but they acted like they didn't hear and Hogan kept trying to turn my head away.


Sudden infant death syndrome is what the doctor said.

"Nothing you did to bring it on, and nothing you could have done to stop it," he said. He was an old man, and he looked sad. I wanted to ask for another doctor, maybe somebody younger, who knew more, but it didn't matter anyway. She was already gone, and I was already fallen into a hole inside myself.

The coffin was tiny, with pink roses painted on the white enamel handles. Hogan picked it out. He did everything. I was so tired it was just about impossible for me to hear the Scriptures that were read or to trudge through the snow to the grave.

Grace was buried in a new part of the cemetery, and we had to walk a long way. Hogan's brothers Giles and James carried the coffin on their shoulders. They came up from Tennessee and didn't know how to dress for the cold, so that their ears were flaming red and their big bare hands stuck to the coffin handles.

*She wasn't even old enough to know she was alive*, I kept thinking to myself. The thought got stuck in my head the way a boot gets stuck in creek mud.

Hogan and me walked with the preacher behind the casket. When someone stumbled, we didn't turn around. When an airplane flew overhead during the prayer and forced the preacher to stop, Hogan and me didn't even look up.

*Damn the world. Damn you, God.* I didn't even feel sorry for thinking it.

My daddy and his wife didn't see their way up to pray for a life so short-lived, but Aunt Fay, she was there. After the burial she knocked on my bedroom door and came in real quiet without waiting for my answer.

"It's Aunt Fay, Lynelle. I've just come to sit awhile."

Five or six blankets were piled high on top of me, pulled up over my head and wrapped around my shoulders. It seemed I could not cut the chill in my bones. As warm as I was while carrying, I was twice as cold after Grace was gone.

"I made you some tea, sweetie. Real tea I grew in my own garden. Chamomile, mint, and lemon. It'll soothe you."

I pulled back the blankets. Aunt Fay was wearing a black cape dress. I could barely see her face in the dim room, but I could smell her Chantilly and I could see her lips set in a sad line. She never looked like my mama, on account of her chubby cheeks and light brown hair, and I was glad for that.

"Lynelle, I'm so sorry for you, baby. I wish your mama could be here to help you, but she's not. I'm a poor second, I know it, but I'm going to try anyway, just to say what I might."

That yawn and lump of weeping came up in my chest. She took a sip of the tea herself, and we sat quiet awhile.

"All babies are still part angel, Lynelle. God gives them flesh, but their souls have strong wings and they fly straight back to heaven if they don't take hold of the body.

"It makes us sad and grieving and even angry, sometimes real angry. But other children live. Others of yours will live."

She took my hand. Her fingernails were painted bright pink.

"I carried seven babies, did you know that?"

I shook my head.

"Only five made it all the way to being born."

Her eyes were shining, the whites glittering above my face.

"The ones who live give up their wings slowly. We watch over them more carefully. I think God takes them young sometimes as a mercy. We can't know, honey, we can't know."

I cried a good long while. Aunt Fay lay down and put her arms around me. The press of her skin and the smell of Chantilly kept me knowing I could find my way back to her when I was done.


Two days after the funeral my milk came in. It came in hard as rocks, with nowhere to go and no one to take it. Aunt Fay and everyone was gone, and Hogan was sitting at the kitchen table eating toast. I sat up in my bed and called up the hospital.

"I'd like to talk to that nurse please—"

"Which one, honey? We got sixteen on round here." The voice was kind but tired.

"She showed me how to feed my baby. She was like a granny."

"You must mean Earlene. She's not here till Thursday. Maybe someone else? Is there a problem with your baby?"

I hung up. Hogan was next to me in a flash, holding a book out and showing me where to read. There was two pages on what to do when your baby dies. It said to rest and give myself time. It said to pump myself like a cow and let the milk go down the drain. I read it with Hogan standing over me and then went back under the covers to wait. I knew I was waiting, but I wasn't sure what for. Waiting for time to pass, I supposed. Waiting to believe it, waiting to cry, waiting to stop crying. Waiting for night, for sleep, for dawn. I remembered waiting for Mama, how the waiting followed me the rest of the year when she died. I waited through my birthday, through Thanksgiving, Christmas, Easter. The feeling that something-should-be-happening-but-wasn't-but-soon-would-be stayed until I was old enough to know that I was waiting for her to come home, to kiss me good night, to flour the whole top of our kitchen table and roll out sugar cookie dough. Even after I knew in my head that Mama was never coming back, I waited for her inside of myself.

I knew this time I couldn't wait for Grace. I knew she wasn't coming back. If I was waiting for anything I was waiting for the chance to be alone, to rage and scream and then slip away from my own life.

Every time I looked at Hogan I could see that waiting inside of him, too. He just kept standing next to me with that grief in his eyes, waiting for me to see it, name it, call it up and comfort it. On top of that was the way he was right there every time I went to cry, or go to the bathroom, or look at something that was part of Grace he was there, my name on his lips, that fur ball of sadness in his eyes.

"Go on and cry, Lynnie," he'd say, or else he'd say, "Don't cry, Lynnie," or "I'm sorry, Lynnie. Tell me what to do, Lynnie," until I couldn't stand it anymore and finally at the end of that day I turned on him coming up on my heels in the bathroom. "Goddamn you, Hogan, get off my tail."

He was wearing his animal skin vest, a straggly patched-together bunch of shearling scraps that somebody in his family hand-stitched a long time ago. I hate that vest, have always hated it, and the way it was draped over his shoulders made it easier for me to yell at him.

"There isn't a damn thing you can do for me except get off me. Can you bring Grace back? Can you take away this hole in my heart? Can you make the damn sun come out or the sky blue or the world something different from what it is?"

The stricken look on his face wasn't enough to stop me, nor was the way he backed away from the bathroom into the living room, stumbling over the loose strip of molding at the edge of the linoleum floor. Even his hand swinging up and grabbing at the wall for balance, as if my words were knocking him over, just gave me steam to keep on going.

"For three days now you've been following me around like there's something you can do for me, Hogan, but you can't, do you hear me, there's nothing you can do. My baby's in the ground and the weight of the world is right here in my chest pulling on me like I'm some kind of cow, so unless you want to do something about it, unless you want to find me a baby to suck me some relief, then you better get away from me."

At that I slammed and locked the bathroom door, tore back the shower curtain with a map of the world stamped on it in bright colors, ripped off my bathrobe, and stood under the blasting hot water sobbing, sobbing, squeezing my two swollen breasts between my fingers and watching the milk swirl down the drain.

That's when I knew I had to get away.

# CHAPTER 2

## $\mathscr{A}nnie$

### Oak Park, Illinois

STARCHY steam hit Annie Thompson in the face as she poured a pot of cooked noodles into a colander, and she felt her cheeks flush, a pool of perspiration shimmy down the notches of her spine.

Annie was an attractive woman with a figure slightly plumped by three children and a beautiful face that had held on to its delicate features and clear skin through the years. She was dressed now in the loose clothes she'd worn after every pregnancy, and there were droplets of red tomato sauce along the front of her salmon-colored shirt.

Outside her kitchen window, early winter twilight was pulling the unusually mild day to an end. The bare trees that separated her yard from the neighbors formed a stark, dark latticework decorating the graying sky, and her daughter, Sophie, swung on the wooden swing set near the garage. Sophie's legs folded and unfolded under her, pulling the five-year-old's long blond hair behind her in a golden fan as she flung herself toward the sky, and fell back to earth again.

Through the window Annie saw her daughter's lips forming the exaggerated *oohs* and *aahs* of someone singing without inhibition, her voice flying through the air like a gift to the fairies and angels that Sophie believed collected in the garden at the end of each day. She heard the high notes and Annie smiled, remembering that she, too, had once lived in a world full of cherubs and elves and leprechauns that danced under ribbons of color if only you *believed*.

Even now, at thirty-five years old, Annie still had faith. She believed in the goodness of others and in the ability of one single person to change the world, which is why she volunteered at a shelter for battered women and was working her way slowly toward a master's degree in social work.

Her husband, David, and her sister Christine called her naïve, but Annie preferred that kind of innocence to the hard bitterness she saw in the world around her. Such an accusation couldn't really bother a woman who'd grown up adored by her father and secure in the way only pretty girls can be. She'd gone through school easily, married her college sweetheart, had three healthy children, and lived now in a four-bedroom Victorian house on the outskirts of Chicago.

Nothing bad had ever happened to Annie Thompson, and she knew it. She knew it especially when she saw frightened women with black eyes and scars, women living out of their cars, women running from men who'd just as soon see them dead as free.

But sometimes, especially lately, Annie felt confused about her life even when she was standing in the very midst of it. Lately, when she had her hands in a sink full of dishes, or her foot on the brake pedal at a red light, Annie found herself wearied by the very people and places that filled her days.

She loved being a mother, she was sure of that. Annie loved learning about ice hockey with Nick and braiding Sophie's hair so it swung down her back in one long yellow rope. She loved holding Dylan against her bare breast and she loved David, especially in the morning when his suit was fresh and his cheeks smelled of shaving cream. She loved watching him toss a tennis ball into the air, and when he cupped her chin to kiss her she always felt young.

But there were other feelings: vague dissatisfactions, sharp boredom, and sudden sadness. The almost tangible sense that she was trapped by the very foundation of her life and wasn't sure exactly how she'd come to be living here in this particular house with berry bushes that tracked into the living room in the spring, breathing the night air next to this particular Minnesotan man, responsible for these three children who depended on her for every meal, every permission slip, every homework assignment.

"Live in the moment," she reminded herself aloud, repeating a mantra she'd read in a book given to her by a friend. Live in the moment, rather than worry about what should be or what was to come.

At this particular moment, Annie saw, her spaghetti sauce was about to burn, and the noodles would get cold if she didn't serve them soon.

Letting a small groan escape her lips, Annie banged on the kitchen window and waved for Sophie to come inside. When the girl skipped in, Annie was pale-faced and round-shouldered, stooping over the sink to splash a little cool water on her face. The child noticed only the bright warm overhead lights, the reassuring presence of her mother in the kitchen, and the smell of food filling the air.

"Take off your shoes," Annie said as Sophie tracked mud across the tiled hallway inside the back door and dropped her coat on top of it. After a few steps the girl kicked off her blue sneakers and dropped them against the wall next to the dog's water dish. It was just a few beats short of direct obedience, but good enough for Annie.

"Wash your hands upstairs, and tell Nick it's time for dinner, sweetie."

Annie filled two white plates with thin spaghetti and spooned red sauce over them, sprinkled on Parmesan cheese, and put the plates on the kitchen table, where they sat, steaming, until Nick and Sophie clattered down the stairs and settled into their chairs.

"Is your homework finished?" Annie asked Nick.

"Yup," he answered without looking up at her.

"Nicky?"

"Hmmm?" His mouth was full of spaghetti, the sauce marking the edges of his lips red, as if they were cracked and bleeding.

"Can you look at me when I ask you something?"

This time her nine-year-old tilted his face up to her, nose slightly smudged with something that resembled blue ink, brown hair cut in a buzz style that hung flat and straight across his forehead.

"Yeah, Mom?"

He was a good boy, Annie reminded herself, good as a third-grade boy can be in a town where his peers are already having their ears pierced and rolling their eyes whenever a girl walks by.

"Nothing, honey." She ran a hand down the side of his head and felt him pull away, a gesture that still surprised her, even two years after it had begun.

"I finished my homework," he said.

"When's Dad coming home?" Sophie asked.

"Late, I think."

Annie fixed herself a small plate of spaghetti and was standing at the counter raising a forkful to her mouth when a soft, distinct gurgle wriggled through the baby monitor next to the sink.

"Squirt's awake," Nick said.

"Why do you call him Squirt?" Sophie asked.

"Change his diaper and you'll know why." Nick rolled his eyes.

"When did you ever change his diaper?" Annie asked.

"With Dad." Nick grinned and shrugged.

Annie looked at Nick and thought of those times he'd held Dylan's small hands in his own, dwarfing the baby's fingers, singing a lullaby in a voice full of crooked notes.

"That's so sweet," she said, watching Nick squirm under her approval. "I bet you could take great care of Dylan if you had to," she added, but Nicky was already pushing his food into his mouth, ignoring her with determined nonchalance.

Upstairs, Annie was greeted by the last of the day's dim light spilling through the window into Dylan's room, the sweet talc of his powder and the soft scent of Ivory Snow mingling in the air.

She crept quietly to his crib, feet sinking softly into the deep green carpeting. Dylan was a child who watched the light move, always turning his face to the sun or staring wide-eyed at shadows that danced across the walls of his room. But at dusk there were no shadows, and when she got to his side, Dylan was staring at a plastic banner of black-and-white shapes hooked on to the slats of his crib.

"Hey, baby." His head snapped around to face her, his eyes lit up with recognition. "How are you doing, sweetie?"

Dylan's hands bent into little fists curled against his face. He wriggled his body. His legs started pumping, his mouth moving.

"Oh yes, you're so happy to see me." The joy in Annie's face matched Dylan's as she lifted him up, held him straight in front of her. "What color are your eyes today?"

They were slate gray to match the light, but in a moment Annie snapped on the lantern on his dresser, and Dylan's irises gleamed light green.

"My little chameleon child," Annie whispered as she unsnapped his velour snuggly, ripped open his wet diaper, and slid a clean one under him.

A gurgle passed Dylan's lips as Annie took him easily back into her arms. From downstairs she heard clamorous noises, as if Sophie and Nick were getting ready to argue, and she walked over to the baby monitor, put her mouth right against it like a microphone.

"Hey," she said, deepening her voice instead of raising it, so she wouldn't startle Dylan. "No fighting."

She heard the clatter of forks, cups, and plates come to an

abrupt stop. She imagined Sophie and Nick looking at each other in shocked disbelief, and Annie chuckled as she sank into the rocking chair near the window.

A hushed peace came over the room as Dylan began to nurse. If living in the moment was the goal, Annie thought, then this was the perfect moment to live in, the weight of Dylan a solid reassurance in her arms as he sucked quietly, milk spilling over into the corner of his lips and then disappearing when he swallowed.

Instead of the frantic categorizing of her daily duties, Annie's thoughts meandered like a stroll along a river. She thought of a fairy tale she'd read to Sophie that morning about a boy who could drink the sea. She thought of the rooms at the shelter, the way they looked like gloves waiting for hands when they were empty, and the way the women filled them with nervous energy and jagged courage. She thought wistfully of how good it had felt to buy a cup of coffee and drink it at her desk in the morning.

Annie looked down at the puzzle of blue veins running along her pale skin, disappearing inside Dylan's mouth. His eyes were open in small slits, but she knew he was looking into the other-world where babies live. Annie shut her own eyes just as much, leaned back against the chair, and let herself see the colors dancing across her eyelids, the welcome blank wall inside of herself.

Dylan was her easiest child, the one who nursed without tugging, who cupped his small hands against the sides of her bare breast gently. So quiet, so sweet. And the only child she hadn't planned. The one she'd been most reluctant to bring into this life she was struggling to claim as her own.

When Annie thought of not wanting him it was with a guilty marvel, as if she had actually looked upon him complete and perfect and almost given him away. But it hadn't been that way at all. The puffiness in her belly, the bloating of her breasts, the sluggish nausea in the morning, and her missed period had come as a complete surprise. Annie had gone to the drugstore in a daze eleven months earlier, brought a pregnancy test home, and left it on David's dresser. She'd felt a tightening in her chest every time she thought about having another baby.

"What if we didn't have it?" she'd whispered to David before she even took the test.

It was a Friday night. They were lying together under their bedcovers, shadows from the television dancing dark and light across their faces. Nick and Sophie were asleep, and a soft spring wind blew the bedroom curtains open and shut, open and shut, so the house itself seemed to be breathing.

David turned to Annie. He was almost six feet tall. His head was propped up under his hands, long elbows spreading out from either side of his head, taking up a lot of space for himself in their queen-sized bed. His blue eyes were sharp behind wire-rimmed glasses, and when he spoke she smelled minty toothpaste on his breath.

"You mean get rid of it?"

She nodded. When she allowed herself only the narrowest thread of perception back then, Annie could almost believe it was no more than an uncomfortable bloating in her belly, an un-welcome mass of tissue that could be blamed on a few minutes before dawn on St. Patrick's Day, when David had rolled on top of her humming an Irish jig, tickling her belly as he pulled up her nightgown.

"Abort it?"

"Well, I guess that would be the option," Annie said, although she'd felt herself flush when he spoke the word aloud.

"I don't think that's much of an option." Someone on TV laughed, and David turned his head away from her, letting his sentence float up to the ceiling and mix with the scent of lilacs coming in with the wind.

"David, I'm asking you something."

She shook his arm, and he twisted his long body under the sheets to look right at her. His bare thighs pressed against hers, his voice was gentle. "Annie, honey, we've talked about this before. I don't think we should abort a baby when we have every-thing in the world to offer it."

"But it was hypothetical when we talked about it. Now it's real. I mean"— she glanced over at the pregnancy test—"it's almost real."

"That's right." He looked at her hard in the gray-lighted room. "If you're pregnant, then it's real flesh and blood. That's exactly the point."

Even in bed, even in his underwear, David spoke as if he had no doubt. He spoke, as always, as if he were standing on a pinnacle, inviting her to come up and have a look. His self-assurance was something Annie held on to, letting it bolster her in moments of doubt, giving her the backbone she needed to meet the world. But on that night she blinked back tears, feeling powerless, as if the decision were being made without her.

Of course she'd known David would have such a response. He believed in keeping quietly to the moral high ground, a holdover from childhood in Minnesota, where decency was expected and reticence was a virtue. Far back, two generations or more, his family had been Calvinists who believed in predestination, and David still had that belief stuck in the back of his psyche like a popcorn kernel lodged between two teeth. The Calvinism gave him an air of entitlement that helped make him a success in business. But his efforts to take matters into his own hands and make things turn out as he desired were what gave David his steadfast strength and kept him always in control.

On that spring night with the scent of lilacs floating on the breeze, Annie felt her own convictions and fears fluttering in her chest, caught in their chrysalis and struggling to open. But David was already an eagle, his wings lifting her up even before she could begin to try out her own. She'd always loved his strength, but on that night she hated it.

"You're a great mother," David said, rolling over and propping himself on one elbow, cupping Annie's chin between his thumb and forefinger. "We're a good family, Annie. Why can't we share that with one more person?"

Annie blinked her eyes away from his stare. She was tired. Tired of bleach, tired of the kitchen sink, tired of answering questions. She was tired of incomplete thoughts, of days spent in the Toyota buckling and unbuckling seat belts and car seats. Tired of being distracted by the repetitious details of motherhood that seemed to slip her mind until they turned up as burnt peas, lost library books, and rotten apple cores shoved under the living room couch.

"One more person is a lot," she said, thinking about her schoolwork and her job at the battered women's shelter.

After years of searching for something she could fit into her life besides babies and laundry and play dates in the park, she'd found her place at the shelter. In the beginning, her volunteer work there had seemed a bit too much like housework: straightening magazines in the lobby, arranging toys for the kids who came in with their mothers. Then one afternoon, when Sophie was a toddler in nursery school, something had happened.

It happened on a warm day when Annie was sitting at the reception desk and a skinny young woman wearing clothes from the Salvation Army opened the front door. The body of her yellow cotton sweater was wide and short, her hair was long and tangled.

"Hello." Annie stood up, her fingers still touching the papers in front of her. She couldn't take her eyes away from the young woman's face. A stirred-up face, eyes going in both directions, mouth moving with no sound coming out.

"Are you alone?" Annie asked.

"I think so. I mean, I don't know. I came here alone."

The other woman spoke in a high, shaky voice. She pulled down her sweater sleeves so that they covered her wrists and the backs of her hands. Her body was wedging the front door open, her blue jeans were washed white at the knees and baggy on her hips.

"Can I come in?" she whispered.

Annie had the sense then that something was happening that

would soon sweep her in, but for twenty seconds more she held herself apart from it.

"Come in," she finally said.

As if she'd been pushed from behind, the woman stumbled toward a soft easy chair next to a coffee table. Annie walked across the lobby, closed the front door, turned the dead bolt shut.

The girl was trembling, her arms twisted across her lap, fingertips working the frayed ends of her sweater.

"Do you need a doctor?"

She shook her head no, pressing her chapped lips together. Annie knelt down next to her, close enough to smell strawberry shampoo and cigarette smoke in her hair. The smoke made Annie think of dirty ashtrays and bar stools.

"Can you tell me your name?"

"Dee."

"Dee? I'm Annie. I'm going to try to help you."

The phone rang on the reception desk. It rang four times, then the call bounced to an upstairs office.

"Dee, can you tell me why you're here?"

"Look. Look at me." Dee lifted her arms in front of her, pushed up the sleeves of her sweater.

Annie stared at Dee's arms. Angry lines in circles the size and color of plums rose in welts on her skin. They were shining, oozing, and pink around the edges, covered with some kind of salve or lotion. The shape of her wounds was almost recognizable, the word was on the tip of Annie's tongue.

"He bit me." Dee began to wail. Annie's stomach churned, and she couldn't turn her eyes away. She wanted to weep, to throw her arms around Dee. A shock ran through her, and the shock touched something inside of Annie.

It was Annie's secret pain that she often felt as if she were looking at everything through a glass, pressing her nose against it and watching other people confidently make their way through the world. Sometimes she was almost overwhelmed by a sorrowful isolation, a sense of failure. But then David would come up behind her and kiss the back of her neck, or Nick would rush into the house with a bloody knee, and she would shake herself back to her customary good cheer.

That day in the shelter, looking at the wounds on Dee's arms, Annie felt a rattling of the glass. She glimpsed what it would be like to live right up close to the powerful forces she knew churned somewhere beyond her own easy life. That glimpse sent a shock through Annie, and on the energy of that shock she'd enrolled in graduate school, increased her hours at the shelter.

For almost two years she'd been racing through her days from graduate school to prekindergarten and back, writing research papers late into the night, helping find safe shelter for women who didn't have anywhere else to turn. She felt exhilarated, tapped into something that mattered. But a baby would change all that. A baby would make her new life nearly impossible.

"A baby, David." Annie said the word and immediately felt the child uncoiling inside her, winding its way into her breathing and the rhythm of her heartbeat. "A baby is a lot of work. How can I have another one and keep going to school and working at the shelter?"

David rubbed his fingers along the muscles in her arm. The limb was tense and sinewy.

"Look, Annie, you can take a year off school, can't you? You could even hire help after the baby is born, within reason, so you could go right back after a few months."

"I don't want to take a year off." Annie tugged her arm away from his touch, working hard to keep her voice from shaking. "I don't want another baby. I'm just finding out who I am. If I have another baby, I'm going to lose that."

"What are you talking about?" David smiled, she could hear it in his voice without looking at him. "You're Annie. Wife and mother, future savior of battered women if you must be. But right now you're a beautiful woman who may or may not have a new baby on the way."

They did, of course, have another baby on the way. The pregnancy test told them so before seven o'clock the next morning. And although Annie spent the next seven months in a kind of numb denial, she never seriously contemplated aborting again. Not once it was a fact, in white and pink, on the testing rod in her hands. Not after David had said what he did about flesh and blood. And certainly not after the doctor showed her the first ultrasound, the small black-and-white snapshot of what was living under the frame of her flesh, a beating heart and tiny fingers, an egg-shaped head with eyes that would someday open into the world.

Biting back tears, she'd pulled old boxes of maternity clothes out of the attic, bought herself some outfits that were new and black and stretched like mad, and counted calories so she wouldn't have to diet for the rest of her life to get back down to a semblance of her former self after the baby came.

And now she had him in her arms. Dylan, a boy with a peaceful soul. A boy who drank until he was full and then gazed at his mother's face as if to say thank you.

"You're welcome." Annie smiled at him. It wasn't his fault he'd interrupted her plans, pulled her back into the world of laundry and diapers. "You're always welcome."

Annie was pulling down her blouse when the telephone rang. Without letting go of the baby, she walked into her bedroom, picked up the phone, and propped it between her elbow and chin.

"Dad had another stroke," Christine blurted out before she even said hello. "And Mom's hysterical."

"When? Why didn't she call me? How bad is it?"

"Don't panic," her sister said in a voice Annie didn't care for. A courtroom voice, a lawyer voice, a voice that said she was in control of herself and suggested that Annie might not be. "It was a little stroke, I called the doctor myself to find out. But he was driving the car, that's the problem."

"Jesus." Annie felt nausea wash over her. "Did they have an accident?"

"No, thank God. He swerved into the oncoming lane but there were no cars."

Nan and Joe Verducci had sold their Long Island home four years earlier and lived now in a community near the beach in Florida, in a place called Singing Island.

"Think about all those roads that run right along the water down there."

"Exactly," Chris said. "The doctor said Dad shouldn't drive anymore. And you know how Dad's taking it."

"What can we do?" Dylan wriggled in her arms, and Annie hefted him onto her other shoulder, patted his back to bring up a burp.

"Mom asked me to go down there, but I can't," Christine said. "I'm in the middle of a case, and there's no way I can get away until it's finished. It's a copyright infringement, it's really complicated."

"Sure." Annie nodded, annoyed again at her sister's tone.

"Well then?" Christine's voice crackled across the wires. "What should we do?"

"I guess I could go down."

"That might be a good idea. After all, you're the one who wants to be a social worker. Can you go without the kids?"

"I don't think so," Annie said. "Dylan's still nursing. And it's almost their spring vacation."

"In February?"

Annie sighed. "I don't make the school calendar, Chris, I just follow it."

"So you can all go down. It's not like Dad's contagious or anything. I just think one of us needs to calm Mom down, and find out what's really happening."

When she looked at herself in the mirror at night, Annie often saw the signs of age she was able to ignore during the day: tight lines around her lips, the gray strands running through her dark hair. Leaning close to the bathroom mirror in her nightgown that evening, Annie recognized her mother's pessimism in the downward droop of her mouth. She frowned, then lifted the corners of her lips in a kind of mock smile. Lips first, to raise the spirits.

"You don't always have to do what your sister says." David's voice startled her. She looked at his reflection in the mirror. He was staring at the open palm of his hand, picking at a callus.

"Sure. Sometimes I can do what *you* want me to do, right?"

David was a tall man who had once set his sights on becoming a tennis pro. Now, at thirty-six, he was on the fast track at McDonald's, putting together marketing plans and unrolling ad campaigns. But he still played tennis hard, and wore the evidence across his palms, in the lean tug of muscles in his thighs.

He looked up from the skin of his hand and met her gaze in the mirror, arched an eyebrow at her. Annie softened her tone. "Maybe we could go down next week, for the kids' break?"

"Do your parents really need you? I mean, you have enough to do here, don't you think?" He reached around her to open the medicine cabinet, and Annie watched her reflection slide away.

"David, this is my dad." She turned to face him. He was wearing a maroon pajama top and gray boxer shorts. They were so close that her breasts brushed against him when she turned. "You know how my mother can be. She takes control of everything, and it only makes him more uptight."

"And you think you can change a lifetime of fishwifery in one visit?"

"Hey." She reproached him with a syllable. "You'd do the same if your family needed you.

"Nobody ever knows how bad a stroke is," she added, hinting at her real fear, a fear she was afraid even to speak aloud. "Nobody ever knows when the next one, or the really bad one, will come. It could be fifteen years from now, it could be next week."

David was flossing, his mouth gaping open over her head, the green threads running between his molars. She looked away, reaching for a bottle of hand lotion on the windowsill.

"I guess I could check out a few corporate stores down there," he said as he leaned over the sink to rinse his mouth.

"It's not like we couldn't enjoy ourselves. The beach is right there," she said. "I just want to see my father. You can understand that, can't you?"

"Sure." David kissed the top of her head. "I'll let you know tomorrow, okay?"

"Thanks, hon." Annie reached for his arm, and he smoothed down her hair. She leaned against his shoulder, and for just an instant, Annie felt as if she weighed nothing at all.

# CHAPTER 3

## Lynelle

### SINGING ISLAND, FLORIDA

I SPENT three days chewing on my hair, looking out the window at the snow falling across the rooftops, squeezing my breast milk into the bathroom sink. What was on my mind were dark thoughts of death and big spaces of empty sky, a feeling that I was going crazy from grief. I got it in my head that sunshine was what I needed, sunshine and time away from my apartment, time away from the telephone and doorbell ringing and the postman bringing cards that me and Hogan kept shoving into the closets because we couldn't bear to look at them.

"I need to go away," I told Hogan. "I need to see the sun and walk by the water."

He looked at me a long time, and I don't know what he saw, maybe the pain in my eyes, maybe the way I was fading away from him fast.

"I can't take you noplace, Lynelle, honey. I need to get back to work. Maybe you could visit your daddy or Aunt Fay."

"You know me, Hogan. You know I need to be alone."

It's always been that way, from so much time alone when I was a girl I suppose, and that's why Hogan let me go, why he got me the free airplane passes from work and made arrangements for me to stay at a motel run by his friend's uncle in a place called Singing Island.

On the morning I was to leave, Hogan gave me a box with a long yellow skirt inside.

"I got it mail order," he said. He had a catch in his throat, it was all he could do to drive me to the airport and put me on the plane. "I want you home in two weeks," he said, his tongue working back and forth furious between his teeth. I hugged him, and then I was gone.


When I got to Florida I knew right away it was what I needed, the thick air folding me up and the palm trees a welcome sight for my eyes. I didn't think anything could round out the flat feeling inside of me, but the warm air puffed me up a bit, made me remember my arms and legs as something that could swing and slide out of a taxicab and move across a path of smooth square stones.

The Hideaway was a row of small white cottages with pink flowers in big clay pots, and old people walking around real slow. A kindly brown-skinned manager wearing a turban hat smiled at me through round glasses and said his daughter would set coffee and donuts on the table outside my room every morning, as long as the weather was good.

"That's nice," I said, but it hurt me to think of something so simple as filling my belly. When I remembered the choke of my sorrow, it was twice as thick with the guilt of having let go of it for a minute, of having forgotten my girl.

My room was a nice size, everything white and pale green. I poked around long enough to find a little refrigerator and sink behind a tiny wall, and a stand-up shower with a door that wouldn't close all the way. The place suited me just fine. Anyplace halfway clean where I could be alone would've been just right by me.

I hung my new yellow skirt over a wire hanger in the closet and put my underwear in the top dresser drawer. Then I sat down on the bed and kicked off my heavy shoes. I opened the night-stand to put away my fanny pack with all the money Hogan had gave me, and inside I found a Bible with a hard black cover. It smelled like the drawer, cedar and dust and a little bit of trapped ocean air. It was a long time since I held a Bible in my hand, but I remembered what Aunt Fay said to me about children and angels and thought I might find myself a bit of comfort in those pages. In spite of my anger and my doubts, I was still drawn to look for the comfort of God.

I opened up the book to wherever it might fall, which was right to the story of Moses. A baby given up and raised to be a king did not suit my mood, although I would certainly think of it later on when I saw that little baby boy laying alone and peaceful in his stroller.

I turned the pages looking for something that might tell me what I needed, and the stories I saw there drew me in like a stream running with blood and grief. People dying, killing each other, taking their sisters' wives into their beds. It wasn't what I remembered, as I was raised on the Good News and the goodness of Jesus, but it was more like the truth than anything I'd ever learned in church.

Jesus as a baby, that's what I learned in Sunday school. Jesus as a boy, so we believed in him like we believed in ourselves. I used to believe in a kind and loving Lord and Jesus. I believed in anything worth wearing my white Sunday shoes for, anyone whose birthday meant everybody giving and getting presents. Church holidays made Mama's face shine and gave her the freedom to sing loud in public with her face tipped up to the sky. Until she died I believed without thinking about it. I believed because God was in a place where all our voices were so loud that there was no need to listen for one special voice above the others.

Then my mama died, and Daddy didn't take me to church anymore. For a long time he was in shock, a shock that hung his jaw and left him staring into the closets, his hand on the doorframe, his eyes stuck and glassy. When he got back to his old self he was softer and sad, and on Sundays we went bowling or fishing instead of going to church. Daddy didn't talk about Mama and so I didn't either, but I prayed at night and waited in the dark for my mama's spirit to visit me. It didn't do any good. Mama didn't answer, and the lines of her face, the feel of her hands on my cheeks, all of it faded so fast it scared me.

I got it in my head that I had to be in church to hear what I needed, and finally I walked there alone one Saturday afternoon. Mama had been gone four months. My heart was heavy and my brown shoes were too tight for me, bringing blisters up on my heels, but I thought the pain would help Jesus notice me so I bit my tongue and kept going. To make the steps easier on my feet I walked off the road, under big oak trees hung with moss that combed across my face, tapping me on the shoulder as I walked.

When I finally reached the Covenant Baptist Church it was rising out of the dirt like a big white ghost. No sound coming from the windows, no doors swung open. Just a white wooden building with peeling paint on the handrails and steps worn brown, swept clean in the center, a thousand foot grooves stepped into them over the years.

Inside I had to blink against the darkness. The church was hushed. Yellow-lighted. I walked up past the empty seats, right up to the altar, and kneeled down.

"Jesus. I want to hear my mama in heaven. I want her to tell me it's all right."

My heels hurt. The gray stubby carpet folded over the kneeler at the altar made pockmarks in my skin. My knees went cold and numb. My fingers, squeezed together in prayer, cramped up.

I closed my eyes. Opened them, closed them. Fluttered them, hoping I might see something moving in shadows. I knew about shadows from my dead granddaddy, knew they could have a power of their own.

When the side door to the church creaked open and threw

step the mud fell from my shoes, and every time I bent to scratch it up the clumps fell apart in my fingers. Mrs. Dale followed behind me saying not to worry, waving those yellow flowers against my back. It was a good-bye to everything I had once believed, and a long time before I could even think about praying again.

When I woke the next morning in the Hideaway my breasts were heavy with milk. I had fallen asleep still in my traveling clothes, with the light on next to the bed and my face pressed up against the pages of the Bible. The front of my blouse was stained, and the bedcovers were wet in two dark, sad, sour circles. I pumped myself in the shower without crying, and when I was done I dried myself with a blue towel, patting carefully along the stitches between my legs.

Dressed in my new yellow skirt, white shirt, and tan weaved slip-on shoes, I slipped out the door into a quiet hushed morning. The soft rain that sprinkles Florida during the darkness was still misting the air. There was no sound but the seagulls, and no one but me walking out on the road.

I walked to the ocean in morning twilight, following the smell and sound of surf coming over the high dunes. Sky, sand, sky, sand, and then there was the ocean, spreading out everywhere. Bare and gray-blue and so big it could swallow me up and I'd never be missed. The water's edge sprayed my face with salty sea tears.

I felt small. Not like a child, but like a woman who can't do anything to keep from being hurt. Suddenly all my anger came up inside of me. The sea was louder than me, bigger than me, and it kept on coming and coming. I could scream and it would swallow up all of my pain without a trace, it would take it and just keep on coming.

I screamed just a little at first, to see how it would feel. The ocean sucked it in. I screamed louder. Then I looked around. There was no one to see or hear me. I could let it go. I could sharp daylight across the altar, I bolted my body upright and clamped my eyes shut tighter.

"Jesus, Mama, Jesus, Mama, Jesus, Mama."

I felt like I might fly up into the sky. Then I heard my name spoke soft-like.

"Lynelle? Is that you, Lynelle?"

It was the preacher's wife, Mrs. Dale, walking toward me with a bunch of yellow flowers in her hands. There were big black spots in front of my eyes.

"You all right?" she asked. She came right up close to me. I tried to stand, but my knees were locked up.

"I was just saying a prayer," I said.

Mrs. Dale had very white teeth which some said she kept in a glass by her bed. She was older than my mama. I didn't want her to touch me.

"I expect I got to get home for supper," I said. In her face over the bunch of flowers I could see Mrs. Dale taking pity on me. Getting ready to put out her hands and hug me. I unlocked my knees against the pins and needles, wobbled when I stood. Something snapped in my leg, loud enough for us both to hear and draw our eyes down to my feet.

"Lynelle, look at that mud," Mrs. Dale cried. Shame-faced, I stared at the mud cakes my shoes had become. I looked behind me. All the way back down the aisle to the front door was mud dropped like pieces of a cracked shadow.

"I'm sorry," I said. "I'll clean it."

She tried to be kind, but I wouldn't meet up with her watery eyes.

"No need, Lynelle, it's time to vacuum in here anyway."

Over her stiff gray-blue hair I saw the cross in front of the altar. I wanted to move, but with each step I took the dried mud fell off to the floor in flakes. Mrs. Dale must have seen I was going to cry.

"The side door," she said, like it was a wonderful discovery, "just go right on out the side door. Don't worry about the mud."

It took ten giant steps for me to reach the door. With each

howl. I opened my mouth to scream my baby's name, but what came out was *Mama.*

"Mama. Mama. My baby's gone," I screamed. I screamed. I howled. I screamed into the waves, I screamed up at the sky. The birds didn't even fly over me. The tide pulled at my feet as if it wanted to hold me there and take me under, but I wasn't afraid. I wasn't afraid of anything, not anymore.

"I let my girl die," I screamed at the ocean, screamed with my arms reached out wide, my knees bent up, my body doubled over, my arms finally wrapping around me in the only woman-hug that could keep me from going under.

I screamed and wailed until I was all tired out. It might have been ten minutes or two hours. By the time I stopped the sand was up around my ankles and water was lapping at my skirt, making a dark golden lace stain all the way to my knees. I pulled my feet loose and gathered up the yellow material, wrapped it like a washcloth and squeezed out what I could. Having nothing else, I lifted the hem to my face and wiped my cheeks cool. I blew my nose on the inside of the hem. I had to blow so many times that I disgusted myself, which shook away the sorrow that was threatening to slam me back down like something loose in the tides.

I started to walk then, walk like my life depended on it. I was desperate as a madwoman walking down the street gnashing her teeth and pulling on gray hair, only my mad was hid underneath my skirt and a long steady stride of walking and walking.

I left the beach as the first few people came out with their hats and colorful shirts. The bright sun was making me squint, walk with one hand shading my eyes. I'd forgotten how strong the sun can be, how horrid it is to feel sad on a sunny day. For a minute I wished I was back home in my own bed, the snow and gray sky covering me over. But there was the bassinet and the tiny clothes, the toys Hogan made and Hogan himself, dressing for work, looking at me through the reflection in our bedroom mirror, not knowing if he should smile, watching me.

He would put away the bassinet and put the clothes in boxes, mark them "baby things," as we had agreed on, but suddenly I feared he might throw some things away, the things made with his own hands, because when he held them he could remember the joy of expecting, the way he ran that wooden rattle over my belly, the polished wood smooth and chilly, me giggling and him saying, "Here it is, little baby, here's the toy Daddy made for you."

I walked as far as I could along the ocean and then up through a big spread of dunes and long grasses, past the service entrance of a fancy hotel with its smell of bacon and the clang of pots in the kitchen.

There was a bunch of shops just down the beach from the hotel. They were built up on a small wooden boardwalk with flags hanging from all the light posts. I went in one that had the door propped open, picked out a pair of dark black sunglasses marked at half price, and chose a postcard showing a sunset over the water. I used the change to buy a stamp right there, from one of the machines where it costs double. As there was nobody in the store except the girl behind the counter, I leaned over next to a display of fish magnets and kids' toothbrushes to write out my postcard. I wrote, "I'm fine. Save the toys. Don't throw anything away." The counter girl came over and smiled at me. She looked to be about my age. "You here on vacation?"

I looked at her, and for some reason I remembered the way we used to tell dead baby jokes in grammar school. Dead babies on a pitchfork, dead babies in a truck.

"Sort of," I answered.

I licked the stamp and stuck it down. When I looked up at the girl, she was reading my postcard. I stuffed it back into the bag, pulled out my new sunglasses, and snapped off the tag.

"I been there," the girl said. Like we shared a problem. Like she knew something about me.

I left the store, dropped the postcard in a mailbox, and walked back to the Hideaway.

There was no TV in my room, but I didn't miss it. When I was a little girl we had a black-and-white TV that stood on four wooden legs in a corner of our living room. It was broken more than it worked, and Daddy was forever hoisting it out the door to Bill B's repair shop. Mama never minded, she would just as soon have music in the house. We liked Crystal Gayle and Doris Day and Julie Andrews in *The Sound of Music*. Mama didn't like to dance, said she was too stiff for it, but when she sang loud she sounded better than the radio and she looked prettier than anybody on TV.

*Que sera, sera. Whatever will be, will be. The future's not ours to see, que sera, sera.*

When Mama sang along with Doris Day she waved her hands and twirled like she was onstage, but when she sang that same song at bedtime, her voice was a soft, sweet lullaby.

"Mama?"

"Yes, Lynnie?"

She took the braids out of my hair slow, and pulled the white chenille bedspread up under my chin.

"What will I be when I grow up?"

"Whatever you want to be, little girl."

"But, ma'am?"

"Yes?"

"Will I be pretty?"

"You already are."

"Will I be rich?"

"It doesn't matter."

"When you were little, did you used to ask your mama what you'd be?"

"I did. And here's what she said to me . . . *que sera, sera.*"

I begged Daddy and Aunt Fay to have that song sung at Mama's funeral. Our house was filled with food people left on our doorstep. Crumb cakes, fruit pies, biscuits, corn bread, chicken fried and baked, roasted and casseroled.

"You tell that Preacher Dale I don't want no brimstone," Daddy whispered. Before Mama passed he sometimes used to yell, but after she died Daddy was quiet.

"My wife was a good woman," he said to Aunt Fay, "she deserves soft prayers."

I was sitting on the floor under our kitchen window with a pot holder loom in my lap, pushing colored loops over and under, under and over, weaving pot holders the way my mama showed me.

"Well then, Bobby, you got to tell the preacher what things Gracelyn loved, so he can talk about them," Aunt Fay said. She wore black shoes, and had her legs crossed at the ankle. She was only four years older than I am now, but I recall her bent like an old woman.

"She loved me," I said. The two of them looked down at me. "And she loved that song. She loved 'Que Sera, Sera.' Why don't they sing that at the funeral?"

But they wouldn't hear of it. On the day Mama was buried I stood next to my daddy in the Covenant Baptist Church and listened to a skinny lady singing sad, slow songs I never heard before, songs that pushed away every happy picture I'd ever carried in my head, every good dream I ever took to bed with me at night, and every song I ever heard my mama sing.

Mama's face and voice and the brush of her fingers loosening my hair faded, and that song went the same way as the other memories.

Then one night in Florida, it came back. It was like it came through a window. I can't say it brought me comfort, but it brought me energy that sent me out into the damp mornings before dawn and kept me up at night with the Bible spread open and my breasts two swollen mounds of anger stuck onto my chest, the words of God mixed up with that song humming around me. *Que sera, sera, whatever will be, will be.*

# CHAPTER 4

## Annie

IT took a dozen phone calls to arrange the Florida trip: calls to the travel agent, the airline, the car rental service. Annie needed someone to watch the dog, she had to stop the newspaper, have the mail held, bring Dylan in for a two-month checkup before taking him on an airplane. She had to climb into the attic and bring down the summer clothes, launder them, and shop for larger sandals, T-shirts, and other things Sophie and Nick had already outgrown since August.

Annie saved the call to her friend Liz at the women's shelter for last. It was a snowy February morning filled with boots and snowsuits and bowls of hot oatmeal when Annie dialed her number.

"We're going to Florida for a week," she said.

"Tough life."

Annie imagined her friend sitting behind her desk, chewing on a pen, looking over domestic violence reports, shuffling through court documents.

In her kitchen, where she stood with the phone cocked under her chin, breakfast bowls were piled in the sink, and the baby swing was clicking back and forth even though Dylan was napping upstairs in his crib. Annie reached out her hand to steady the swing.

"My dad had a stroke."

"I'm sorry." Immediately Liz's voice changed; Annie could almost hear her friend's concentration fine-tune itself.

"A small one," she added. "But everything is chaos for my parents. I'm going down to see if I can help."

"Let me know if I can do anything."

"I'll be fine. But thanks."

There was a silence on the line. Annie walked away from the sink so Liz wouldn't hear the slosh of water, the clink of dishes.

"When are you coming back?" Liz asked.

"Saturday. Next Saturday."

"No, Annie. I mean when are you coming back here? Dee's been asking for you. And we have a new family. Cop's wife. Two kids, two broken arms."

"I'm coming back," Annie said. She remembered the way midmorning light streamed into Liz's office from the south window, illuminating dust as it floated through the air above her head like a splintered halo. "I want to come back. I think I'm coming back. I'll call you when I get home, and we'll talk."

Annie hung up the phone and two pictures flooded her mind: her father, as her mother had described him, with trembling hands and a lost look in his eyes. And herself, always taking care of people, always standing at the kitchen sink watching the patch of grass and trees in her backyard slowly change with the seasons.


The five Thompsons flew out of Midway Airport early on a Thursday morning in mid-February, leaving behind six inches of snow and a wind chill so severe it was dangerous to touch a car door handle without gloves.

Dylan traveled with the same wide-eyed silence he brought to everything, snapping his head around each time the pilot turned on an overhead sign or sent his voice through the intercom system, whimpering for only a minute during takeoff and landing.

They reached West Palm Beach Airport without incident, and after much juggling of luggage and children and keys for the rental van, Annie and David stepped out of the air-conditioned airport into a sultry Florida day, loaded their minivan, and were on their way.

David drove slowly, rolling down all the windows to give the warm air a chance to blow through their hair. In turn each family member smelled in the breezes salt water, something like fish sitting in baskets on a dock, coconut oil, chlorine, and the plastic scent of beach balls unwrapped in the parking lot outside Kmart.

"Why does it smell funny?" Nick asked as a whiff of fish odor passed through the van. His new sunglasses, bought by Annie at Walgreens the week before, were pushed up on his head, and pieces of his hair were sticking straight up behind them.

"Can Grandpa walk yet?" Sophie asked.

"Yes, honey." Annie twisted around in the front seat to answer, worried that she'd frightened Sophie with the sudden plans for the trip, the late night phone calls to her mother. "There's nothing wrong with Grandpa's legs, he's just a little weak, that's all."

"Grandpa can walk, dummy, he just can't sing," Nick said.

"Who told you that?" Annie asked.

"Grandma, she said he ruins every song he tries to—"

"She means he can't carry a tune," David said.

"What's that mean, 'carry a tuna'?" Sophie asked.

"It means he can't sing," Nick said firmly.


When they drove over the Palmetto Bridge onto Singing Island, where the turquoise bay was dotted with white sailboats and the glimmering Atlantic Ocean spread softly across the horizon like blue wings, Annie felt something inside her shift into low gear, settle down and breathe deeply. Even with her father's health on her mind, she felt the quiet strength of the ocean begin to do its restorative work.

"Sparkling Waters," Nick read aloud as they pulled to a stop in front of the blue-and-white mosaic gateway at the entrance to Joe and Nan Verducci's condo complex.

The road leading into Sparkling Waters was blocked by a large white gate. David picked up a security phone, dialed his in-laws' extension, and waited for Nan's voice to blare through the speaker.

"It's us," he called into the black box. "David and Annie."

The gates swung slowly open. Nick and Sophie unsnapped their seat belts.

"We're here," Nick called out. Sophie joined in. Dylan kicked his feet against the edge of the car seat.

Nan was already standing outside, waving her hand, as they pulled up. Her hair was coppery auburn, fresh from the salon.

"Halloo, halloo," she called.

"Is your mother actually saying *hallooo?*" David muttered under his breath as he cut the engine.

"Appears to be true," Annie said through a stiff smile. "Must be a Florida thing."

Nick and Sophie leapt out of the van, jumping onto hard blades of grass, and stomping so their light-up sandals sent patches of color splashing underfoot.

"Give me a hug," Nan demanded, her hands on Sophie's head, fingers catching the neck of Nick's T-shirt, "give me a kiss."

Annie climbed out of the front seat, and Nan pressed her cheek against hers. She smelled of hairspray and nail polish, a scent that made Annie's nose itch.

"Oh, baby, it's so good to see you, you don't know what it's like down here alone with your father," Nan said.

"Where is Dad?" Annie asked, looking over her mother's shoulder at the front of the house.

"He's dozing on the porch," Nan said, her hand tight on Annie's arm. "He fell asleep a while ago."

David came up behind them, carrying Dylan in his portable car seat.

"Oh my God, look at him." Nan reached for Dylan, her ten lacquered nails grabbing onto his small hands, brushing against his cheeks. "He's just beautiful." Her voice rang out, jumping nearly an octave with the syllables of the word, *be-au-ti-ful,* in shrill singsong. Dylan stared at her, transfixed by the colors, the sounds, the motion of his grandmother.

"Grandpa!" Sophie shouted a greeting, and Annie swung around to see her father moving carefully down the porch step, using a cane for balance. They all watched as Joe took the single step slowly: cane first, left leg, then right, each limb moving stiffly, his body bent at the waist, the top of his gray head tipped toward them.

"How are you doing?" David called slowly and loudly to his father-in-law.

"I'm just fine." Joe looked up when both feet were on the ground, annoyed at the way they were all staring at him, annoyed at the trembling in his hands.

For three decades Joe Verducci had owned a tailoring shop on Long Island. Over the years his back had curved from sitting at the sewing machine hour after hour, but he had remained spry and sure of himself until the stroke.

Now Annie saw what her mother had been watching day after day: Joe Verducci was an old man, old before he'd expected to be. Old without warning.

She wrapped her arms around her father and squeezed him, noting with satisfaction that he still smelled of Barbasol shaving cream, he still felt solid in her arms.

"He's a beautiful boy," Joe said, reaching for Dylan. Everyone watched as he leaned forward and kissed the boy on the head. Nothing shaky about his lips and the way they landed right on Dylan's cheek. Nothing sad about the way Dylan reached his hand up, lightly whacking Joe in the chin.

"Hey, hey now, young man." Joe grinned. Annie smiled, and Sophie clapped her hands.


During the next twenty-four hours Annie watched her father for signs of exhaustion and weakness. He was cautious in movement, which was to be expected at least for a few months, until the physical therapy did its deepest work. It saddened Annie to see her father's hand moving slowly toward Nick, the boy's eyes following the fingers as they advanced toward him through the air. But what troubled Annie more was the way her mother hovered.

Joe held Sophie's hand as she skipped into the house, and Nan was right beside him, warning him against strain. Joe sat down in the living room with a newspaper open in his lap, and Nan warned him against taxing his eyes. He stood to walk down the hall, and Nan called after him to slow down.

"I think you may be stressing Dad out," Annie said.

It was the day after their arrival. They were making tuna sandwiches to bring to the pool, standing at the kitchen counter slicing and spreading, wrapping and stacking.

"The doctor said he has to take it easy."

"What do you want him to do, Mom? Lay in bed all day?"

The knife slipped from Nan's fingers and clattered onto her linoleum floor.

"For goodness' sakes." Nan bent to pick up the utensil. "You know your father, you know he has trouble taking it easy."

Annie bit her tongue. What she knew, what everyone knew, was that Nan had trouble taking it easy.

"What did the doctor tell you to do?"

"Doctors." Nan waved her hand, a dismissive gesture. The knife, coated with a thin layer of mayonnaise, waved past Annie's face.

"You don't like the doctor, Mom?"

"I guess he's all right." Nan shrugged. "He gave us a folder full of instructions, typed so small I can barely read them."

"Maybe I can take a look at it for you. When's Dad's next doctor appointment?"

"Tuesday. Every Tuesday."

"Do you mind if I go with you?"

"Why should I mind?" Nan said, twirling the lid back onto the mayonnaise jar. "Your father, he'll probably mind."

She stopped midway to the refrigerator and held the jar aloft. "You know, when I was young, we used to put mayonnaise in our hair to make it shiny. You should try that, it could add luster to your looks."

Annie turned her eyes down to the task at hand. "I'll think about it," she said.

From the bedroom she heard Sophie and Nick giggling, and the loud growls of David playing his mock water monster routine to a captive audience.

"Now what are they doing back there?" Nan asked, shutting the refrigerator and frowning. "They'll upset your father."

Annie snapped on the radio as her mother left the room, and Sinatra filled the kitchen with a song Annie remembered from years ago—the years when her mother used to keep the books for Joe's tailor shop and groan over their bankbook as if they were rubbing their last two dimes together.

"Joe, where are those slipcovers?" Nan's voice came back to Annie from three decades past. "Joe, you need more work. Joe, you're too soft, you're too kind, you don't charge enough, you shouldn't give anyone credit, we have to eat, don't we?"

They'd lived in a small Long Island town then, a place where the salty musk of the ocean followed Annie from her bedroom, around the corner to her father's tailor shop, where bells jingled whenever the front door opened.

"What a pretty girl," her father's customers always said when they saw her. She'd look up at them from under her long, dark lashes and they'd pull nickels out of their pockets, slip quarters from behind their ears, they'd press little pieces of candy into her palms.

Christine would come into the shop with a book in her hands and smudges on her glasses, eye the candy, and say, "Sugar is a stimulant. Mommy doesn't want you eating candy in the morning," and the customers would turn their heads to one side, look at Christine with a crooked smile, and murmur, "What a smart little girl." But when no one was looking they slipped the treats into Annie's hands again.

When the shop was empty Annie watched her father work, sucking on peppermints and fruity candies that melted away into soft jelly centers. She loved the starchy smell that came from the steam press, the row of scissors and tape measures, the steady clacking of the sewing machine, the metal thimbles lined like shields on wooden pegs, the rainbow of threads, the pins her father slipped between his lips and into pincushions, the needles that slid into the flat pile of the gray rug underfoot.

"Watch it," her father said whenever she walked barefoot through the shop, or sat somewhere without first looking for the sharp edge of sewing scissors, the surprise of a straight pin in the seat cushion.

She learned to look carefully at her father's lips, checking for pins before kissing him. And she listened. She listened to the radio on his windowsill, the hum and clack of the sewing machine. She listened to the way people talked to her father about the secrets in their lives. She watched a chubby bride twirling in front of the three-way mirror, glowing with joy at the way the billowing white dress hid her hips. She watched skinny old ladies smiling at pleats her father added to their dresses. She saw how hard people worked to hide their flaws: how happy her father's work made them.

And she listened to the rude ones, too. Women who haggled over prices, nitpicked at a missed stitch or a hanging thread. Women who made her father rip out hems, get down on his knees and start the job over again.

She watched as her father brushed dust from his trousers and unbent his body at the end of a long day. She listened to the slow crackling of his bones and joints as he moaned, "Oh, Annie, I'm getting old," and made her giggle with his grimaces.

Annie's eyes stung, remembering the way he used to look with a hank of dark hair hanging over his forehead, his dark eyes glowing in their deep sockets, the easy way he walked along the sidewalk holding her hand while she skipped beside him, and the way his voice sounded when he told her, "Don't ever treat people like you're better than they are, Annie. Will you do that for your old man?"

With one eye on her father and the other on her children, Annie fell into a familiar routine in Florida, going to the beach in the morning, eating lunch at the condo, spending afternoons at the pool, then showering in time to go out for an early dinner. There were plenty of nearby restaurants to choose from, with hamburgers or chicken fingers on the kids' menu, early-bird specials for the adults, and spicy Bloody Marys that David ordered and Annie sipped at.

Nick and Sophie went to bed easily at night, drawn into slumber by exhaustion from sun and sea and sand. Even Dylan went down quickly, nursing from only one breast and dozing with his cheek pressed against Annie's chest.

"Look at him," Annie whispered. It was Saturday night, and she'd ordered herself a glass of white wine with dinner, then sipped away half of David's Bloody Mary, too. The warm air coming in through the open window felt like a caress on her bare breast. Dylan's breath pumped cool moist air across her nipple.

David leaned over her, put his finger between the boy's lips and Annie's body, and separated them with a soft, popping sound. He lifted Dylan and lay him carefully in the portable crib next to the sofa bed in the room where the three of them were sharing quarters. David's movements were tender and careful.

"What color do you think his eyes are?" Annie whispered, but of course David saw only the blue veins in his eyelids, the sucking movement of his lips.

"Blue, aren't they? Or light green?"

"Who does he look like?"

All their babies looked the same to David, small faces, pudgy limbs, tiny fingers that bent and unbent as he willed them. He strained to remember Nick as a newborn, and could only remember the red at the back of his throat when he howled.

"He looks like you, honey," David said as he put his arm around her, smelling the yeasty scent of Annie's body, milky and round and sweet.

Annie could still feel the wet tug of her son's mouth on her nipple, and so it came as a surprise when she felt a long muscle of desire rippling in her belly when David kissed her.

David's beard, which hadn't been shaved for two days, stung a burn across her cheek. Annie pressed a hand over her breasts to keep the milk from trickling out, and ignored the dryness between her legs. It had been months since she'd felt desire, and she wanted to feel David's sureness, the thing she loved best about him, crushed against her chest and hips as he rose and fell above her, whispering her name.

They made love quietly, quickly, listening for sounds in the hallway as David slung off his underwear and lifted Annie's nightgown. When they were finished they rolled apart, and Annie listened to the quiet around them. She was relieved when there was no patter of small running feet, no child whimpering.

"That was nice," she whispered.

"It was," David said, but he was looking at the ceiling when he said it, and she knew his mind had already slipped away.

Pushing the sheets gently off her body, Annie sat up and pulled on her nightgown. David lifted one hand and stroked the small of her back, and she waited for his hand to drop before easing herself slowly out of bed.

She stood and walked to the open window. Drawing in a deep breath, Annie smelled the sweet scent of hibiscus threading the night air. She inhaled again, feeling the welcome blankness that could come at the end of a busy day, willing herself to think about nothing but the rhythm of the ocean she could still feel against her legs, the rhythm of David rocking above her, the rhythm of her own heartbeat in her chest.

It was then Annie heard the sound.

She froze, one ear turned toward the window screen, and listened.

"Do you hear that?" she asked in a soft voice.

David opened his eyes a crack. "Hear what?"

"That sound. Like children crying."

David listened. He heard a car door slam and the noisy chug of his infant son breathing in the crib across the room.

"I don't hear anything."

Annie strained to listen. With a shift of the wind the distant whimper was gone.

"I think I'll check on the kids," she said.

In the bedroom down the hall, Sophie lay bundled under a blanket, hair spread across the pillow. Nick slept in the narrow bed across from his sister, limbs spread in four directions, blanket and sheets kicked onto the floor.

Moving his legs together, Annie covered Nick with a smoothed sheet and stood for a second to gaze at his parted lips, the straight line of his nose. She felt his forehead, pressed her lips against his cheek, smelled shampoo in his hair. She did the same at Sophie's side, pausing to watch the way the little girl's eyes were moving in her sleep, following a dream across another world.

Satisfied the children were safe, Annie pulled the door halfway shut. She stood in the hallway outside her parents' room for a moment, but again heard only the slow rhythm of their breath filling the air.

Wrapping her arms around her torso to ward away a shiver, Annie padded back into the room where the baby and David slept. She curled around her husband and listened to the night sounds of people playing cards, shuffling the deck somewhere close by. In the distance she could swear she heard the sound again, something like a cry, coming and going. But it was so faint and far away, surely it was only her imagination.

# CHAPTER 5

## *Lynelle*

I DIDN'T talk to anybody on those long Florida days. I just
walked and walked and thought about Mama coming back to
me in pieces and Grace leaving me all at once. I walked and
sang and looked out at the ocean and let my mama come to me
with her hair pinned up from the heat, her hands smoothing
down the flyaways during a thunderstorm, her mouth smiling
down at me through the shadows from long-ago leaves. I
strained to see her whole face. I waited and watched for comfort.
And I walked.

One morning when I was walking down the quiet road that
runs behind the Singing Island post office, I saw a silver pin in
the shape of a starfish laying in the weeds at the cracked edge of
the sidewalk. The silver was dull and the clasp was all bent, but
something about it reminded me of Mama. I picked it up, rubbed
it between my fingers, put it in my pocket without really knowing why.

After that I started finding other things. Bobby pins, little colored barrettes girls wear in their hair. A white comb with sand
stuck in between all the little teeth. One small blue baby sock. It
is amazing what you can find if you cover enough ground and

keep your eyes open. There was no rule or rhyme to what I picked up on those sandy roads. I walked as long and as hard and far as I could, picking up scraps off the street to fill the long pockets in my yellow skirt, singing the song to myself that Mama used to sing. *Que sera, sera.*

I tried not to walk by the ocean when I knew people would be out playing on the sand, but I saw them anyway. Girls my own age with smooth bellies and bright lipstick. Little boys in tiny white baseball caps. Little girls with ruffled bathing suits bending to pick up seashells and chasing waves. When I saw them I shaded my eyes and walked the other way. I walked along the road by the bay, past the marina, as far along the peninsula as I could go until I reached the bridge crossing to the mainland.

By the time I reached the bridge in the late morning I was wet from heat and walking, my legs shaking like suddenly I had no blood left in my body. I had to sit there until I could get up the energy to walk over to the little fishing store at the edge of the bay and buy myself a 7-Up, which I drank down in one swallow, waiting for the dizziness to pass. While I waited I sat down on a patch of dry sandy grass and emptied my pockets, looking over what I found, touching each thing like it might be a memory.

On those days I was sure that I would never get over my pain, never close my eyes without seeing Grace's gray face. Sometimes I kept my eyes open, not even blinking, so that I wouldn't have to see those little pads on her chest, or remember that ambulance speeding through the darkness.

I'd held her in my arms only a few minutes, and I ached remembering the way I whispered in her ear without staring at her, without committing it all to memory. I ached for the way I'd held her whole lifetime in my arms without knowing it, thinking more about the milk in my breasts than about the light of heaven coming at me in her eyes.

Night after night I cried, sometimes stuffing the sheet in my mouth to stop from screaming. I wondered what was wrong with me, why I didn't want Hogan there to hold and comfort me. But I didn't.

I needed to cry alone and then listen to the sound of not-crying, to feel the way a sorrow fills the room and sucks everything else from it.

If there was one thing I wanted with me on those long nights, it was a baby. A small baby curled up against my skin, lulled to sleep by the rhythm of my heartbeat. I thought about that for two nights, about how it would be to hold a little baby in my arms. I even prayed for it, prayed that somehow I could have a baby next to me, prayed that somehow I could be comforted by something small and very much alive.

Yet in spite of my prayers, I didn't plan ahead. I didn't go out looking for a baby. I just woke up hungry that morning, put a jelly donut in my pocket, and walked and walked like I did every other morning.

It was a foggy day. There was just me and the sound of my feet hitting the street, stopping while I picked up a rock or something that caught my eye.

When I reached the bridge, the fog hung so low that the top of the bridge was swallowed up in haze. It looked like a bridge that went nowhere, and it called out to me. I ate my jelly donut and then I walked right up into the fog. I couldn't see a thing except for my own hands, my own arms, my own feet. It was quiet. There was steamy air all around me, and the fog seemed to have fingers that reached up under my skirt and caressed the tips of my braid, too. It was like being in a cloud, or flying on an airplane with all the windows open.

I was eleven years old the first time I ever flew in a plane. My mama's mother, Grandma Pynch, passed away, and I went to her burial up in Georgia. Daddy didn't go with me. He had a girlfriend named Tammy, who worked with him at the juice factory.

"You should send the girl, it's the only right thing," Tammy told him. She could tie one of those red cherry stems into a knot using her tongue. She could twist anything to sound like it was an idea for the good of others.

"Her mama would want that," Tammy said, though of course she didn't know diddly about my mama.

When I was going to bed in the trailer that night Daddy came into my sleeping place. He didn't come all the way in, not really. Once I was old enough to wear that training bra from Aunt Fay, he never came all the way into my sleeping space.

"Do you want to go?" he asked. I was holding a nightshirt in my hand.

"I guess. I don't know."

"Your Aunt Fay can pick you up right from the airplane," he said. "It would be right, and I mean to do right."

"Okay then."

I recall most clearly how I felt when that plane lifted up in the air. It rose in a sharp angle that pushed me back into my seat, and as we left the ground those fans that keep the air moving in the plane stopped whirling. The lights went out and it got hard to breathe. I looked out the window and saw nothing but white clouds. It took me the good part of a minute to realize we were inside a cloud, where I once believed angels sat looking down on the earth. Of course I'd already learned that clouds are just rainwater waiting to spill out, but still I looked into the cloud and wondered if that was what my mama saw in heaven.

I sat back in my seat and thought maybe that's what it's like to be dead. To rise up without effort. To lay back, feeling my body lifting off the earth, seeing only clouds around me.

I recollected all of this while I was standing on that silver bridge leaving Singing Island, and I thought that maybe sometimes living is harder than dying. Maybe slipping into the water, letting the fog and the sea swallow me up, might be easier. Might be what I wanted after all.

I felt for what was in the pockets of my skirt. That day I had picked up a round rock, a perfect gray circle that fit right into my palm. What was I thinking? Water swallows up people, earth swallows us up, air can swallow us, too. Would I die if I jumped off the bridge, or would I just need to swim?

I held my hand out over the handrail. Opened it. Let the rock fall. It was swallowed right up.

"Hey," I cried, but the fog took that, too. I couldn't hear anything but a foghorn in the distance. I was alone in the world. Me and whatever was in my pockets.

I was aching inside and outside, too, aching with almost more strength than I had before. I needed to put a baby to my breast. I needed it. I tried not to think about it, tried not to think about that big round rock sliding under the water without even a splash. I tried not to think about jumping.

I started dropping things into the water, the pebbles that were in my pockets, smooth pieces of sea-worn glass that were fogged up like the day and would have made great jewels. The bobby pins in my hair, they went over. Everything went into the white air, waiting for a splash that I never heard, waiting for a wind or a sign.

I could jump. I came close to it. I slipped off my soft shoes and felt the concrete under my bare feet. I could jump and be swallowed up or float to the surface, whichever God might choose for me.

Or maybe God would be looking somewhere else, looking out for some girl who prayed even when she didn't desperately need something. Maybe, for whatever reason, God was looking elsewhere and my life would depend on what was below me in the fog, on whether I would sink down or float, on whether or not there were angels in the white steam rising off the water after all.

I dropped every single thing I didn't need. I dropped the napkin from my donut. The key to my room at the Hideaway. I opened up my fanny pack, took out the wallet. I dropped the card from my doctor's office, a card from a warehouse store, a calendar from the man who sold us car insurance. There wasn't any wind to blow back the cards. They floated like feathers, out of sight just below the roadway of the bridge. I even threw pennies over the side, saying, "good-bye, good-bye," every time I let something go. I dropped everything but the bunch of bills that Hogan gave me for the trip, and I didn't cry, not once.

When I was done I felt like I might never cry again. I felt like something had closed up over me, like I was changing into somebody else. I looked at the name and picture on my driver's license. Then I dropped that over, too.

I wasn't scared. I was freeing myself.

My baby was dead. I thought of it like that, something not part of me but just a fact like my name is Lynelle, my baby's dead, my breasts hurt, I just ate a jelly donut, I'm listening for something in the fog and I hear nothing. I'm dropping rocks into the water, I'm emptying my pockets, I'm going to keep on living because I'm afraid that if I hit my head and die that there isn't anything else but the fog, there are no angels in the clouds and no God in heaven to catch me so I'll live. I'll just live.

# CHAPTER 6

## Annie

ANNIE was surprised when she woke Sunday morning to see David dressing in chinos and a button-down shirt.

"Are you going to church?" she asked as a joke.

"Nope," David replied.

"Well, then?" She stretched, feeling the slow luxury of her bare toes rubbing against clean cotton sheets.

"I'm going to check out some of our stores."

"On Sunday?" Her voice rose sharply, and she looked quickly over at the crib. Dylan still lay quietly, his face turned toward her, his cheek pressed against the mattress, eyes closed and mouth half open.

"It's a cloudy day, not a beach day." David nodded toward the window, and Annie followed his gaze through the half-opened blinds and beyond, to a cloudy sky. "Sunday's the best day, anyway. The store managers are usually off, it's a good time to see how the crews operate without the top guns around."

Annie flopped back in bed, feeling a dull disappointment.

"Anyway, aren't you going to that craft fair with your mother?"

Annie nodded again.

"Well then, you don't need me," he said. "I'll be back after lunch."

The craft fair was across the bridge on the mainland, on a wide green lawn adjacent to a church. Nick went along reluctantly, tugging on his seat belt and kicking the back of the seat as Nan turned her car into the parking lot behind a statue of a shepherd extending his arms east and west.

"It's gonna be boring," Nick groaned as the car came to a stop in the gravelly lot.

Annie pushed Dylan's stroller over the bumpy lawn, holding Sophie's hand and trying her best to ignore Nick's sulking and the way his shoulders slumped under the long white T-shirt that clung to his thighs when he walked. The way the word *boring* came out of his mouth sounded like a threat.

"I wanted to go with Dad," Nick moaned.

"Well, you're with me," Annie said, hardly looking at her son. "Please make the best of it."

By eleven-thirty the long rows of canvas booths were crowded with women in white pants and men in sandals, families fresh from church still dressed in their linen best, loud women exclaiming over dried-flower arrangements.

"I'm worried about your father," Nan said. They were standing in front of a stained-glass collection, pastoral meadows and orange-hued sunsets casting geometric colors across their arms and their clothing.

"Of course you are, Mom. We're all worried about Dad."

"I mean now. You know, I'm worried about him being home alone."

"I read through that folder of instructions, Mom." Annie heard her voice heave in annoyance, she didn't even try to disguise it. "It said stress relief is one of the most important aspects of recovery. I think being alone in the house is good for Dad, it'll give him a chance to unwind."

"You sound awfully snippy." Nan adjusted her sunglasses, wide black ovals that cast a gray shadow over her cheeks. "Is something bothering you?"

Annie felt the disconnection, the confusion, the underwater murkiness of her days well up inside of her, clouding her thoughts. Maybe it was weariness. Maybe it was hormones, reversing themselves in afterbirth, or the way young couples in their twenties walked arm-in-arm past Annie in a world of their own. Maybe it was Nick, dragging his large feet in his man-sized sandals across the lawn, or the way David had rushed out before breakfast, not even offering to take one of the kids along.

Whatever it was, Annie felt a stab of ill humor cutting into her day, she felt the hours weighing her down like a physical ache.

"I'm tired, that's all." Tears stung her eyes, a moment of self-pity overtaking her. Annie felt her fingers tighten around Dylan's stroller. "I'm just tired."

"Well, three babies is a lot more than two," Nan said in a low voice, a conspiratorial tone, so the children wouldn't hear. Annie let go of Sophie's hand, and the little girl skipped ahead.

"But Dylan is so easy. I swear, sometimes I almost forget he's there." Annie looked down into Dylan's face. His eyes were open, watching the people moving past him. "It's not Dylan," she said, thinking of the peace that spread over her every time she held him in her arms.

"But it's something else?"

"I don't know." Annie shrugged. "Sometimes I guess I'm just sick of it."

"Sick of what?"

"You know, sick of dishes and laundry and of telling the kids what to do." She ran her hand across the colors of a stained-glass box on the table in front of her as she spoke. The tips of her fingers glowed as she traced the delicate web of colored glass. "I'm tired of breaking up fights and losing things and trying to keep Nick from tumbling into adolescence with that sullen look on his face."

The words spilled out almost without Annie hearing them, a letting go of something she'd held in so long it was welling up inside of her, pressing on her chest. But when she looked up and saw her mother staring into the distance as if she were trying to puzzle out a memory, Annie was sorry to have said so much. This unhappy feeling always passed. Now, with the words spread out in the air between them, flung into the cloudy day that was clearing overhead, she feared the feeling would be there longer, lingering into the afternoon.

Annie tried laughing. She shrugged her shoulders, one hand on Dylan's stroller, the other still trailing across the colors under her fingertips.

"I'm being silly, I guess." She looked at her mother out of the corner of her eye. "I'm just tired, that's all."

"Are you unhappy?" Nan's voice rose just when Annie felt it should fall. "Is that it? Maybe it's postpartum depression. I've read about that. You know, it's a real thing that happens with hormones."

"No, Mom." Annie put two hands on Dylan's stroller. "No, Mom, I'm not unhappy, I'm not depressed," she said. "You're making too much of it. I came here to help you and Dad, not to have you help me. I'm fine, really."

Annie pushed away from the stained glass, past the original watercolors in bamboo frames that stretched from ground to sky, moving toward the stuffed bunnies where Sophie was standing. She pushed the stroller vigorously, calling "Sophie" to the little girl as she moved ahead, calling "Nick" into the crowd of people around them. Nick was standing in front of a small booth and spun around when he heard his mother's voice.

"You okay?" she asked, coming up alongside him. The day was warming up, the air growing sticky, and Annie felt suddenly breathless as she eyed the table he was looking at. It was filled with small gadgets, key chains and pocketknives, fancy corkscrews, letter openers and ornamental wine bottle stoppers.

"Mom?" Nick peered at her with his eyebrows raised, a look

she recognized from the toy store. Expectant. About to ask for something.

"What?" She looked at the display table, casting about for something to lighten the tone between them. "Do you need a new letter opener?"

"No, Mom." He groaned but didn't grin. "I want . . . you know." He gestured with one hand, a simple movement.

"What?" Annie looked at the sharp objects. "You want a knife?"

He nodded eagerly. In his left pocket he had his hand wrapped around twelve dollars saved from his allowance.

"No way." Annie shook her head, she started to turn.

"Please, Mom?"

"No, I'm sorry." She pushed the stroller away from the booth. "I'll buy you a T-shirt, I'll buy you something with a creepy bad guy or the goriest-looking animals you've ever seen. I'll buy you any beach toy under the sun. I'll even buy you one of those giant supersoaker water guns. But I can't let you have a knife. Sorry."

She pushed away from the booth. Nick rolled his eyes, his face dropped back into a sulk.

"Anyone hungry?" Annie asked.

"I'm thirsty," Nick mumbled, mopping a hand across his fore-head, pushing his hair up in the air.

"Come on." She looked at her watch. "It's almost lunchtime. Let's get something to eat."

"I have to go to the bathroom," Sophie said at almost the same time. She crossed her legs and jumped up and down, tugging on Nan's hand.

Only Dylan was quiet, playing with his feet and not seeming to mind the heat or the way Annie had filled a bottle with water and propped it against the side of the stroller in order to keep it in his mouth.

"Look," Annie said to Sophie, "Grandma's going to take you to the bathroom, and I'm going to get Nick a soda."

"I really have to go, Grandma," Sophie whined. Nan looked

down at the little girl, her own startled expression matching Sophie's. "Let's go then," she said.

"We'll meet you right here, Mom," Annie called after them. They were at the edge of the crafts booths, near a tree by the parking lot.

She looked at Nick. He looked a bit flushed. "Do you feel okay, honey?"

"I'm bored, Mom. And I'm hot."

"Look, Nick, why don't you wait under the tree with Dylan?" Annie said, feeling the need for a moment of solitude pressing against her like humidity. "I'm going to run over and get you a soda, and just pick up a quick gift I saw for Grandma. I'll be right back."

She wheeled the stroller across the bumpy lawn, into a shady spot under the elm tree.

"Okay?"

"Sure." Nick leaned against the tree. "Can't you just think about the, you know?"

She looked at him from head to toe—the long baggy shorts, the grown-up haircut—and wondered what she'd been thinking, to let him dress like that. David was right, he was growing up too fast.

"No, you're not getting a knife. I'll get you a grape soda if they have it. And a hot dog, if you're hungry."

"Fine."

"You just stay right here with Dylan," Annie said. She lifted the bottle of water, which had rolled away from Dylan's mouth, and shook a drop onto her arm. It was lukewarm, almost hot. And there was very little left. His cheeks were flushed, but he felt cool enough to her touch, and his eyelids were beginning to droop.

"He's probably going to fall asleep anyway," she told Nick. "He'll be fine. And I'll be right back."

Glancing once over her shoulder before she turned a corner, Annie didn't stop to look at the photographs or gold-sprayed picture frames; she breezed right by hand-painted T-shirts and dried-flower centerpieces, going directly to the booth where the man was selling scented candles in the shapes of seashells.

There she took time only to inhale the soft waxy scent of patchouli, orange blossom, seascape, spring garden. She picked a lavender-scented conch shell for her mother, a peach-scented one for home, and a plain vanilla scallop shell for her friend Liz. Then she dashed to the food stand, buying orange sodas for Nick and Sophie, and a hot dog for each of them.

With the candles wedged under her arm in a brown paper bag, and the food and drinks stacked in her two hands, Annie retraced her steps along the perimeter of the fair, using the high-reaching elm tree as her guide.

# CHAPTER 7

## *Lynelle*

W HEN I walked out of the fog onto the other side of the bridge I felt lighter. I was moving faster.

I turned onto the main road and walked past a hairdresser's and a thrift store with old brown couches in the window. The fog lifted and the stores got nicer as I went along. I passed an art gallery and a couple of restaurants before I got to the craft fair with fancy wind kites blowing out onto the sidewalk and people selling all kinds of stuff. There was pottery, paintings, dried-flower centerpieces, and a man with all different kinds of seashell candles and baskets full of ocean-scented bubble baths.

"The perfect gift for mother or wife, all the ladies love these beauties," the man was saying to anybody who'd listen.

I tried not to see the mothers and children, but they were everywhere. One little girl in a pink sundress even ran over and pointed at my skirt.

"Pretty," she said. It came out *pwitty*, but I knew what she meant and I remembered to smile at her just before I heard a baby crying.

That sound. It was a little lamb sound that turned on my breasts like somebody opened up a spigot. The milk came in strong.

I turned a corner, away from the people and away from the sound of the baby, away from all the mothers with their children looking up at me. I walked behind a booth with a lady selling silver necklaces, and that's when I saw it: a little blue stroller, sitting under a tree.

Just a stroller alone, like a boat left in the water. A blue stroller with a white blanket draped across the top of it. Not four feet away from me. Too close for me to turn away. Alone, like I was.

I got right up next to the stroller and looked inside. There was a baby in there, surrounded by air and light.

I leaned over real slowly, half-expecting someone to come up behind me, but the only thing to touch me were the baby's eyes. A shock of green eyes, wide awake and staring back at me. Cool, deep, pond green eyes. They locked me in.

I reached out to touch him, to touch that place where his gaze began, and suddenly I had him in my arms. Lighter than I expected. Quiet. Pressed against the milk in my chest.

My heart started pounding a drumbeat in my head. If anyone had called out or screamed, I wouldn't have heard it. I didn't see anybody either. The whole world just about fell away soon as I was holding that sweet warm little body in my arms.

I walked directly away from the fair, away from the parking lot and right across the road, right through whatever cars might have been turning or driving by my way. I crossed without looking and certainly without thinking, for I didn't think of anything but the baby pressed up against my chest and me bursting to feed him.

I looked down into his face. His eyes were staring up at me, then past me, to the sky. He had olive-white skin, and the lids of his eyes had tiny blood vessels right on top, almost purple. He looked more like me than even my own girl. He looked like my own child.

# CHAPTER 8

## *Annie*

WALKING back to the stroller, Annie squinted up at the clearing sky, where the sun was sending stubborn yellow streaks through thinning clouds. She was thinking about heading home for the afternoon, wondering if David would be back as promised, when she turned the corner and saw Dylan's stroller standing alone on the shady patch of grass.

"Nick?"

The stroller was empty. She lifted her sunglasses. Her voice flared into a loud cry, a mother's call in the wild. "Nick, where are you?" she shouted.

Annie looked right and left across the grass. Behind her were the white canvas backs of the vendors' booths, in front of her was about fifty yards of faded grass, and beyond that, the parking lot and the church.

"Nick Thompson," Annie shouted again. "Nick Thompson, where are you?"

"Mom?"

Annie whirled around. Nick was behind her, his hands in the pockets of his green shorts. The front of his hair was sweaty and sticking straight up.

"Nick, I told you to stay right here. Where's Dylan? Did Grandma take him?"

Nick's mouth fell open. He dug his hands more deeply into his pockets, balled them into fists. "I don't know."

Hot dogs and sodas spilled onto the ground as Annie ran over to Nick and grabbed him by the shoulders.

"What do you mean, you don't know?" She shoved her face right down into his and saw his sullen expression shatter like glass.

"He was there a minute ago," Nick managed to stammer.

Annie shook his thin body. "What are you talking about? Did you leave him alone here?"

Nick hung his head.

"Look at me." She grabbed his chin and pulled his head up. "Did you leave Dylan alone here?"

"I guess." It was barely a whisper.

"Oh my God." For the rest of her life Annie would remember the way the world went off kilter in that instant, grass tipping overhead, the church steeple plunging into the clouds underfoot, the statue of the shepherd, arms reaching east and west, coming at her like a demon.

Spinning Nick around by the arm and dragging him behind her, Annie stumbled over the food and ran into the nearest row of vendors' booths.

"Did you see a baby? A little boy in a white blanket?" she asked as she pushed through the shoppers, scanning the ground and looking into the arms of everyone she passed.

Annie's head was pounding. Her chest felt empty, then too full, and the lump of fear in her throat made it almost impossible to breathe as she moved through faces and bodies that seemed to weave and fade in front of her, like lights flashing on and off.

"Mom has him, Mom has to have him," she chanted as she ran. The fright was so bad it was a blinding light, then a black mask over her eyes.

"*Look* for him, Nick," she said when she saw Nick was staring at the ground, watching the movement of his own feet. "Damn it, look up and look for your brother."

Annie saw Nan from a distance and waved her hands, a frantic gesture that shuttered across her field of vision.

"What happened?" Nan called, her voice instantly shrill. "What's the matter?"

They came face-to-face. Nan was holding Sophie by the hand. Nick was twisting away from Annie, feeling something sour rising in his throat.

"Dylan's gone." Annie reached for her mother's sleeve. The package of candles under her arm fell onto the ground. "Mom, Dylan's gone. I left him with Nick and now he's not there."

The blank wall of sky stared down at them unblinking and nearly blue now. Annie grabbed Nick by both wrists and shook him.

"What did you do?" she cried. "You walked away from him? How could you do that? What were you thinking?"

# CHAPTER 9

*~*

# $\mathcal{L}ynelle$

THERE is no cure for dreaming and praying but waking up and walking through the dream to find out where it leads.

I walked with that baby like I was walking through a dream until the silver bridge came up in front of me, the long stretch of it shining in the full sun of late morning. The fog was gone. I was holding a baby that would surely be hungry soon, would need clean diapers and a place to lay down.

My heart had stopped thumping and the world came back at me. I didn't think yet about what I'd done, but I recall noticing cars all around me, horns beeping, a siren wailing behind me, and a bus, the Number 22 bus, pulling right to a stop in front of me.

The bus doors opened and the driver looked down at me from under the brim of his hat. I jiggled the baby over to one shoulder, felt in my fanny pack for some money, stepped up, and let the doors close behind me.

The bus was cold with air-conditioning, and I worried the baby wouldn't be warm enough. He was dressed for summer in blue shorts with the dimpled skin of his knees poking out. His legs were the sweetest, plumpest, happiest things I'd seen in a very long time. I wanted to gobble up those knees, to put their

chubby happiness inside me, to protect them and warm them. Then the bus jerked back on its way and the bus driver said, "Twenty more cents," without looking at me.

I was relieved to find two dimes in the bottom of my fanny pack. I dropped them into the box, and walked down the aisle until I came to a seat with empty places all around it. I sat down and pressed that baby tight against me. My breasts were just about weeping warm milk all over his face.

I unbuttoned my blouse and pressed myself against his mouth. He turned to me and opened up, latched on, drank me in. He must have tasted longing and loss in that milk, he must have tasted the salt water of my tears splashing on him like rain, but he drank anyway, drank and drank until he had to pull back for air.

Then he looked at me. Looked right at my own eyes. Squirmed. Opened his mouth and made a sound. A coo.

I smiled at him. Laughed through my tears. I blew air onto his face and felt the humming in my chest grow into a song just looking at him, his cheek resting against my breast, his little fingers wrapping around one of my own.

I wasn't thinking about what I'd done. Instead of thinking right from wrong, I was filling my head with a list of things I needed to take care of a baby: onesies, sleepers, diapers, wipes, and a way to carry him. I was thinking like crazy when I looked up to see the bus driver talking right at me. Looking at me in his big mirror, and scratching his head with the edge of his hat.

"Two more stops to the end of the line," he said, and it seemed like he'd said it before.

I looked around. Me and the baby were the last ones on the bus.

"I'm the next stop," I said. The bus slowed down. The side street sign said Alabama Road. It didn't look like too bad of a place.

"Alabama, that's me."

I smiled at the bus driver as I walked by, holding that baby tight as I dared. Two steps down, and I was on the ground. The bus door didn't close behind me right away.

"Thank you kindly," I called, remembering my manners. I thought I could feel the driver staring at me, but I didn't look back. I walked up to the nearest store window like I had somewhere to go, and stared at nothing until I felt the whoosh and hot wind of the bus moving away.

It took me a minute to see that I was standing right in front of a spirit shop. Statues of Mother Mary, Joseph, and the Christ child lined up in all sizes, some with white skin and some with brown. There was a statue of a fat old Chinaman with his feet folded under him, and about a dozen little black stick figures lined up like something for witch magic.

Hanging right over all of them was a wooden sign with letters painted white on top of light blue. It said, SOMETIMES THE SPIRIT FINDS YOU, AND SOMETIMES YOU HAVE TO FIND THE SPIRIT. Soon as I read those words, I was moved.

"That's just it," I said to the baby. He was looking right into my face. His eyes had been green when I found him, but right then they were blue like the sky. I squeezed him, kissed him on the cheek.

"I prayed for you," I said, "I guess that's what it means when they say sometimes you have to find the spirit."

I liked it better than anything I'd been reading in the Bible. The words on that sign were all I needed to believe I was on a path intended, and that I had a right to hold that baby in my arms. He was the answer to my sadness and my prayers.

Just up the road was one of those stores that sells a bit of this, some of that. There were metal bars across the front window, and the girl behind the counter was painting her fingernails while she watched an itty-bitty red television set next to the cash register.

She looked at me for just a second, then went right back to her show.

I picked out what I needed and put it on the counter. I still had at least two hundred dollars tucked away in my fanny pack. I regretted throwing my credit cards over the bridge, but then again I was glad I had nothing with my name on it. I wasn't Lynelle with no mama and no baby anymore. I was nobody, and I was anybody. With my charcoal eyes and dark hair, I was just another mother, out walking with her baby in the Spanish part of town. I was invisible. The girl at the register hardly even looked at me.

I slipped a candy bar and a pack of gum into the pockets of my skirt while I was waiting.

When I was a teenager I went through a time of stealing things from stores. To be good at shoplifting it helps if you're easy to overlook, which I was. I was quiet, just the right size for my age, of average height, with coloring only a little darker than other Florida white girls. I wore my hair long and neat, and was usually alone when I went into the shiny new drugstore at the edge of the town of Frostproof, where I lived with Daddy and his second wife, Stevie.

Until I started stealing I just about never did anything wrong. It was Stevie who drove me to it. She wore all kinds of jewelry and makeup, and hid everything away when she wasn't home. Used a key to lock her jewelry box and a tiny silver lock on her closet. Said it was in case of robbery, and my daddy just let her do it. It took him two years to see past her bleached blond hair and know what a nasty one she was. Until he did, Stevie made me feel dark and dirty and in need of things like Maybelline and Cover Girl and Sun-In hair lightener, which put orange streaks in my hair so that I had to wear a hat for almost all of eighth grade.

The year I was stealing things I got more and more bold, smiling at store clerks while I stuck Life Savers up my sleeve, looking over my shoulder in the mirror of one powder compact while I stuck another one into my pocket. I filled a big old sanitary napkin box in the back of my bedroom closet full of stolen stuff, and got away with it until the pipes in the wall sprung a leak.

The leak was right in my closet. It sprung on a Saturday afternoon while I was out on a so-called shopping trip, and my daddy emptied everything from the closet so he could take a look at the pipes.

What a shock his face must have had when my carton of girl things split open and out came piles of eye shadows and Almay skin stuff and rhinestone jewelry with the price tags still on them. I didn't even like rhinestones, I just liked to hold them in my hands.

Daddy was waiting for me when I got home. "What the hell are you doing, Lynelle?"

He kept pushing back his brown hair and biting on the filter of his Marlboro. My heart was pounding. I was always so good, I wasn't used to getting caught at something.

"You selling this stuff? Giving it to your friends?"

I started to cry. In my knapsack I had a stash of new stuff, and I was terrified he'd find it.

"Speak up, girl. Turn off that faucet and speak up."

By the time I got out the words—"I stole it"—I was so ashamed that the thrill of taking each thing became something to choke on.

"You know right from wrong," Daddy said. "We don't steal things. We're not trash."

I dug the toe of my sandal into a wet spot on the floor of my room and cried some more.

"She's faking it," Stevie said from behind my back. I looked up and saw my daddy's face go real hard.

"You mind your business," he said through his teeth, in a low and scary voice. Stevie blew air out of her lips, but she said no more.

Daddy made me put everything into two brown paper bags. We drove to the Goodwill box behind the Catholic church, dumped everything in, and I didn't steal anything, ever again, until I got to Florida.


Me and the baby came out of the store at the hottest part of the day. The sun was glaring, and my arms were straining with everything I had to carry.

"Hi, baby boy," I said. It was so good to have a small somebody to hear the sound of my voice, somebody worth making it dip and sing for. I talked to him while I put down my packages and balanced him on my hip.

"What's your name, baby? Is it Andy or Billy, is it Charlie or Pete?"

I'd bought a new blue sheet in that store, and right there on the sidewalk I looped it around my waist, tied it in a square knot over my shoulder, and slipped the baby inside. Fitted just the way I wanted, and ready for walking. We were going to be moving. I didn't know where we were going yet, but I knew we'd be moving.

"Are you Rick or Sam or Danny?"

He pressed against me with his arms going around my ribs and his face looking up between my breasts. A darling round face, bright eyes turned blue as the sky on that afternoon.

"I'm so glad you're with me."

He started to squirm, drumming his little feet against my belly.

"What is it, baby? What do you need?"

The boy reached up and tugged on my shirt, sending a tingle right through me, a tingle that filled up my breasts and almost turned a giggle in my throat. My body was working the way it should. I let the giggle go.

"You're hungry again!" I nearly shouted with that laugh, and believe me when I say that it turned my heart a lighter color. I went from black and blue to lavender with that giggle. From midnight to dawn.

I looked around for someplace where I might sit to feed him.

The sidewalk was growing weeds between the cracks. There was a smashed soda bottle on the ground, old garbage all over the place, and three men in long pants talking together across the street.

The boy started to whimper. My chest, I knew when it was getting ready to leak.

"Okay, baby, okay, I'll find us a place."

I turned off the main street onto a side road, walking past crumbling houses with windows wide open without screens or anything. Wild boys ran in the yards, little girls with their toenails polished bright red swung their dirty feet back and forth off the small stoops.

"Don't worry, little one, I'm gonna take care of you, you were meant for me," I said to the baby, walking, walking, until I saw an open lot up ahead, filled with old tires.

"Heaven-sent, that's what you are, I should call you Heaven, or Angel."

I sat myself down onto a hot black tire, whispering to him, singing him little pieces of song, lifting up my shirt, and putting my swollenness into his mouth.

"There you go, angel, there you go."

What was around me was no mind. I didn't care. Everything fell away. Something shot through me, soon as he started sucking. Like there was peace and sleep and soothing right in the milk I made. I looked at his face, and I just kept saying in a low voice, "Angel, you're my angel."

I liked the way it sounded. I closed my eyes and whispered myself into a sweet little reverie, and when he was finished eating I just sat letting the sun soak down on us, until I felt someone standing there. I looked up to see a girl with a belly full of baby staring down at me, smiling sort of funny. I smiled back.

"Angel, that your baby's name?"

I nodded. It seemed right. The spirit that found me, what else is that but an angel? In my head I got a picture of a heaven full of angels, waiting for mamas who need them.

"This one here"—she looked down at her belly—"this one here I'm gonna name Destiny. I already got me a girl named Summer at home."

"What if it's a boy?"

"Ha," she laughed. "None of us have boys. My mother, she has six girls. And I got five nieces. No brothers. No nephews. But you should see my Summer, she run around like she may as well be a boy."

She talked like I knew what she meant. She talked to me like one mother to another.

"Angel, I like that name."

She tested out a tire with her foot, then lowered herself real slow, holding out her hands for balance.

"Whew." She laughed when she sat down. She had brown slippers and blue socks on her feet, and a plain white T-shirt stretched over her belly. "I'm a sight, don't I know it."

The baby was still in my arms. We both looked down at his face.

"I ain't seen you around here before," said the girl.

"No, I come from south a ways." I flattened myself out inside, getting ready to tell lies.

"I'm going to my mama's, up north," I said. "She's the one person in the world I want to see right now."

At least that part was true. The person I wanted to see more than anyone else was my mama, standing in the kitchen of our house, or sitting on the edge of the bathtub rinsing shampoo out of my hair. Helping me care for my baby.

"My mother kicked me out on my ass when I come home with Summer," the girl said. "She say, 'You got into trouble, now you make yourself a boat that'll float in shit.'"

The girl laughed. She had a gold tooth in the back of her mouth. I wondered how a poor girl like her got a gold tooth.

"She got a way with words, my mother does."

"Well my mama, I don't even know if she'll be there," I said.

Of course I didn't think I would really find her there, in the flesh. But maybe in the spirit. Maybe the spirit might come to me there.

"You tell her you're coming?"

"No. She doesn't have a phone."

"Oh yeah. I know about that. Damn phone company." She kind of spit-laughed.

"She know you got the baby?"

"Oh yeah, she knows."

"She like the daddy?"

"I guess."

"Well then, she be happy to see you," the girl said. "My mother, she don't like Summer's daddy. But then, I don't like him no more either." She patted her belly. "Now this baby here, she got a nice daddy."

I thought of Hogan for a minute, but it spoiled the way I felt and so I pushed him from my mind. Two little boys playing in the tires ran by, hardly giving us a look.

"How far you going?"

"Just to Gainesville. A town outside Gainesville."

"You getting the bus?" She stuck out her chin, pointing toward the main road.

"Yeah," I said. My mind was made up, just like that. It didn't even seem crazy, no crazier than anything else that had happened to me so far.

I never was much for pretending Mama was alive. But with that baby in my arms, it didn't seem so crazy to try to walk backwards in my life. To try and pick up the pieces one at a time, going backwards like a video on rewind, back to the beginning. Back to Flaglerton.

"Well, I best be going to see about my Summer," the girl said to me. She looked at the baby. "He's happy."

"Yeah, he is. I best be going, too."

We stood up slow as two old ladies, and laughed doing it. Neither one of us could help the other.

"Which way is the bus station, again?"

She told me the way.

"Go past the new courthouse and turn left toward the water," she said. "You can't miss it."

"Bus to Gainesville runs at two o'clock," she added. "I got a sister there, that's why I know."

"Y'all take care now," I said.

"You too. And that baby. Angel."

We waved good-bye. She shuffled off. I set out toward the bus station with a new intention inside me.

# CHAPTER 10

## *Annie*

B ENT at the knees, fists jammed into the pit of her stomach in a pained and whispered prayer, Annie unfolded herself as a silver sedan and a police squad car skidded to a stop in the parking lot. Two men in tan pants got out of the sedan without closing the doors behind them. The driver was chubby and balding, wearing a blue blazer. The other had big forearms sticking out of a short-sleeved shirt, and slick hair that looked wet.

Annie ran toward the cars on wobbly legs, moving headlong through the circle of onlookers that parted to let her pass.

*My baby is gone, my baby is gone.* She heard the words pulsing inside her but wasn't sure if her lips were moving, wasn't sure if the sounds were inside her mind or in the airwaves around her.

"Here we are." Annie's hand flailed overhead, her voice shrieked along with Nan's. "Over here."

She'd been waiting for the police the way a drowning person prays for a life raft, but when she saw the slow gait of their walk, the way the men searched the scene with their eyes, she knew their arrival would not save the day. Annie balled her fingers into a fist, rammed it against her bottom teeth, and bit down.

The chubby policeman closed the space between them.

"Lieutenant John Herrara," he said, fishing something out of his jacket pocket and flashing a badge at her. "You're the mother?"

Annie nodded. No one had yet said, "Don't panic," and although the thought had passed through Annie's mind, she could see that there was every reason to panic. She felt it in the nerves of her arms, in the very thickness of the air passing through her windpipe, in the empty space in the stroller that still had the small imprint of Dylan's body pressed against the blanket.

"Who saw the baby last?" Herrara asked.

Annie pointed at Nick. There were spots in front of her eyes, her voice came in a breathless rush.

"My son. I already asked him, he didn't see anything. He says he didn't talk to anybody."

The cops followed the point of her finger and stared right into Nick's eyes.

Nick looked down at the ground and pushed his back into the telephone pole behind him. His hands were shaking, even shoved into his pockets they were trembling. There were people standing around in a circle, and Nick felt everyone looking at him.

"Nick, I'm Lieutenant Herrara." The cop was wearing brown loafers. Nick stared at them. "I need to get some information from you, buddy. Do you know what happened to your brother?"

Nick nodded. He hated when men called him buddy.

"Why don't you tell me, then. I mean, try to tell me in your own words what happened to him."

Nick cleared his throat before answering. He kept his eyes on the cop's brown shoes.

"He disappeared."

"That's right." Herrara nodded. He had two teenage girls of his own, and he knew how to talk to kids without pushing them. "It looks like somebody took your brother. My job is to find him. In order to find him, I have to find out who took him."

Nick moved away from the guy just a little bit. He tried to do it without lifting his feet, but his back was pressed up against the telephone pole.

"That's where I need your help," Herrara said. "Did you see anybody near the baby? Did anybody talk to you? Did anybody approach or say—"

A hand grabbed the top of Nick's hair and yanked up his head. His mother's face was inches away from his own, her eyes bulging and scary.

"Answer him, Nick." The spit of Annie's words stuck to Nick's skin. "I want you to answer him, I want you to answer him."

When Nick's jaws didn't open, Annie's fingers tightened. She shook his head. *Thump.* It knocked into the telephone pole.

"Answer him, damn it," Annie cried. "Tell him what you saw."

*Thump.* Nick's head banged against the pole again. Tears sprang up in his eyes and he clenched his teeth together to bite back a howl.

"Annie," Nan called a warning cry that didn't reach her daughter's ears. She pulled Sophie toward her, turning the girl's face away from what was happening.

"Mrs. Thompson." Herrara wrapped his wide fingers around Annie's wrist and applied a small bit of pressure.

"He was with him, he was supposed to stay with the stroller," Annie wailed.

"Mrs. Thompson, I'm sure Nick is as upset as you are. Let's give him some space here, okay?"

Herrara used his fingers to pry Annie's hand loose. He waved behind him, and Officer Carlos Molina came up and put a hand on Annie's arm.

"Who are you?" she demanded, looking up at the rookie's dark brown skin, his mustache. "Get your hands off me, I need to find my son."

"That's what we're going to do, ma'am. One thing at a time," the rookie said, silencing her with words she couldn't remember later, soothing her with something in his eyes.

Nick was left staring up at the patch of blue sky next to Her-

rara's head, his eyes watering and the splintery wood of the telephone pole pressing into his scalp.

The ride to the police station was a blur of wailing sirens and
scattering traffic. Annie and Nan rode shoulder-to-shoulder in
the back of the silver car, the kids on either side of them, the bitter taste of fear drying the insides of their mouths.

A red light spun on the dashboard. Annie dropped her head
down onto her chest, pulled at her hair.

"Holy shit," she said under her breath. "Holy shit, holy shit,
holy shit," she chanted into her lap.

"The children," Nan said to her daughter. "You're scaring
them."

Annie looked up, blinking at the light dancing on Nick's face.
The boy looked at her, and tears slid down his face.

"I'm sorry, Mom." Nick's bottom lip was turned out, trembling. "I'm sorry."

"Oh, Nicky." Annie wrung her hands together. "Didn't I
ask you to watch him?" she wailed. Nick's head moved in a
nod, the tears splashed dark spots onto the front of his shirt.
He'd looked so old before, so sullen and mature. Now he
looked like a child, a frightened child. Tears fell across
Annie's cheeks, too.

"I told you to watch him, Nick, didn't I?" she said again, this
time in a whisper. "I shouldn't have asked you, I shouldn't have
thought you were old enough."

"It's my fault." Nick put his fingers in his mouth and bit down
on the ends; he could barely keep himself from doubling over
with sobs.

"It's nobody's fault," Nan said, her voice coming to Annie and
Nick from a distance. She slid one arm around Annie, stretched
her fingers to stroke Nick's rounded shoulders.

"It's not your fault, Mommy," Sophie said, in a louder
voice. "It's nobody's fault. Maybe Dylan learned to walk and

walked away. Do you think maybe that's what happened, Mommy?"

They followed Herrara through a rear door of the Palm Beach Police Headquarters, entering a long hallway dotted with small wooden doors and glass windows looking inward toward each other. Phones rang in the distance, but the hall was empty.

"Mommy, I'm scared," Sophie cried. She clutched at Nan's hand, her face pale and twisted.

"I'm sorry, honey, I know you're scared." Annie bent to put her arms around Sophie. "I'm scared, too. But the police will make it all better. The police will find Dylan for us."

Annie looked up and saw Herrara watching them with no expression on his face.

"Is there someplace my mother can take the kids?"

"I need your son to come with us," Herrara said, "the little girl and your mother, they can go upstairs with Officer Molina."

"I'll be right here, Sophie," Annie said as she watched the cop lead them away. She reached for Nick's hand, but the lieutenant stepped an inch between them.

"Nick's going with Detective Romalho," Herrara said. "We'll be right across the hall in my office."

Annie looked at him blankly.

"We find people remember things better when they're not distracted," Herrara said, putting a hand on her arm.

"Mom." Nick sniffled. "Mom, please."

She wanted to comfort him, knew he was scared. But she was scared, too.

"We have to do what the police tell us to," she said as the detective led Nick into a small office. "I'll be right across the hall."

In Herrara's office Annie sat down, putting her purse with diapers and wipies at her feet. Black spots dancing again in front of her eyes. Panic numbing her fingertips.

"Your husband's on his way," Herrara said. He was leaning against the front of his desk, arms crossed over his chest.

"Oh." Annie pressed her palms against the sides of her face. "Was he home? Did you reach him at home?"

"I didn't make the call. I just know he's on the way, Mrs. Thompson." Herrara put a hand out toward her. There was hair on the backs of his knuckles, she noticed. The hands of a stranger. Hands like the ones that might be holding Dylan right at that moment.

"May I call you Anna?"

"Annie. Everybody calls me Annie."

"Okay, Annie, I need you to answer some questions," the lieutenant said gently. "They might not be easy questions. But I have to ask them."

"Go ahead," she said. "I'll tell you anything you want to know, whatever you need to find my baby."

"Let's start with the reason you're in Florida."

Annie told him about her father's stroke, about coming down to help take care of him. She felt her knees trembling as the cop took careful notes, questioned her slowly.

"Okay," he said at last, watching Annie shred her fingernails between her teeth. "How about the last twenty-four hours? Tell me as much as you can remember, beginning with noon yesterday."

With her eyes closed, her heart pounding, and the picture of Dylan asleep in his crib floating across her vision like a mirage, Annie talked about the pool and the beach, the tuna sandwiches, the trip to the drugstore for suntan lotion and the sunburn on the backs of Sophie's legs.

"Everybody went to bed early last night," she told him, and as she said it Annie remembered the sound she'd heard through the window. The cry, like children moaning. It sent a chill through her, and she shivered.

"You're going to find him, aren't you?" she asked. It was a plea. Annie's hands were folded together as if in prayer, and there was blood at the edges of her fingernails.

Herrara's face twisted into a frown. "I wish I could say yes, but I just don't know. I can tell you that typically a missing child turns up with a family member."

There was a moment of silence as they looked at each other. Annie did her best to meet the lieutenant's eyes, seeing the steadiness of his gaze, the way he held himself perfectly still. Then gently, as if he were slipping the question into her drink like a sedative, he asked, "Have you left your children alone before?"

Annie felt the sting of his words. She winced.

"I didn't leave them alone," she said, "I left them together." She rolled her thumb against her teeth, felt the salty taste of blood on her tongue.

"And how old is Nick?"

"Nine. He's nine. I already told you that at the fair."

"Your son is nine years old. Is he a truthful boy, generally?"

Everyone had seen her grab Nick by the hair, Annie thought. She was probably some kind of a suspect.

"He's a good boy," she stammered. She tried to think clearly. Did Nick lie? Was he honest and forthcoming? "He's my first."

"Your first?"

"My firstborn. My first baby. I used to sing to him every night."

Herrara nodded, encouraging her to go on.

"I used to sing to him every night. I thought it would make him a gentle person." Tears came up again, they spilled over onto her cheeks. She wrapped her arms around herself and rocked in the chair, bent her knees toward her chest.

"And is he?"

"Gentle? Yes." Annie remembered the feel of his hair in her fist. She'd seen him flinch when she grabbed him. Seen the set of his jaw. "He's a boy. He has his moments. But he's a good boy."

"What grade is your son in now, Annie?"

"Third."

"Is he a good student?"

"Yes. Why? Why are you asking me all these things about

Nick?" Annie twisted in her chair and stood to look across the hall through the window in Herrara's office, but all she could see was a blank glass.

"This isn't Nick's fault, you know," she said, feeling a fierce loyalty for her son flare up. "It's my fault. It's my fault."

"My purpose here isn't to find fault. My only goal right now is to find your son. Nick was the last one with Dylan, right? That's why we're talking about him."

The lieutenant's voice went from gentle to firm, and Annie jabbed her fingers into the flesh of her arms. She nodded. If she'd thought getting down on her knees and begging would have done any good, Annie would have done it.

"Okay," she said. "Anything to find Dylan. Just find him, please, please find him."

"Please don't take offense," Herrara said. "I'm trying to understand your family in the shortest amount of time possible. Just try to imagine if Nick could have done something to your son, maybe as a practical joke, maybe accidentally."

"Nick couldn't have hurt Dylan." Her shoulders twitched as a new wave of fear washed over her. "Anyway, what makes you think he's hurt? Do you know he's hurt? Is there something you aren't telling me?"

"No." Herrara studied Annie. "All I know is what you know."

"I don't know anything," she cried. "He was there one minute, and gone the next. That's all I know."

David was pale and drawn when he stepped into Herrara's office, his feet slipped into moccasins, his eyes bright blue behind his glasses.

"Christ, Annie, what's going on?"

"David." She stood to put her arms around him, and he grabbed her elbows, held her at arm's distance to look down into her face.

"I was stupid," she cried, the pain in her chest a searing ache now, her heart racing, her skin burning and tingling. She struggled for breath, but her lungs wouldn't open. "I'm sorry. I was stupid. I wasn't thinking."

"What happened? Tell me what happened."

She couldn't look at him. She couldn't breathe.

"I left Dylan with Nick. I told Nick to stay with him." Her voice came through a tiny opening in her throat, and it was closing up, she was struggling for air.

"Why did you do that?"

"I don't know." She walked to the edge of the office, looked into the hallway where the air was cooler, and sucked in a breath. "I didn't think he'd walk away. I thought he'd stay there. I was only gone a few minutes."

"A few minutes too long," David said, almost under his breath, just short of reproach. But his words wounded Annie.

"Where's your mom and the kids?"

Annie stuck out her chin, indicating the room across the hall.

"Mom's upstairs with Sophie," she answered. "Nicky's across the hall."

"He was the last one to see Dylan?"

"He's so upset, David. I'm frightened."

"We're all frightened, Annie." His voice dropped, it sent a shiver through her. He was on his moral high ground, looking down at her. Annie felt herself shrivel.

"We're all frightened, but that's not going to get us anywhere. It's remembering what happened, step by step. It's a plan of action"—at this he looked at the lieutenant—"isn't it?"

Herrara nodded, studying David carefully. "Your son's across the hall with one of our detectives," was all the lieutenant said.

Moving Annie out of the way with a hand on the small of her back, David crossed the hall.

"David, please," Annie called after him weakly. "He's frightened. Don't frighten him any more."

Striding into Romalho's office, David stepped in front of Nick and knelt down so his face was eye level with the boy's.

"You were the last one to see him, Nick," David said in a level voice. "That makes you the most important person in the world right now. You're the one who has the clue, the clue that's going to help us get Dylan back."

Nick looked at his father with blank eyes, but no words came to him.

"Did you see anything?" The volume of David's voice dropped into a modulated intensity that Nick recognized as anger. "Tell me, Nick, did you see anyone suspicious? Anything?"

Detective Romalho stood up and moved around the desk.

Annie stepped into the doorway. She heard the heights of David's voice falling, crashing. David was scared, she realized with a shudder, and with that realization her own terror intensified.

"Think, Nick," David was repeating, rocking back and forth on the balls of his feet as his legs tired of squatting. "There must be something you're forgetting."

Nick blinked, his eyes filled with tears.

"Honey." Annie put a hand on David's arm, she could feel the current of his emotion like a charge up her limb. "David, honey," she said again, gently.

David let go of Nick's arms and stood to face her.

"Don't say 'honey' to me." There was rage in his voice and it struck against her, it pushed her back against the wall of the small office. "You left the house with our son this morning, and you're coming home without him. Jesus Christ, Annie, don't say 'honey' to me."


"What's your wife like, generally?" Herrara asked David when they were alone in his office.

"She's levelheaded most of the time. Takes on too much, you know, always doing twenty things at a time, but she's never done anything like this. Jesus." David clawed at his hair with his hands, pushing it away from his face. He felt the very ground under him was shifting.

"What do you think happened here?" was all he could manage to ask.

"I'm not sure what happened," Herrara answered him. "That's why I have so many questions."

David nodded, feeling the fury mounting in him like nausea. Fury at Annie, fury at his helplessness at this critical moment. Feeling he might throw up at any second, David clamped his lips together.

"Has your wife been troubled lately, under too much pressure?" Herrara kept his voice neutral, a tone he'd perfected over the years. "Forgetful or angry, depressed maybe, anything like that?"

"I don't know." David stood. Annie and Nick were in the office across the hall looking at mug shots on the off chance they'd recognize someone from the craft fair. "Maybe three really was too much for her," he said.

"What's that?"

"Three, you know, the third baby. Dylan was something of a surprise, and Annie was worried it would be too much for her. I guess it was."

David could see Annie staring blankly at the book of mug shots. Nick was slumped in a chair next to her, holding a dirty fist against his cheek.

"You're upset, Mr. Thompson, that's understandable," Herrara said. He appraised David, looking for nervous tics or the stiff-backed posture of a liar.

"Of course I'm upset. I don't even know what to do first, I feel like I should be doing something. Anything, you know, maybe driving around the city looking for him." David turned his face to Herrara, and the lieutenant saw his fear.

"First, you need to focus as best you can. Everybody in your family needs to work on staying calm and focused, so you can help us."

"Help you how?"

"While we're out there on the street, you can get us started with names, lists, people, places. Anybody and everybody in your life who could want to cause you harm, I need to know about them."

David was still standing. He paced the small length of Herrara's office, hands working the air.

"Did my wife tell you what she does for a living?"

Herrara nodded, silent. David rubbed a hand across his eyes.

"She works with battered women, helps them get away from their husbands. How many pissed-off men do you think are out there with a grudge against my wife?"

Herrara saw the clench of David's fists, the tight set of his lips.

"Could be something," the cop agreed. "But don't overlook those people closer to home, either. Disillusioned siblings, angry in-laws, stepparents, lovers. Those things."

David looked at Herrara. "I don't like what you're suggesting," he said.

"I don't like it either, I can tell you that. But right now my primary concern is your son's whereabouts and safety, and I'll do everything I can to find him."

"You'll get your list of names," David said. "You'll get everything and anything you need from us, I can assure you."

Herrara nodded.

"We called in a doctor, he's going to check out your wife and offer her a sedative. It can be helpful at a time like this," the lieutenant said. "How about you? You look a little pale."

David shook his head, waved his hand away. "Just a little nausea." He watched through the glass window as a woman cop leaned over Annie and said something. Annie nodded. She began to rise.

"This is a nightmare," David said.

"It's a nightmare all right," Herrara echoed him. "And we need to work together to get through it."


In a private cubicle on the second floor of the police station, Annie accepted a sedative injection. It was the next best thing to dying as far as she could tell.

"If you're a nursing mother, I'd also recommend a lactation

suppressant," the doctor said. He looked at his watch as he prepared the injection.

"What happens if—I mean when—what happens when I want to nurse again?"

- "There shouldn't be a problem," the doctor said.

On the other side of the partition walls Annie heard phones ringing, and someone yelling for a roadblock up north. The doctor wiped her arm with a cold, wet cotton ball.

"This will make you relaxed, but not confused or groggy," he said.

"I don't want to be groggy," Annie said as the needle cut into the skin, but the truth was that she wanted to hold her head underwater until Dylan came home, or take a knife and stab the pain from the middle of her chest.

In the front seat of Herrara's silver sedan on the way back to Sparkling Waters, David's mind spun and flashed with colors and fear, caution yellow, red for danger. He'd been raised to believe all things have their cause and effect, their moral dimension and consequence, and as he cast about in his mind for an explanation, he turned a spotlight on these questions: *Why hadn't he been there to watch over his son? Why had Annie been so careless? Why had Nick walked away? Who would have taken Dylan and why?*

Behind him Annie sat in the backseat chewing her fingernails, while Nick wept silently, catching his tears in the cup of his bottom lip. Nan sat between them holding Sophie on her lap, nervously braiding the little girl's long ponytails.

They were the wounded, the sticky dampness of their legs holding them together like Band-Aids, the thump of their hearts loud in their throats. If they moved, if one of them shifted away as Nick did when Nan tried to reach for him, the others pressed more firmly together. Even Sophie slumped her head on her grandmother's shoulder and wrapped her hair round and round her wrist, kicking one foot lightly against the front seat until her grandmother pressed it still.

"Maybe Dylan's playing a trick on us," the little girl said as the car turned off the highway and Palmetto Bridge spread before them. "Maybe when we get back to Grandma's house he'll be there waiting for us."

"I don't think so," Annie said without turning.

As the car rolled over the metal grates at the center of the drawbridge, Annie shut her eyes and saw her son's small body floating alone through space, blue sky around him, clouds blanketing his belly. He was reaching out his arms, reaching for her. He was crying, his face twisting. He was afraid.

"Oh, Dylan." Annie reached out her own arms, her voice a gruff whisper. "Oh God," she said as her fingers hit the back of the front seat. "Oh God, my baby's lost somewhere, he's out there, God, oh, Dylan, I'm sorry."

Nan put her hand on Annie's back and patted her, but there was no comfort in her mother's touch.


At the condo Annie ran up to her father, caught his hand in hers, pressed it against her cheek.

"There are some cops here already," Joe said.

She peered over his shoulder. Inside, men in plain clothes were setting up a telephone tap. There were black boxes and wires stretched across the kitchen counter, their dark shapes waving like flags in Annie's mind, expanding and shrinking as she tried to hear the technical explanation Herrara offered for each piece of equipment.

"We can listen to any calls you receive," he said, moving around the condo as if it was a public forum and not a place for their private grief. "The only thing you have to remember is to let the phone ring three times, so our device is activated."

"I can't just wait," Annie said. She moved around the kitchen, stacking up the styrofoam cups and tossing them in the garbage, running her fingers along the thick black wires. Her hands felt foreign to her, fake limbs moving without her will.

"I want to do something. I'm not just going to stand here, I'm going to do something, I'm going to do something."

She opened kitchen cabinets, shut drawers, picked up envelopes her mother had piled in a corner next to the refrigerator and shuffled them, folded the *Palm Beach Post* into a small square, rearranged the salt and pepper shakers next to the toaster. She didn't even see what was in front of her as she moved.

"I have to do something, Lieutenant," she said, her voice urgent and not her own, her voice a plea and a cry at once. "Tell me what to do and I'll do it."

"Annie," David said. "Sit down."

Annie flinched at the hard edge in him. He was standing next to Herrara, the two of them looking at her as if she were about to fling something through the air. She picked up the newspaper and slapped it down again. "What should I be doing?" she asked.

David sucked in a long breath. He pushed at the front of his hair in an angry, mowing gesture and looked at Annie with an eye that seemed to pass right through her.

"We should be doing whatever the cops tell us to do," David said, turning to Herrara, trying to take stock and control of the chaos around him. "What are you doing, anyway? And what can we do to help right now?"

Herrara resisted the impulse to crush the empty soda can in his hand. He looked into David's blue eyes, bright with loosely corked fear. "We're doing everything we can to find your son," Herrara said. "We've got emergency manpower out there watching the roads and airports, and they'll stay out there all night if they have to."

"What about TV? Don't you want to put Dylan's picture on the news?" David handed him a recent picture of Dylan, one that Nan had put in a silver frame.

Herrara took the photo. It looked like any one of a thousand babies.

"I'll have it faxed to all the departments around the state. Tomorrow, if we're still status quo, you and your wife can make an appeal on television and radio for your son to be returned."

"We'll do whatever we have to do," David said.

Annie leaned against the kitchen wall, feeling woozy and far away from her own words. The bruised faces of women from the clinic popped unbidden into her mind, the bone white images of victims mesmerized by the microphones pushed in front of them.

"We'll do whatever we need to do," David said again.

Herrara dreaded the crank calls that media brought, but the truth was they didn't have a thing to go on, and with every passing hour the chance Dylan would be found by nightfall grew dimmer. Once the sun set it was easy for people, whole groups of people, to vanish in Florida. There were waterways, back roads, swamps, Indian lands he couldn't get onto without a special permit. There was no way to watch the whole coastline.

"You've got nothing," David said to the cop. "Nothing at all. You haven't got a clue, do you?"

The lieutenant's instincts were to dislike David. He was thin, and thought he was smarter than everybody else. But hell, the guy was going through an ordeal, one hell of a crappy ordeal.

"I'm not going to lie to you, David, it's not an optimal situation. But we're just starting our search, and we'll stay with it for as long as it takes." Herrara looked from husband to wife. "If your son isn't home by tomorrow evening, the FBI is going to be all over this state. The best thing for you to do is stay calm, keep your kids calm, and try to think of any information that might help us."

"Why can't you bring in the FBI now?" Annie asked. "What are you waiting for?"

"Just getting everything in order," Herrara told her. "If you think we've invaded your home now, just wait until the feds come in here. It's like army central."

"Army central's fine with me," Annie told him, closing her

eyes. "As soon as I can manage it, I'm going to call everyone I know."

"Everyone you know is up in Chicago or New York," David said. "Everyone you know won't do us any good down here."

"No," Herrara pitched in, "your wife's right. Call everyone you know. But first, get me that list."

# CHAPTER 11

## Lynelle

THE bus station was gray and empty, a sad old building stuck at the end of a pretty street, with its back to blue water and four long rows of hard plastic chairs inside.

I pulled open the door and an old black lady looked up from her seat next to the soda machine. She checked me over from head to foot, taking note of the way I was carrying my things in plastic shopping bags and the baby in his sheet. I got scared for a minute but I held the baby close and remembered the feel of him drinking my milk. He was mine. I smiled at the lady and walked up to the ticket window. I was lucky, my bus was due in less than an hour. I bought a ticket to Gainesville for thirty-four dollars and another one from there to Flaglerton. Then I sat down to wait.

"How old is your baby?" the lady asked across a row of seats.

"Three months." I took a guess based on the size of his hands and the way he pulled on my shirt when he was hungry.

"So new to this world. So beautiful." She stood and came to sit down next to me. She smelled like gardenias and was holding a fine-quality handbag on her lap.

I saw her eyes take in my wedding ring and little chip of diamond. Hogan's face flashed in my mind. He was frowning.

"Is it a boy or girl?" the lady asked, smiling.

"Boy. His name's Angel," I told her, for I'd decided to call him that.

"Angel. Nice eyes you have, Angel." Right then his eyes were deep gray and green, like the sea on a stormy day. "You have your mommy's beautiful dark coloring."

She went on that way, smiling at the baby and asking questions that I soon tired of answering. The strain of thinking up lies made me weary.

"And where might you be going, ma'am?" I asked finally.

"Down past Miami. I'm going home." She said it proud. "My family is waiting for me, my daughter and her three little ones. Though, of course, they're not little anymore."

Her old eyes lit up when she talked about her grandchildren. I couldn't help but think how there was nobody in the world to sit and talk about me that way, getting all puffed up with pride, digging photos out of her wallet and showing them off to a stranger.

"This here is Melody, and this one is Scout." She held the pictures up for me to see. "He's a football player."

I was looking at a picture of Scout in his uniform when the baby started to fuss against me. I stroked his cheek, jiggled my legs underneath him, but soon he was crying outright, his little face scrunched up like an old tissue.

"Excuse me," I interrupted, "I'm sorry, ma'am, but I think it's time to change his diaper."

"Oh but of course, dear. The baby comes first." She looked me over when I stood.

"That's a lovely skirt," she said. "Nice bright yellow." She kept talking while I walked to the washroom, even though the baby had started bawling.

"I can watch your things, dear," she sang out.

"No, I don't want to trouble you." I carried the two plastic bags into the washroom and breathed the smell of ammonia and unclean toilets soon as the door shut behind me. There were real tears going down Angel's face, and his hands were bunched up into little fists.

"It's okay, it's okay, little one." I tried to soothe him and stay calm at the same time, reminding myself that babies cry and that changing a diaper is easy, but still my hands shook as I laid him on the blanket.

"It's okay, sweetie, it's okay."

Soon as I got the diaper off he stopped crying. He stared up at the light on the ceiling and gurgled, waving his chubby little legs in the air. When I had him all put back together I sat him up and held one hand on his belly, another on his back.

"What do you say, little boy? Can you sit? Can you sit up for me?"

A smile, I swear it was a smile, tugged at his lips. He sat for a second or two before tumbling over sideways into my arms.

"That's okay, I don't mind holding you, not one bit."

I tucked him back into the blue sheet tied around my waist, then walked around in that smelly bathroom singing and passing the time until I could go stand outside in the sunshine and wait for my bus.

"You have a good trip, ma'am," I said to the lady as I walked through the waiting room.

"Same to you, dear. And good luck with your little boy."


The bus was just about empty. I sat near the back so I could nurse the baby in private, and soon as we were on the highway I slipped the baby out of the sheet and held his face up to the window. I looked at everything like I was seeing it through his eyes, the yellow stripes glowing against black pavement, bright cars whooshing by, sun glowing and the sky the color of robins' eggs, shining right back at me in that baby's eyes.

I held a robin's egg in my hands once, a long time ago. I was six years old, and Mama and me were walking through the thick of trees near the Peace River. We were watching the ground as we went. There was always so much to watch out for, tree roots, rattler and copper snakes, brush piles where hornets might make a nest, busy patches of fire ants, mud slicks, and the cold spots of air where a spirit might be hanging about. With all of that on my mind and a bucket for early gooseberries to carry besides, I wasn't listening to the birds singing, or to Mama's humming, or to the tap-tap dance of our shoes on the ground. I hear them now better than I did then.

"Lynnie," Mama called, "look, Lynnie."

I was ahead of her on the path, and I swung around to look while holding on to the thick leg of a banyan tree.

Behind me Mama was stooped over, half in and half out of sunshine coming through the tent of leaves. She was wearing a pink dress, her hair caught up in a pink-and-white bandanna. The more it comes back to me, the more it seems like a perfect minute in my life, a time when I was thinking of nothing but the feel of banyan on my palm and the picture of Mama with a look of wonder on her face, bending to pick something up from the ground.

"It's a robin's egg," Mama cried. She held it in the hollow of her hand. I crossed back over my own footsteps and set down the tin bucket next to her feet.

"Hold out your hand," Mama said.

Can I be only imagining that her voice was a song, an angel's breath upon my cheek? That she always talked to me so sweet and touched me with the careful tenderness she did that day as she showed me how to make a bowl with my palm, then poured the egg from her hand into mine?

I rolled the egg across the line the bucket handle had made in my palm, back to the crease in my fingers, from pinkie to thumb. I couldn't believe the color, such a brilliant blue, the color the sky ought to be all of the time.

"It's beautiful," I breathed in a gush.

The egg was so lovely, I just had to hold it up to the light dancing between the trees.

"Be careful," Mama said, but it wasn't warning enough, for as I held it between my fingers the egg cracked and a clear liquid spilled out.

"Oh no," I wailed. Mama cried out, too, not a word but a moan as she watched me trying to catch what was falling from the center of the shell. What I caught were crumb-sized specks of blue and the beginning of a bird-body, all creamy white with little gray eyes that couldn't see a thing.

"It's all right," Mama said when she recovered herself. She took the pink handkerchief off her head and wiped my hands. "It was far from the nest anyway. Goodness knows we don't get many robins around here."

"Can we save it? Can we save the shell, at least?"

"No, no, sweetie. That's all there is. It belongs back where we found it."

Mama shook out the kerchief, sprinkling little flecks of blue sky into the dirt, rubbing it into the ground with the tip of her shoe. Her face, which was heart-shaped and lovely, was turned away from me, giving no glance or glimpse of sorrow or comfort, anger or regret.

I watched her foot until all the blue shell was blended into brown, and then we went quietly on our way. We never talked of the bird's egg again, but many times after that when the sky was a perfect color blue I remembered how the egg just disappeared into the dirt. I remembered it exactly on that day in the bus with Angel, riding toward home and watching a perfect robin's egg blue sky rolling outside the window glass.

"Listen to this, little boy," I whispered in his ear, and then I sang him the song my mama used to sing me. "*Que sera, sera*, whatever will be, will be, the future's not ours to see, *que sera, sera*."

I'd been thinking only of the dead. Now I was holding life in my arms. Praying, reading, walking were nothing compared to holding a living, breathing child in my arms. Singing to him was a prayer. Holding him was like holding a sky blue piece of heaven.

# CHAPTER 12

# $\mathscr{A}nnie$

A NNIE stared at a pad of paper on the kitchen table. The page was swimming with names, blue ink on yellow paper, Liz at the top of the list, followed by schoolmates and social workers, neighbors, Nick's hockey teammates, women she knew from Oak Park, and even old friends from high school, girls whose faces she knew as young and untroubled, fresh and unlined.

It was after the dinner hour on the day of Dylan's disappearance. There was a half-empty bowl of soup in the sink, some crackers on a napkin with Sophie's bite marks turning them into half-moons. The police were gone from the condo, but the outline of their shadows remained on black boxes linked to the telephones, a patrolman sitting outside in his squad car.

Annie chewed the edge of the pen and read over the list. It was full of names she'd pulled from memory and numbers she'd copied from the address book she carried in her purse. She stared at the paper, but what she saw were blank pages, empty sheets, a carriage without a baby in it.

"The battered ones." David's voice startled her from behind, coming sharp across her shoulder. "Those are the names the cops need. The women and their husbands."

She could smell the rank of his armpits, the sour echo of his breath.

"What?" Annie turned to see him looming over her. She felt a flash of recognition, as if this was what he sometimes looked like to his children, large and scary, with a booming voice uttering commands.

"That's the list, isn't it?" David walked around the table now and stood in front of her. Annie nodded.

"Well, I think you need to give the police the names of those women. The women you work with at the shelter."

David heard his words come from his mouth, he knew they sounded calm and rational. He looked away from Annie, down to the paper in front of her.

"I can't do that," she said slowly, as if the sentence were the saddest thing she'd ever uttered. She pictured Dee with her bite marks, the cleaning woman with a broken nose whose husband had threatened them both in family court, the mother who took her two toddlers and ran away from her boyfriend when she was six months pregnant. Mostly they were poor women, and the chance one of their husbands could have hatched some elaborate scheme that involved airfare and sleuthing and doing her harm seemed so unlikely to Annie, so impossible to imagine, that she couldn't justify betraying them.

"It's all confidential. Those women are hiding, David, or else they're getting ready to run away. I can't put down their names and phone numbers."

"What do you mean?" There was no logic for him in what he heard, nothing that pertained to him and his family. Nothing about Dylan. "Write their names down, Annie."

Annie closed her eyes. "I put Liz on the list, and the people I work with, you know they'll do whatever they can. But for those other women it's a matter of life and death."

"*This* is a matter of life and death." David smacked the tabletop with his palm. "This is our life and your son's life."

"I know. Don't you think I know that?" She bit down on the

edge of the pen so hard it cracked in her mouth. She dropped it on the table, and wiped at the spit in the corners of her lips.

"Eight hours." David's voice was deadly low, it washed over her like the dusk settling outside. "It's been eight hours. Do you realize what can happen in eight hours?"

The names on the paper blurred in front of Annie. Her tears fell onto the page, drawing spidery blue lines of ink from the words she'd written.

"Think about the reasons someone steals a baby." Nightmare visions waved like ugly effigies across the back of David's mind. "What do you think is happening to our son right now?"

"Please stop it, David. I couldn't feel any worse than I already do."

"Then write down their names." He pointed his finger at the pad, hitting the spot where her tears splashed. His voice softened, as if he were trying to coax a child. "Go on, write down those names so the police have something to go on. Somewhere to start."

"Stop it," Annie cried. She gripped the table. She shoved her chair backward and stood, feeling all the energy course through her body and come up into her fingers, spelling rage and fear in new sign language her skin understood.

*Fear. Fear.* Her hands clawed at her face.

"What's going on? What are you two doing?" Suddenly Nan was in the room, pressing herself between them. "Both of you, please, you need to be together now, not fighting one another," she cried.

"That's right, Annie." David's eyes glistened bright behind his glasses. "Listen to your mother. We need to be a team now."

Annie saw only the red cavern of his mouth, the lash of his tongue as he spoke down at her.

"Look at this, Nan." David picked up the pad of paper with Annie's list and slapped it with the back of his hand. "The cops asked for a list of people we know. I think Annie needs to give them those women she works with at the shelter."

"This is what they asked for." Annie tried to tug the pad out of David's hand.

"Oh sure." His face twisted. "Carol Bismark just might have taken a plane down here with her own three kids to snatch Dylan. Or here's a good one"—he looked at her—"Julia Mirano the music teacher. Culprit if I ever saw one."

He bore down over her again. "You're not being logical here, Annie. If we're not rational and logical, all is lost."

They all heard the words, but they heard them as David meant them: if we're not calm and rational, *Dylan* is lost.

"You don't know," Annie cried. "It's not for you to decide what names the police do or don't need."

"You know what, Annie?" David's voice dropped three decibels into a flat, deadly, low pitch. "This list is bullshit." He threw the pad onto the table. The cracked pen went flying. "This whole thing is bullshit."

"Don't say that word, Daddy, that's a bad word."

David spun around. Sophie was standing at the crest of the kitchen in a pink nightgown, with Joe behind her. At the sight of her, sweet and pink and looking up at him expectantly, David felt something crumble inside of him. He dropped to his knees and wrapped her in his arms, breathing in the fresh talc powder and soap from her bath. She smelled so full of hope, he felt he would weep right then and there with his chin buried in her wet hair.

"I heard you say a bad word, Daddy," Sophie said. "*Bullshit* is a bad word, and you don't want to say bad words because that won't help us find Dylan."

Annie slapped her hands over her ears. "I can't stand this," she cried.

"Where's Nick?" Nan asked, looking at Joe. "Isn't he with you?"

Joe shook his head. Everyone froze. Annie's heart leapt into her throat.

"Nicky," she called his name.

"Hey, Nick," David shouted.

He didn't answer.

They ran out of the kitchen, down the hallway, each to a different bedroom. It was already dark outside.

*Nick. Nicky. Nick. Nick,* they called, and their voices rose up to the sky, they floated on clouds, they washed out to sea.

# CHAPTER 13

## Lynelle

A s the bus rolled over the highway I watched the landscape change from green and white to tan and gray, the colors I expected to find right before reaching the thick swamplands of my home. We were heading into the place where I grew up, the land between beaches and tourist spots, and I could feel how much I'd already put behind me.

When I put my face against the bus glass I could almost smell the air coming off the swamps and dark waters ahead. The road underneath me was black as the river and it was singing, too, calling the way the ocean called me, pulling me home the way a river will, with a stream as steady and silent and necessary as blood in the veins.

I almost let myself believe that when I got back to Flaglerton my mama would be there. In my mind I saw her hair grow longer, the way it did right before she got sick. She traded her dresses for pants and her face aged long beyond the time she'd ever spent on this earth. She grew wrinkles that she called laugh lines, and her hair got gray. We went walking by the river, me holding the baby and her singing. We talked about how I'd need to teach my child to watch for snakes, to jump over the brush piles, and to stay away from the trees at night, especially the banyans with so many thick branches that could catch a soul and hold it there, and the cypress with their knobby knees that could hide an old swamp witch and her black magic.

I rode through Florida with those thoughts in my head, and by the time we got to Gainesville it was already dark.

"Don't you worry, we'll be out of here in no time," I said to the baby. My plan was to settle down in a motel, sleep deep, rise early, and catch the first bus to Flaglerton. The rest of my plan was loose and small. I was aiming to find our old house on Pebble Road, and when I got there I was going to pray for Mama's spirit to find me. It wasn't much of a plan, but I couldn't think of what else to do or where to go.

I thought Mama was the only one who would understand, and I believed in the lightest place in my soul that I was doing the only thing I could. As for the dark corners, the doubts, and the beggar man with no legs who grabbed at my skirt bottom asking for money inside the bus station, well, I wasn't thinking about them. I turned my back on everything dark, on the tunnel of grief and everything attached to it, and I walked past two policemen, out into the middle of the city.

Night was settled and the air was cool. I was cold and hungry, and feared Angel would feel the same. I stopped on the street for a minute, looking up at the signs for hospitals and colleges, but soon the pocket of empty space around us was filled with cars honking and girls with big baggy shorts and black cherry lips bumping into us, and I had to move on.

I went into McDonald's and got some food to go, and then picked a motel I could see from where I stood. The lady at the desk was glad to take my money without making small talk, and I felt a great relief when I got to my room.

I ate, then nursed the baby. The hum of the air conditioner drowned away all the noises from outside.

"You're a hungry boy," I said. Angel reached up and played with the end of my braid. He drank from one side until it was empty, and started a funny kind of whining until I switched him over and let him drink the other side dry, too.

After a while I set him down on the bed with pillows all around him. He was happy to play with the empty white bag from my food, crunching the paper up in his little fist, flinging it back and forth like crazy for a minute.

I couldn't get enough of watching him. I put my face up close to him and watched his eyes lock with mine. I smiled, and he smiled. He gurgled, and I gurgled. I laughed, and he kicked his feet and smiled, and then I kicked my feet and laughed some more. Oh my God, it was just like I hoped it would be, having him all to myself.

# CHAPTER 14

## Annie

ANNIE found Nick under the bed he'd slept in the night before.

"Nicky?"

He sniffled, stifled a whimper. Annie knelt beside the bed and put a hand under the bedspread, brushing against the carpet, reaching for his damp arm, the crook of his elbow. "Honey, what are you doing under here?"

"It's my fault," he said, carpet and dust filling his mouth. "It's all my fault."

Annie lay down on the floor and lifted the bedspread. Her cheek pressed into the beige carpet. "It's not your fault, Nick."

He was turned away from her, facing the wall. She patted his arm and rubbed the fine hair on his forearm, but didn't try to tug him out. "It's not your fault, it's really not."

"It is." His voice sounded like it was coming through a paper bag. "I heard you and Daddy fighting and I know it's my fault and what if somebody kills Dylan, what if somebody hurts him?"

Annie took a deep breath. For a brief period in college she'd had a spate of anxiety attacks that caused her heart to race and kept her attention focused on the dark caverns of fear in her chest. With the help of a counselor she'd learned to breathe deeply in times of stress, to focus on the breath entering and leaving her body, lifting and falling inside her belly until it calmed her.

She did that now, touching Nick, hoping she could calm him, too. One son was missing. She couldn't lose the other to heartbreak.

"Annie?" A stab of light filled the room, her mother shrieked over her. "Are you okay?"

Annie turned, looked at Nan's white tennis shoes. "Mom, it's okay. Nicky's here, we're talking."

"Is he all right?"

"Yes," she snapped, "I just need to talk to him alone."

"Oh." Nan's feet stayed there.

"Mom, you need to leave us alone. And tell everybody he's okay."

"Right," Nan said. Annie's fingers caressed Nick's arm. She watched Nan's shoes turn to leave the room, then hesitate. "Do you need anything?"

"No, Mom. Just close the door behind you."

Nan left, pulling the door shut, taking the spear of light with her.

"Nicky, are you thirsty? Can I get you a drink of water?"

Nick's mouth was full of dust, his eyes hurt, but most of all his heart was aching, his belly was on fire. He was terrified.

"Nicky, I'm going to lay here with you all night if that's what you want, okay?"

"Are they going to find him?"

"I hope so," she said, her voice cracking. "I'll tell you the truth, honey, I don't know what's going to happen. But I do know one thing. I love you, and I'll always love you, and I'll always love Sophie and Dylan, all three of you."

Annie bit her lip to keep from sobbing. She wanted Nick to feel safe even when the world was proving no one was safe, not even a baby, not even her child.

"What about Dad?"

"Daddy doesn't blame you, Nick. Nobody blames you."

"I heard him yelling. Are you always going to love Dad, too?"

Annie squeezed her eyes shut. She said, "Daddy loves you. We both love you, we're always going to love you."

"How can you?" Nick turned his head, showing Annie the gray shadow of his eye sockets, his cheeks dark and wet with tears. "How can you love me? It's my fault."

"No, Nick, it's not your fault."

Annie shoved herself as far under the bed as she could get, but the frame was low to the ground and her shoulders wouldn't fit.

"Nicky, please come out here, I need to hold you."

She tugged on his arm, and he inched forward this time, sliding across the carpet until his face came close to hers. A young face full of anguish.

"Mom, I'm scared," he sputtered, his breath feverish as it washed against her cheeks.

"Oh, Nick."

He crawled into the bridge of her embrace, and she held on as tightly as she dared, squeezing him to keep from slipping away.


David stepped into the night. The screen door shut behind him.

"Evening," the cop said. It was Carlos Molina, the rookie who'd been on the scene that morning. David didn't recognize him, but nodded a greeting and looked up at the sky. Somewhere out there Dylan was alone. Even in Minnesota the sky had never seemed so big.

"What do you think?" he asked the cop.

"Sir?"

"What do you think about this? Do you think we'll find him?"

David kept his face turned upward. A plane flew overhead, then a cloud, and another cloud, blocking his view of the stars.

"If he's here to be found we'll find him, Mr. Thompson."

"What the hell does that mean?" David looked Molina full in the face.

"I mean if he's in Florida, if he's in our jurisdiction, we'll find him. We're combing every inch of this county, sir. We'll find him if he's in this area, that's what I mean."

David nodded.

"If it was a kidnapping for money, wouldn't we have gotten a call by now?"

Molina thought for a minute.

"I don't know about that," he said finally. "It's late. Maybe they'd call in the morning, or maybe they'd wait until the middle of the night when you're feeling most vulnerable."

David felt the cop scrutinizing him.

"But honestly, I don't have any experience with ransom calls. This would be my first incident of this nature."

David pushed his glasses up his nose, sucked in the night air.

"I'm making up some signs, you know, with a photo and a reward. Using my laptop," he added. "Think your bosses will object?"

"Can't say for sure, sir. Sometimes reward offers attract all kinds of undesirable interest."

"I hadn't thought of that."

On the ground the night remained thick and still, but the clouds overhead were roiling and rolling in the high wind moving above the trees. A low, distant moan cut through the air. David snapped his head up like a dog on a scent.

"Did you hear that?" he demanded. Indeed, Molina had heard. He put a finger to his lips, silencing David. It came again, a soft moan from the direction of the sea.

The hair on David's arms stood on end. He was feeling weak and nauseous from the day, had eaten only a few crackers since breakfast. He glanced at the rookie to be sure it wasn't just his own imagination he'd heard cut through the air, but Molina had the same look on his face, the look of someone attuned to something delicate and far away.

They stood in silence. The sound came and went. David's knees began shaking, his hands went clammy.

"It's the tides," Molina said at last. "A trick of the tides. The island is famous for it."

"The tides? It sounded like a voice. Some kind of moan, something human."

David jutted his chin toward the squad car parked at the curb. "I think you should get on the radio, ask them to check it out," he said.

"But they'd be following the sound of the tides," Molina protested.

"They'd be following a hunch, right? What else do you have right now?"

"It's like chasing a ghost in the night," Molina said. He knew the myth of Singing Island, knew the story of a storm that had wiped out all the children of a village and turned the island into a peninsula.

"Look, I'm going myself." David turned toward the ocean. "My son's out there. I don't have time to wait for you."

David's legs were moving before he even finished his sentence, his arms working, his feet slapping the ground.

Molina stood still, torn between his orders to watch the family for signs of suspicious behavior and his duty to protect them. As David turned out of sight, the rookie walked to his squad car and called the desk sergeant for backup.

Annie pulled her arm out from under Nick. It was past eleven, and he was asleep in his clothes on top of the bed. She tugged off his shoes and slipped his legs under the covers.

Walking into the bright hallway, she knocked softly at the doorway to her parents' room and tiptoed in. Nan was sleeping cheek-to-cheek on the bed with Sophie. The little girl's mouth was open, her eyes moving rapidly as if she were looking for something in her dreams. *Dylan*, Annie thought, *she's looking for*

*Dylan.* She bent and kissed her head, knowing the girl wouldn't wake.

"Annie? Are you okay?" Nan's voice was gritty.

"It's okay, Mom, nothing's happening. You may as well rest."

"Where's your father?"

"Probably in the living room. I'll check on him if you want, I'm sure he's fine."

"Any word?"

"Nothing."

They spoke in stage whispers across Sophie's face, across the quiet of her slumber.

"Stay with Sophie, Mom. That'll make me feel better," Annie said. "I'll let you know if anything happens."


On the highway along the ocean, David stopped to catch his breath. A car passed, and for an instant the whole night was lit, then plunged into deeper darkness. Listening to the silence in the car's wake, David heard the sound again in the distance. It was a sound like wind chimes, or singing, or the wail of a small child.

*Dylan.*

The chill ran through him, turning his intestines to water. David doubled in pain, he moaned out loud. He covered his ears and heard nothing but his own heartbeat. He took his hands away and listened to the wind, the scurry of small lizards, the wide swell of quiet, and beyond it a jingle, a wail, a cry.

David twisted his neck right and left until he felt sure of the sound's direction. Then he ran down the side of the road. There were no streetlights, but he ran by the light of the stars, heading toward the narrow end of the peninsula. Sand kicked up under his shoes. He crushed hard weeds and small, thick leaves on the ground. His chest opened up, and David felt something rip loose inside of him.

It was hope, blind hope, the featherweight of hope, rushing through him. His heart pounded. He stopped again. Listened.

The sound was gone. The night was quiet and the road was empty. His chest was heaving. He held his breath, but heard only silence.

"God damn you," David screamed at the phantom in the silence. His own words echoed and were swallowed by the dark cave of the horizon. He heard the roar of the ocean from one direction, the soft clang of the boats in the harbor from another.

Forced to choose between the wide empty sea and the silver boats in their slips, David turned toward the marina, going on intuition, hoping the boaters might have seen something, imagining he could grab someone by the collar and hold on until he heard the truth about Dylan.

Fighting a pain in his side, he trotted down a road of small dark houses, moving toward the hazy harbor lights that glowed and flickered like candles in the distance.

He ran until his feet hit the wooden dock. The figures of the boats stood like dark mountains on the water, and he smelled the gasoline pump at the edge of the pier, heard murmuring voices and the low strains of music. But nothing else. No child's cry or whimper. No moan. No lullaby. He felt both frightened and desperate.

He looked at his watch. It was 11:37. Almost midnight.

"David?"

Headlights washed over him. He turned, and the twin spotlights of a car blinded him. He shielded his eyes in the glare and felt raw terror, like an animal caught in a trap.

"Who's there?" he shouted.

"Officer Molina. What are you doing?"

"I'm looking for my son," David answered, angry and relieved at once.

"Why here?" The voice came from the other side of the lights.

A trembling overtook David's body. He didn't recognize the tightness in his throat, the sudden dizziness as a breath rushed into him without rushing back out.

"Why not here?" A sob ripped through him.

His hands grabbed the air for something to hold on to, something to lean against, and he found Molina's body next to him. He held on to the man's shoulder, squeezed his forearm until he brought up bruises. But he couldn't stop the sobs.

"Why not here?"

# CHAPTER 15

## Lynelle

A
FTER a while I unpacked all the stuff I'd bought at the store.
I had diapers, wipes, baby powder, baby bath foam, and a
new package of little baby sleepers.

I set Angel down on a blanket on the floor right outside the
bathroom door where I could see him, and then I set out all the
bath things very carefully, like a minister in church looking over
each thing, putting it down just where I thought it belonged. All
the while I was murmuring to Angel. I used a towel to line the
sink so he wouldn't slip, and then I turned on the water and ran
it over my wrist until it was just right.

To make sure he wouldn't get a chill I turned off the air conditioner and turned up the heater. I put the shower on hot and
let steam fill the bathroom.

"Okay, Angel," I said. His little legs were pumping, I thought
maybe he knew what was coming. "You're going to take a bath."
I tried making it sound like a lot of fun.

The bathroom was wet and warm, thick as a summer day near
the swamp. I stepped out of my yellow skirt, lifted my shirt over
my head, took off my bra. It felt good to be almost naked, to have
nothing pulling or tugging or binding me up.

I undressed the baby slow, legs first, then arms, T-shirt, and finally the diaper, until he was naked in my arms, the two of us wet as toads in the steam, his skin soft as a daisy petal, a gurgling coming from his throat, a humming from his chest, the purr of a cat.

"Bath," I said again.

When I dipped him in the water I put his foot first, then watched his face as the rest of him slipped down. I used my hands to wash him, touching him so carefully, feeling a catch in my throat like I'd loved him a long time. Under each arm I rubbed him with a white cloth, between each toe with the edge of my pinkie finger, along the curve of his bottom and the hollow of his back, the small line where his ribs met, the small dots of what would someday be a man's breasts.

I expected the sadness I felt, but the joy was its own thing, rising with the shower steam, part of the breath filling and leaving our lungs together, the baby splashing and splattering until the water cleared the mist on the mirror. I looked the way I did right after Grace was born, a high flush in my cheeks, my breasts big and the color of peaches right down to the ripe purple cones of my nipples.

I felt in love with him right there, desperately in love, so much so that I could see myself in his eyes, my braid coming undone from the damp heat, my eyes pleading, Be mine, will you be mine?

I wanted a baby, any baby, just like I'd once wanted a mama. Any mama at all. It's a hard truth, but I've come to see it.

After me and daddy moved away from Flaglerton and set up our trailer house in Orange Grove, I stopped missing my mama and started wishing for a mother to wash my sheets and fold them back when I got into bed, to pull the blanket up under my chin and say something sweet. I wished for a mama to make me a birthday cake, to tell me when my fingernails needed cutting, to come meet my teacher on visitors' day.

Maybe other girls grow up faster without a mama, but I stayed young longer, sitting alone in that tiny square of bedroom in our trailer, saying good night to the Barbie dolls Aunt Fay bought for me, braiding up their long hair, shopping at the Ben Franklin store for colored yarns.

I was shy and spent a lot of time at home, listening to the radio. In secret I taught myself to play the harmonica. I worshiped Crystal Gayle, and when I wished for a mama it was always somebody like her, hard and soft at the same time.

I was glad when Daddy took up with Stevie Knox. She was pretty and smelled good all the time. Ciara, that was her perfume. It made my eyes burn, but I loved it anyway.

Stevie polished my nails one Saturday before we three went out to the Ponderosa for supper. First we scrubbed them, then clipped them and used her nail file to shape them, and finally she polished them pink and pearly. She brought me a new pink shirt, and called me Sweetie. I thought she called me that because I was dear to her.

"Now you're starting to look like a young lady," she said in the restaurant. "Next we'll work on that hair."

My hand flew up to my braid, which I had tied at the bottom with a pink yarn to match my new shirt. Stevie's own hair was silvery blond and fluffy all around her face.

"Lynelle's hair looks just fine," Daddy said. He was chewing on a big piece of steak.

"Bobby, don't talk with your mouth full," Stevie scolded. "Lynelle just needs a little work, that's all. It's not her fault."

I watched everything Stevie did. When she picked up her fork, I picked up mine. When she patted a napkin across her lips, I did the same. When she buttered her bread on both sides, so did I.

That night her and Daddy told me they were getting married, and I was glad for it. I was twelve years old and finally getting the mama I'd been waiting for.

Stevie planned the wedding one, two, three, reserving the VFW hall, having Daddy fitted for his tuxedo, winning me over by taking me to get my hair done and telling me how beautiful I looked in pink. I was to be a bridesmaid, and somehow I got it in my head that I'd be going with Daddy and Stevie to New Orleans for their honeymoon, too.

"What do you think about the French Quarter?" she asked, showing me pictures of cobblestone streets and fancy horse-drawn carriages. "What do you think about this hotel?"

Whenever she talked about New Orleans she said "we" and "us," and since Daddy had never gone away without me in my whole life, it was natural to think I'd be going, too.

It wasn't until Stevie left the wedding party, changed into her travel suit, and said, "You have a good visit with your aunt Fay," that I dropped my jaw and realized they were going without me. I felt dumb as a mouse. Aunt Fay was standing next to me. She was a sad sight then, in between husbands and frazzled to death by slow Turtle and cousin Wilma, who wore a red dress to the wedding and kept going outside to have a smoke and draw bright new lips across her mouth.

"Don't look at me like that, you knew we were going on a honeymoon." Stevie's laugh was hard. She kissed the air next to my cheek, and Daddy hugged me against him.

"You're a real treasure," he said.

"Come on, Bobby, we got a honeymoon suite waiting."

As Stevie whisked my daddy away, Aunt Fay put an arm around my shoulders and said, "What a bitch." I'll never forget the stab those words cut into me. But she was right, of course. Just that me and Daddy didn't want to see it.

The next day I went over to the Ben Franklin and stole myself two fancy gold hair combs with pearls on the ends. I put them in my hair and sat in front of the mirror combing, brushing, and hair-spraying myself to death. Wilma spent most of the visit in front of the TV with her fashion magazines, but when I promised to get her some hair combs like mine she agreed to do me up in her lipstick and eye shadows. I was a stranger to myself in the mirror, but I knew, somehow I knew that if I didn't toughen up I'd have a broken heart for sure.

I found myself a mean streak and I worked it. When me and Daddy moved into the new house with Stevie, I did my best to look like her and walk like her and laugh like her, but it wasn't to win her over. It was to change myself into someone that couldn't be hurt. In private I kept my Barbie dolls and my harmonica and my Crystal Gayle cassette tapes, but I hardened myself on the outside, just like her. And it worked for a while. But inside I was still a sad, good girl, and so my game came to an end a year later, on the day my daddy tumbled all my stolen stuff onto the bedroom floor and said, "We're not trash."

When Stevie and Daddy parted ways I grew my hair long again, but I was changed. I had the same braid, the same pretty dark hair, even the same Barbie dolls lined up on my dresser, but I didn't have the same hopes inside of me anymore. It wasn't until I met Hogan that I started thinking I'd ever have a true whole family for my own.

Hogan. He knows things, I saw that right away. And he understood me in a funny, roundabout kind of way. The only way anyone can understand another person, by looking sideways, around the face we put on for the world.

Hogan once told me about seeing an airplane spin out of control and crash on the runway during takeoff. He said there comes a certain point when the plane is already in motion and there's no turning back. That's how he explained it to me.

I knew what he meant then, and I knew it that night in the motel.

After I got the baby out of his bath, dried him off, and put him into his new little pajamas, I wanted to call Hogan and tell him I was like that airplane, in motion on a dangerous course and no turning back. But then I'd have to give the baby up. Then he wouldn't be there next to my chest, and the emptiness would come up in me even worse than before.

And so instead of calling Hogan I put the baby real carefully in a dresser drawer lined with a blanket. I put the drawer right next to my bed and made sure Angel wasn't smothering. I checked that the blanket was flat and wouldn't slip over his face to choke him in his sweet sleep. He sighed once, puckered his lips like he had something between them, and then he was still.

I turned off the lights and sat on the bed watching him sleep, my head humming, trying to figure out what I'd done. Trying to make sense of it.

For the first time since morning I felt my sorrow blow inside me. I tried to hold it back, to choke it down, but of course I hadn't saved my own girl, I wasn't looking at my own baby, I was watching over a baby who'd grew in some other belly, a baby who was made up of a whole 'nother being and love and family.

I was a girl with no mama, no baby, nobody to turn to, and I was as alone as a body could be, alone with nothing but my fears and my grief watching over the baby along with me. Alone in a strange place with brown bedspreads and the shadows of moving cars passing by in the night, bumpy tan walls and a dark television like an eye waiting for me to blink it open.

I couldn't walk, and I couldn't read the Bible, as there was none anywhere I could see. I tried to pray, but there was nothing more for me to say to God, nothing I could think of except that thing about the spirit finding me. I took a piece of paper out of the side drawer next to the bed and wrote down what I might want to say if I could pray. I wrote down *Mama. Grace. Hogan.* I put a circle around them. It was dark in the room, and I just about had to guess at what I was writing, had to trust that the whisper of the pencil on the paper was putting down the words *que sera sera*, which I wrote, and even tried humming, but it didn't do any good.

I was thinking about what I'd done, at last I was thinking about what Hogan would say and how crazy it would be to try to bring this baby home as my own, to put him in with Grace's pink blanket and all of her clothes too small for him, his little feet with their curling toenails kicking the sides of the cradle Hogan made, and Hogan standing over it saying, "This ain't right, Lynelle, we need to make our own baby and give this one back."

Give him back? When he's drunk from my breast and slept against my belly? Give him back to who? To a silly old carriage where he was laying all alone with nobody to watch over him? Give him back like a lost little puppy when I don't even have any proof he was being cared for?

Wasn't I set out on a journey? Didn't that sign speak to me? Hadn't the sky been robin's egg blue?

Didn't I deserve more? Didn't I deserve a real live baby and a mama, too?

I made up my mind to have that baby on the bus to Flaglerton first thing the next morning, and everything else be damned. An answer would come to me. I had to believe it, so I did.

# CHAPTER 16

## Annie

ANNIE couldn't sleep. She shucked off her bra, changed into a T-shirt and shorts, padded through the house in bare feet. She gently woke her father from where he was dozing on the couch and led him to the bedroom. Several times she picked up the phone to make sure it was working, and heard the dial tone buzz in her ear.

Once she ran outside full of hope at the sound of a car engine, but she stopped short at the sight of David emerging alone from the front seat of a police car.

"Where were you?" she asked. "Did something happen?"

David looked at her as if she were a stranger. "Go in the house," he said, and she did as he told her, feeling stones cut into her bare feet.

"You're scaring me, David," she said as soon as they stepped into the front porch. "Did something happen?"

"I went for a walk." His voice was weary, his glasses spotty and smeared. "The cop brought me home."

"Why'd you go out? Is there something you're not telling me?"

She stepped toward him, but he crossed his arms over his chest, warning her away.

"I just went out to clear my head." His words came in a curved line over his shoulder as he walked into the living room. "And you know what? The cop followed me because we're suspects, Annie. You and me. Prime suspects, I would imagine."

He pulled off his glasses and wiped them on the end of his shirt. The tears had made him tired, the run had drained him.

"Were they questioning you? Did they take you somewhere to question you?" She reached for David's hand, but he pulled away.

"Is that it, David? Were they asking you questions about me?"

He looked at her with blank eyes, then put his glasses back on his face.

A new fear gripped her. "Do you think I did something to Dylan?"

"Jesus, Annie, that's not what it's about."

"But I'm asking you a question, David. *Do you think I did something to our baby?*"

He stepped away.

"No," he said. "No, I don't think you did anything intentionally."

"Intentionally?"

"Annie, you left him alone. Now this." He swept his hands wide, spinning them around the room, pointing to the dark corners, the shadows, the black boxes, the emptiness in Dylan's absence.

She followed the arc of his arms and saw the colors drained from everything, all of it gray and frightening.

"I need you, David." Her voice was quiet, too small to fill the silence.

David felt his back stiffen, he felt his own fear vibrating around him. He put his face in his hands so he wouldn't have to look at her, so she wouldn't see the stain of tears across his cheeks, the red rims of his eyes.

"I feel helpless," Annie said, desperate to say anything that would quiet the white noise between them, cover the ticking of the kitchen clock.

David lifted his face out of his hands. Out of habit he looked at the calluses across his palms, the familiar terrain of his own skin.

"What can we do, David? There must be something we can do besides sit here and wait."

David shoved his hands into his pockets and paced the room, away from her.

"Are you not speaking to me?" Annie looked at her husband's back, the vee of his torso, the sharp jut of his shoulder blades.

"What do you want me to say, Annie?" He spoke with his back to her still. She heard the hush of his words, the anger but not the anguish.

"It's our baby, David. I don't think I can stand it if you blame me."

David took off his glasses. The world dissolved into an impressionist painting, a drab gray nightworld with no stars, only the blur of pressing anxiety, the weight of anger welling at him from inside. The room was fuzzy around him. He rubbed his hands across his eyes. It was late, and he was aware of feeling very unkindly toward his wife.

David tried to be compassionate. He tried to imagine what his own father would have said or done in a similar situation, in this kind of emergency. He saw his father's wide, honest face, the quiet movement of his body, the clasp of his hands in prayer. How many times had David seen his father press his empty hands together? Every Sunday at dinner, every time he lost a customer, every time a new widow called to collect her husband's life insurance, Carl Thompson had folded his hands in prayer.

"A man who's afraid to pray has a false sense of his place in the world," David had heard his father say hundreds of times, shaking his head at the rise of the secular around him.

David realized this was exactly the kind of moment when his father would have shamelessly dropped to his knees to pray out loud, pray reverently, fervently, for hope and understanding. For patience and strength. He put his own hands together and paced once around the room, searching his soul for a place to begin such a plea. But he soon realized there was no prayer in him.

"I'm sorry, Annie," he said, turning toward her, the words coming out in a strangle. "In the morning we'll go over everything again. Some details," he said, and that was all Annie heard as her husband left the room.

Annie sat alone for a long time listening to the clock in the kitchen ticking off seconds like a drumbeat, each one taking Dylan further away from her.

As the night's darkness fell across her in a shroud, the faces of a dozen battered women rose up in Annie's mind, women she'd heard describe the exact moment when the errors of their lives revealed themselves in a bruise that couldn't be covered, a bone that couldn't be mended out of sight.

Annie had believed their stories were as close as she ever would get to chaos and danger. Over and again she'd put herself into the middle of their lives, knowing whenever the emotions got too menacing she could rub the inside of her wedding band and the gold touchstone would carry her back to the safety of her own home.

But what good was that home, now? She was alone, as those women were alone: a victim who felt like a suspect. Caught between fear and anger, confused about who to trust.

If Dylan was gone for good, Annie couldn't imagine how she would go on. She couldn't imagine calmly serving breakfast to Nick and Sophie again, or even brushing her own teeth without sorrow. She couldn't imagine waking with David and watching him turn those blue eyes on her, knowing he blamed her. Knowing it was her fault.

The night wore on, and Annie felt logic leaving as she moved from room to room. Everyone was sleeping or else lying with eyes closed, breathing in the dust of yesterday, leaving her alone with her desperate thoughts.

She'd been fooling herself, of course. All this time she'd thought the constance and cadence of her life was rooted within. How many times had she congratulated herself as the last child was put to bed? How many times had she picked up a schoolbook and pressed its drab olive cover against her cheek while sighing a secret benediction?

She'd believed it was the books and her work that held her up; believed it was by their strength that she had the presence of mind to be a good mother and the ability to help the women who came to the center for safety.

Now she knew it was folly and conceit. What self-deception, to think that it had ever been anything but her children that set the rhythm of her life. The children marked the current she moved with, pulled against, and lately, since Dylan, the tide she'd rested upon. She'd depended on Dylan to be bright when she was dim, to wave his fingers through the air trying to catch the strands of her hair that fell across his face when she nursed him. It was chatty Sophie and Nick, poor Nick with his pained confusion and his teeth blue from grape chewing gum. His blue teeth drove her crazy, but she counted on them, for blue teeth had become a normal part of her days, a predictable color on the palette of her week.

She watched the night soaking colors from the furniture around her and knew there never would be one normal, unbleached moment without Dylan. The darkness that stole the yellow from the kitchen curtains and drew the purple from her shirt was a darkness that would surely be part of her always.

As the clock passed four and Annie knew the dawn was coming, she crept into the bedroom where David was curled on the bed in his clothes, his back to her, his shoulders rising and falling.

Dylan's crib was empty. Annie touched her baby's things one by one: a white T-shirt with a yellow stain on the chest, his red hooded sweatshirt, his bathing suit. The suit was an old one of Nick's, and when she lifted it, sand spilled onto her feet.

Annie wept. This was her punishment for not wanting Dylan, this was her punishment for the day she'd lain in bed with her husband and said she didn't want another child. She gnashed her teeth, the salty tears pouring down her throat, flooding her ears, drenching the pillow. This was her punishment for every wrong she'd ever done in her life, every selfish act she'd ever committed. Every time she'd turned a deaf ear to one of her children or put her own needs ahead of theirs, every time she'd been weak instead of strong, every time she'd wished for a moment of solitude, she'd put the fates in motion.

"Give me my baby," she whispered fiercely to the wide darkness. "Give me back my baby and take me instead. Take me, take David, take my marriage, take everything, but give me back my baby, please don't let anything bad happen to my little boy."

# CHAPTER 17

## Lynelle

$\mathcal{B}$IRDS wake you, the sun wakes you, fear wakes you, and grief wrenches you in the middle of the night, stealing sleep.

But love, the coo of a child, the smell of baby lotion and the burst of my breasts meeting the mouth of a hungry one is the best way to wake that I have ever known.

He nursed as if he was my own again that morning in the Gainesville motel, and when I fed him I saw my face in the centers of his eyes. I was a solo woman in the middle of a circle, sitting in the calm of a storm. I smiled at him and saw the smile returned in his eyes while the sun came up and trucks gunned by and the day woke slowly and my heart sang.

I packed our things into the same plastic bags they came from and got us on the bus to Flaglerton even before the street people had a chance to jingle their cups at me. The bus ride seemed quick, and my heart was fluttering when we pulled into town. My town. I pressed my face against the glass and watched the buildings pass by on Main Street.

The way I remembered, the bus stopped at the center of town right between the stamp-sized post office and the beauty shop with pink-and-black walls where Mama used to get her hair cut.

Beyond that was the everything store called Ed's, the church up past the stand of mangrove trees, Bob's TV repair, and a few more places up the road. Mostly it was houses or forest brush and small pines, and everywhere you walked the smell of the Peace River followed you, even inside Ed's freezer chest where he kept the ice pops.

But Ed's wasn't there anymore. There was a convenience store instead, and what I guessed to be the old empty lot was filled with two trailer trucks and a snarl of weeds growing along a big metal fence.

The town me and Angel stepped into smelled like hot tar and dust, and from where I stood in the gas station parking lot I could see it stretched out in both directions, filled with a diner and a luncheonette, car and boat supply stores, a place called Fanny's Bar, and any number of ugly-looking buildings. Up ahead was a liquor store, a Winn-Dixie supermarket, and the post office grown to twice the size I remembered.

The bus chugged away, leaving me standing near a gas pump. Two men in green shirts and hats sitting in chairs outside the gas station office looked at me. Three boys on bikes rode a wide circle around me and Angel. I heard the *ding ding* of a car driving up for service and I moved on, stepping onto the sidewalk and trying to get my bearings.

I learned to ride my bike right in that town, right next to Ed's, in a parking lot edged with loose gray pebbles. I learned with my daddy running alongside me with a pocket full of money and keys jangling together and him saying, "You got it, Lynnie, you're going now, Lynnie, you're really moving."

I was planting my feet on the ground in the town I'd carried like a dream in my heart for years, and everything seemed strange. Almost nothing looked at all like I recalled, nor did anything ring a bell of memory. Even the old bumpy sidewalks with tree roots cracking up trip spots and triangles of dirt teeming with fire ants were gone, replaced by a smooth cement walkway that didn't hold a trace of mine and Mama's footsteps. My head spun to see the old mixed with the new, to smell the river water mixed with dust.

I clutched the baby to me. The sweat was building between us, and the sheet I used to tie him onto me was soaked. He squirmed and turned his face away from my body, and a true bit of swoon passed over me, weakening my legs and the bend of my arms. Heat will do that to a body, especially when there aren't any trees for shade.

"Excuse me, sir," I said to an old man who was walking by me with a cane. He was wearing a white hat with the brim stuck way up in the air. "Didn't there used to be a place called Ed's over there?"

The man stopped, which is to say he just slowed down his shuffle three notches and his feet came to a stop. He looked across to where I was pointing.

"Ed's? Why sure that was Ed's. And there was Bill's barbershop too, and the hardware store." He had a dusty voice. "But if you're looking for Ed, he's long gone. Gone to Clearwater."

He squinted at my face. "Are you looking for him?"

I shook my head. We stood and looked at each other for a minute, the way people will do in a small, slow town.

"I'm looking for Pebble Road," I said, for that was the road me and Mama and Daddy used to live on. "Just up the way, off Main Street."

The man shook his head slowly. "Road's gone now," he said. "Hurricane washed everything that side of town away about twelve years ago, and them trailer builders bought the land and put up a display yard."

My house knocked down by a big storm? The walls where Mama hung her pictures soaked full of water and running to the river? I was forced to take deep breaths and look around for what I was to do next. Beneath the dust I smelled the river, a dark water thickening the air.

"Pardon me for asking, but who were you hoping to find on Pebble Road?"

"Just the house," I said at last. "The house I used to live in."

"What the hurricane didn't take, the floods whipped away the next year. 'Eighty-seven, it was. The year my Trixie died."

"I'm sorry," I said.

He waved a wrinkled hand, the one that wasn't holding the cane. "It's okay. She was an old dog."

I looked at that man a long time more. I'll always remember his face, and the way the gray hairs on his eyebrows went in all different directions. It was like he was the face of a spirit telling me there wasn't anyplace on earth for me to find my memories.

I'd been thinking I was going home after a long long time, and finding everything changed brought the weight of my journey down heavy upon me. I was tired and weary, for I could see there would be no place for me to settle into, no store where I could just walk in and find the ice pops in the freezer. I'd had the highest hopes for myself in this town, and though they were surely mistaken and filled with the dirt of the dead, I'd held on to those hopes sure as I was holding on to the child wrapped up against me.

"What about the church? Was the Covenant Baptist blown down too?"

The man was rubbing two pieces of money in his pocket.

"It was. Only thing left was the graveyard, and that stayed put, so they built another church in its place. Folks don't like nobody raising their dead."

He leaned closer to me. Maybe it was rye I smelled on his breath, but there was kindness in his old eyes. "Young lady, you look like you need to sit a spell. Why don't you walk over to Ruby's? I'm going there myself for a piece of her pie."

He pointed up the road to the place called Ruby's Luncheonette. Me and Angel didn't have anything else to do just then, anyhow, so we went along.

# CHAPTER 18

## Annie

"A MIRACLE," Nan said to Annie. "Pray for a miracle."
"I don't want to pray, Mom." Annie's head was full of cobwebs, her heart full of pain, her stomach a lead ball.

"God is watching," Nan urged, her eyes growing large, her face a rain cloud floating over the condo. "God is watching."

"Stop it, Mom." Annie thrashed in her sleep. She saw dark hands carrying Dylan away, hands with hairy knuckles holding him by the ankles, covering his mouth with broad fleshy palms.

"No," Annie cried at the waves crashing over Dylan, at the child swinging him by one leg, the man with dirty clothes and bare feet stuffing him into a knapsack, the woman singing him a song, the half-witted girl wrapping Dylan in doll clothes, forgetting to feed him, smothering him with a pillow.

"No."

Annie snapped awake, bolted upright on the couch with a fist of worry already in her stomach, pushing nausea into her throat.

"Mom? Dad? David?" She pulled the blankets back and jumped up, still wearing the shorts she'd pulled on the night before. She stubbed her toe on the doorjamb as she ran from the living room.

Her father was standing in the kitchen waiting for her. "It's okay, Annie," Joe said, seeing the circles under her eyes and the tangle of her dark hair. "It's okay."

"Where is everybody? Did we hear anything?"

Joe shook his head. The clock over his shoulder said 9:35. Outside the sky was a cheerful blue, the sun unblinking, the leaves shiny on the hibiscus bushes with their brilliant red and shocking pink blossoms.

"David's out with Nick," he said. "Mom took Sophie for a walk to the pool."

"Did anybody call?"

"The police came by to check the phone equipment. There's still one officer outside"—Joe tipped his head toward the east— "holding reporters back at the front gate."

Joe looked down at his hands and was surprised to see he had a firm grip on his daughter's arms.

"Sit down," he said, pressing her back toward a chair at the table. "I'll make you some tea, maybe you'll eat a little cereal."

Annie sat. Somewhere, if Dylan was alive, he was waking and he was hungry. She pressed her hands across her breasts and felt a thin trickle of liquid seep from the nipples. Annie felt hazy from lack of sleep, yet pumped with anxiety—full of dread and energy that she didn't know how to use, her mouth full of words and every one of them sounding like "Dylan."

When she reached for the cup of tea Joe put on the table, Annie's own hands looked strange and foreign, the nails painted sheer linen white but bitten to tiny nubs, the knuckles chewed raw during the long night. Everything, it seemed, was happening as if in a dream. Or a nightmare. Happening to someone else. Except that Dylan wasn't there, and his seat was sitting empty in the corner of the room, empty as a shell and piled with toys next to the black wires that ran to the telephone on the wall.

"I had a dream," Annie said in a low voice. "A nightmare."

Joe sat across from her and listened as she drank her tea and spoke in a whisper. His eyes never left her face. He took her hand. Again, the fingers that had been weak since the stroke closed with some force. He squeezed her trembling fingers in his own.

"I think I'm a suspect." She stared toward the yellow curtains on the window, looking out at the cloudless blue sky. "They think I did something to Dylan. Me, or Nick."

"Why do you say that?"

She didn't say anything about David's late night walk, the way he'd spun around and thrown the accusations at her, his voice sure and angry as if the very idea she could have harmed Dylan was something to be hurtled with weight.

"You should have heard the questions the police asked." Her mouth twisted in a rueful smile. "Didn't they ask you questions about me?"

Joe didn't answer.

"Of course they did, I know they did. They said it was protocol, right? They asked me all kinds of questions about Nicky, too."

"They'll know soon enough that you didn't do anything to him."

"How? How will they know?" Annie tried to keep the edge out of her voice, but it was hard to temper everything she was feeling, the double weight of terror and guilt.

"We're suspects, Dad, let's face it. It's so unlikely for this to happen that it's ludicrous, it's almost impossible. It's inconceivable, that's what it is."

Joe sat next to her in silence, searching his mind for something that could be helpful to Annie at a time like this. Something hopeful, but not trite. Something with faith in it.

"You know once, when you were about three years old, I took you with me to the market. It was a weekend, I think, and your mother wasn't feeling too good." He spoke slowly at first, his words picking up speed and timbre as he saw her eyes following the thin spotlight of his memory.

"I was tired, but you were full of energy, skipping along next to me, putting your hand in mine and then pulling it away."

His eyes looked around the kitchen, but what he saw was his little girl wearing a white dress, tugging on his hand.

"Anyway, I lost you in the fruit aisle. One minute you were there, the next minute you were gone." He looked at her, staring hard. "It can happen, Annie. It can happen even when you're being careful.

"You can imagine how I felt. I called for you a few times, but you didn't answer. The store was crowded, and you were so little. I panicked. I ran up and down the aisles calling your name, all those women with their shopping carts turning to look at me like I was crazy. You were missing for about ten minutes. Ten minutes. It was an eternity to me. By the time I found you in the candy aisle I was crying."

"Were you mad?"

"Mostly I was scared, honey. Mostly I was scared."

"I'm scared now, Daddy." Her breath caught in her chest, but she swallowed it back down.

"I know, Annie."

"Do you think they'll find him?" She heard pleading in her voice, as if the answer he gave could change the outcome.

"I do." He nodded slowly.

"You do? Why?"

He looked past her, again seeing a memory, this time Dylan, waving his hands in the air.

"I don't know. I just think they'll find him. Your mother always says I'm an optimist." Joe laughed a little, a sound more like a sputter and a cough. "Well, really she says I'm a fool, but that's because she always thinks the worst. I don't, Annie."

His eyes sought hers, held on to the dark center of her gaze. She didn't see the aging, watery blur at the edges of his irises, but hope and faith and strength.

"I never think the worst. Even when I had my stroke I never thought the worst. I kept hoping things would get better."

Annie looked down at his hand. The grip was weakening, but his hand was steady. Last night she'd seen liver spots and age but now she saw the hand that had taught her to cut a fabric on the bias and sew a straight line. The hand that held hers the night she fell off her bicycle and cracked two front teeth and had to have twelve stitches in her lip. It was the hand that carved skis for her out of wood, the hand that built a cage for butterflies she caught in a net one summer, the hand that touched her cheek and sent her off on her first date with five dollars in her purse and a reminder to call home if anything made her uncomfortable.

She'd chosen differently—married a strong man instead of a gentle one—and now Annie wondered at the wisdom of that choice as she cried with her father's fingers wrapped through her own, catching tears in the cracks and folds of his palms.

"If they don't find him I'm going to die, Daddy, I'm going to die."

"You have two other children, Annie. You won't die. I promise you that. Pain doesn't kill you. You think it will, but it doesn't."


"Do we really have thirty thousand dollars, Dad?" Nick asked, reading the posters in his lap, staring at Dylan's picture and trying hard not to feel the sickness in his belly.

They'd been out in the van since before nine that morning, carrying David's laptop to the copy shop on Blue Heron Boulevard and walking out with a thousand bright green posters with Dylan's picture scanned under the word *missing* and above the words *$30,000 reward.*

"Yup." David kept his eye on the road, his mouth in a firm line.

"In the bank?"

"Nick." David's voice was sharp, a single word that meant *Stop asking questions.* He nosed the van out of the parking lot onto the street, glancing right and left and sidelong at Nick, who was biting his lip, looking down at his lap.

"Don't worry about the money," David said, more gently. "If it comes down to money, we'll get whatever we need."

Charged as he was by urgency, it was all David could do to stop the car every fifty yards, rip off pieces of masking tape with his teeth, and watch Nick run out to mount the flyers on mailboxes and telephone poles. It seemed so mundane, so small in the face of such a vast personal emergency, yet experience had taught David that the way things turned out depended on how the details were attended to each step of the way, each task building upon the precise execution of the one before it.

The police rode in a car behind him, and a television crew alongside them. David did his best to ignore the cameras, but when they were persistent he stopped the van and got out holding a green flyer.

"This is my son." David pointed to the scanned photo. "If you see him, if anyone sees him, please call the police. I'm offering a reward. Whoever has Dylan, please bring him home."

Soon there were people, ordinary people he'd never met, coming up to him with their own rolls of tape in hand, taking fistfuls of flyers and hugging him, promising to take the posters to the far corners of the county and beyond. One older woman, in particular, riveted David's attention when she pressed herself against him. "God bless you," she said, squeezing his hand. "There's a lesson in everything."

For a moment, looking at the peace in her blue eyes, David felt himself relaxing into the idea of a fate beyond his control. It was a soothing memory from his childhood, a belief that all things are in the hands of God. But as the woman walked away and the glare of the sun blinded him, a terror pulsed through David's heart. Soon he was getting out of the van at every block, taping the flyers up himself, quizzing Nick at the same time.

"When you were at the craft fair, did anyone stop and talk to you?"

"No, Dad, I already told you, no."

"Think, Nick. Think back. Did anybody walk by and *look* at you?"

"No."

"Are you sure?"

"Yeah, pretty sure."

David looked down at Nick, saw his eyes flicker.

"*What*, Nick? Tell me."

Nick squeezed his eyes shut so tight he saw dots, but even in between the red and green dots he saw his brother's tiny feet covered with white socks, just as they'd been the last time he saw them in the stroller.

"I'm telling you the truth, Dad, I don't remember anything."

The boy pushed his shoulders back so far the blades almost touched behind him, his neck craned up to stare at his father's face.

"Okay," David said. They were standing on the side of the road, and the police car cruised up next to them. David waved a salute. He put a hand on Nick's shoulder and moved him along.

"How about a car, did you see any cars drive by in the parking lot?"

"The police asked me all these questions already, Dad," Nick said, but he knew enough not to whine, he could see how important the answers were to his father. "I already told them everything."

But he hadn't.

"What did you tell them?"

"I told them about the station wagon that drove by, and a little blue car, too."

What Nick hadn't told anybody—not even his mother when she was holding his hand on the bedroom floor last night—was that he'd left Dylan alone so he could go back and look at the pocketknives, thinking he might be able to buy one without anyone knowing.

"And that's when you went to look for the man selling starfish?" David asked.

Nick nodded. He'd told the police he walked away from Dylan to look for the man selling painted starfish because he wanted to buy one for his mother's birthday. The lie had come suddenly and easily to Nick, who was not in the habit of lying, and there seemed no way out of it now.

"I'm sorry, Dad." He felt tears coming. The weight of the lie was behind his eyes, forcing its way out. "I'm sorry."

They stood on Route 1, in front of a car wash, and David put his arm around Nick's shoulders. The sky was clear, and the red, white, and blue car wash banners were flapping in the breeze behind them.

The television cameras zoomed in. Soon everyone who watched CNN would see the tears glistening on the boy's face, the grim set of the father's mouth as he patted Nick on the back and moved him along the road under a waving sea of red, white, and blue flags.


"I have to do something," Annie said to her father. "I'm going to go crazy if I just sit here waiting."

She was holding the portable phone in her lap when it jangled the first time, ringing so loudly she jumped, jamming her knees into the underside of the kitchen table.

It took a moment for Annie to recognize her mother-in-law's voice, tight with worry, calling from Minnesota.

"David phoned last night, we want to know if anything has changed," Eleanor said. The precision of her diction, the direct way she cut to the point, reminded Annie of her husband's own matter-of-fact efficiency. To this day Eleanor carried small tissue packets and wet wipes in her purse in case of spills or smudges. She always had a needle and thread handy, and never had to use the microwave to defrost anything for dinner at the last minute. Comparing herself with Eleanor, Annie cringed with inadequacy.

"You phone us the minute anything happens, please."

"I will," Annie promised before she hung up, wondering how much of the story Eleanor knew, and how much she blamed her.

"What should I do, Daddy? Should I go down and check on Sophie? Should I try to find David and Nick?" Annie bit her nails, the nubs oozing small dots of blood where she'd bitten through the skin.

"Maybe I should be calling people. Who should I call? Maybe I should call Christine," she suggested at last.

Her sister Christine was another woman who often made Annie feel her own clothes were too wrinkled, her ideas a bit too muddled and far too liberal to be the opinions of a true grown-up. Annie was mentally tallying the reasons she didn't want to talk to Christine, then thinking of all the reasons she should call her sister in Boston, when the phone jangled on the table in front of her a second time.

She gritted her teeth and waited for the third ring, heard the black boxes on the kitchen counter whirring and snapping, the tracking devices warming up.

"Annie, it's Chris." Her sister's voice came in a rush over the phone line, an accusation that took Annie's breath away. "My God, what's happening down there?"

"Chris"—she repeated her older sister's name—"I was just getting ready to call you."

"I'm at my office. I have to be in court in an hour. I can't believe Mom didn't call me, I can't believe someone had to see it on CNN and tell me about this in the elevator this morning. Annie, I'm a lawyer. I work with the criminal mind, I understand it better than you do."

"We have the police," Annie said. She propped the phone between her chin and shoulder and stood up, pacing from nerves. "Anyway, you do business law, Christine, you don't know the criminal mind."

"Annie, do you have any idea why someone would do this to you?"

Without realizing what she was doing, Annie started opening kitchen cabinets, moving aside boxes of crackers and jars of bran, looking for chocolate. "I don't think someone did this to me," she said weakly as her hands fell upon a small yellow bag of chocolate chips. She ripped it open, poured a pile into her palm. "I think this was random."

"You have to give the police a list of everybody you worked with at that shelter, everybody who was ever mad at you."

Annie was sweaty all over, her head was reeling. She sat down, poured the chocolate pieces right from the bag into her mouth. She ignored the way her father was watching her, the pained confusion on his face.

"Look, I'm trying to get down there," Christine said, her voice loud in Annie's ear, as if the connection had been blocked and suddenly cleared.

"Okay," Annie said, gratitude and fear washing through her at the same time, bringing a hot flash that felt like shame to her cheeks.

"I'll call you later if I can get everything arranged."

Christine clicked off the connection. Annie lay the phone down on the table and finished another handful of chocolate chips. Then she pulled a piece of paper in front of her and picked up a pen.

It was twenty-two hours since she'd seen Dylan. Twenty-two hours since she'd noted his flushed cheeks and wondered if he needed a diaper change. Twenty-two hours since she'd propped up the bottle of water so he could drink from it, feeling guilty even for such a small transgression. The books warned against bottle propping, but they never warned against baby snatchers. She was frightened. More frightened than she'd ever been in her life.

Yes, the battered women's names were confidential. But giving the police their names was one more constructive thing Annie could do, and her fear outweighed every other consideration. She pulled the cap off the cracked blue pen and wrote down the name Dee Pulaski.

Dee Pulaski, the woman with the bite marks on her arm. Her husband had seen Annie pregnant when they went to court for an order of protection. He'd glared at her. His name was Tom. Annie wrote his name down next to Dee's.

She remembered looking at Tom's teeth, the way they were stained brown with cigarette smoke, and she felt the chocolate chips churning in her stomach.

# CHAPTER 19

## Lynelle

R UBY'S Luncheonette was a place like any other, with a counter full of glass-covered cake plates and a row of booths running straight to the back. We had our choice of seats as the place was empty just then, and we sat in a middle booth. There was just enough room for me and Dylan to squeeze in together across the red plastic seats.

Ruby herself, who I knew from her name sewed onto her pink shirt pocket, poured us two cups of water into yellow glasses. The water looked green in the cups. The old man said to me, "My name's Chip and you can trust me—that's clean water. Looks green but it ain't." He winked at me and swallowed down his whole glassful.

There was a tall metal fan in one corner of the room making a lot of noise just to blow a bit of breeze across the tops of our heads, a TV stuck on a shelf behind the counter, and a couple of newspapers left open in the booths next to crumb-filled plates. This would be the kind of place where people asked for extra toast to sop up the last bits of runny egg yolks. It was the kind of place my daddy and me used to go on Sunday mornings.

Sitting in Ruby's, smelling the river in the air and feeling the loss of the girlhood ghosts I'd hoped to find, I started missing my daddy real bad. I missed the way he always tried to get me to help him with the crosswords in the newspaper, the way he jumped in the air whenever he bowled a strike or took a spare.

When I was a girl and we went out to eat, Daddy never minded me playing with my dolls or kicking my legs against the seats or asking for a pen so I could draw pictures on the napkins. He'd sit and read the paper or talk to the waitresses. In one place, after he was divorced from Stevie, Daddy had a couple of buddies who bet the dog races. Daddy always had a strong opinion about which dogs to bet, and though he was often right he never bet more than two dollars himself.

"Got a girl to take care of," he told the other men, but after they left he'd say to me, "I ain't lucky, Lynelle. I got no luck."

I was old enough by then to see that sometimes my daddy felt sorry for himself, and with good reason. First Mama, then the bad luck of choosing Stevie, and finally the orange juice job gone on account of a winter freeze and a general depression in the state of Florida. He said it was the best job he'd ever had, too.

"I land on my feet though. You're a Page girl, and just like me you'll always land on your feet."

I wanted to believe him, but right then, sitting in Ruby's, I felt mostly sad and tired and not very lucky. I missed my daddy, missed the way he told me, "We're not trash. We don't steal." His words were big in my head when Ruby came over again and asked what we'd be eating.

"Got good egg salad today," she said.

Despite the heat I had a sudden longing for grilled cheese with tomato, my daddy's favorite rainy day food. Just as I was about to ask for it, Chip spoke up. "Ruby, this girl grew up in town," he said. "House over on Pebble Road."

Ruby looked at me with milky blue eyes. For a minute she looked like the Preacher Dale's wife, but Mrs. Dale would be an old lady already while Ruby was fat and perky and no older than a young grandma.

"No fooling," she said. "What's your name, hon?"

"Lynelle," I answered without lying because I'd already told a piece of the truth and the habit of making up a story wasn't right there on the tip of my tongue.

"Lynelle Page Carter. Carter's my married name," I said, hungry to be known in my hometown. Ruby said my name a few times to herself, trying to see if it rang a bell. While she was thinking the door opened and two men walked in. She called a big hello as they sat down on round stools near the cash register. She asked if they thought the thermometer would reach one hundred before noon, and I was left waiting to see if her face might show some memory of my family.

"My mama was Grace Page. My aunt is Fay Bartlett."

Ruby shook her head.

"Bobby Page is my daddy."

"Bobby? You mean Bobby Page with those dark eyes?" And then she remembered. I saw a whole bunch of memory dance across her face.

"You the little girl?"

I nodded. I could see myself across a great distance, me as a sad little girl.

"You look fine. You look well. Looks like you done good."

"I guess," I said.

"I see you're a mama now. Let me see your baby."

She peeked at Dylan, who I had took out of the sheet and was holding across my shoulder, rubbing his back. He was sucking on his fingers. I could hear it in my ear.

"When was he born?"

"Early February," I said, again without thinking.

"February? You mean to tell me this here's not even a one-month-old baby?"

We both looked down at him together. I bit my lip and nodded. When I looked back up at her eyes, there was something new in them.

"First of the month he was born," I said, wrapping my arms

around the size of his body, trying to cover up my mistake. "Really he's almost four weeks. And he was born big. His Daddy's from Tennessee, and you know how big they grow men there."

I tried laughing a little, as laughter will hide a lot. Then me and Chip put in our orders.

While we waited I could feel my foot beginning to shake under the table, I could feel myself wanting to move on and walk away from all that truth and the tower of lies I was building, a shaky batch of tales. Country folks can sniff out a tale the way they can sniff out a bad fish from a batch of good ones. No sense sitting around and telling a mixed-up tale to somebody who knew so much of my story, I told myself.

But the food was ordered and they already knew my name, and anyway the baby was sitting in my arms, reaching for my hair, and I was thinking it would be time to feed him again soon when Ruby set a plate with grilled cheese, tomatoes, and pickles in front of me.

I ate fast as I dared while the old man Chip kept up a steady account of storms and rains and other things that had battered my old town.

"The worst ones was before you was born, that would be the Hurricanes Donna and Cleo back in the sixties," he said, rattling on about trees torn up by the roots and folks floating down the road on pieces of clapboard or screen doors tore right off the houses, chairs drug out from where they were sitting on front porches with the people still set in them.

I nodded and smiled, at least I think I smiled, all the while wondering what I would do next. I pictured in my head just how much money I had left and what I would do when it ran out. I thought of my daddy, of Hogan, of Aunt Fay sitting in her hot tub under the Ozark sky that she says is filled with more stars than anywhere on earth, and I felt a longing for the living, a longing for a whole family surrounding me and my baby, whatever baby that might be. That was the last thing I thought before the front door to Ruby's place opened again and the sheriff stepped in.

He was a black man with glasses and silver hair, nappy and shiny like it was freshly oiled. He had wide shoulders and long fine fingers. I recall that detail, the way he touched his hand over the gun in his holster, how pearly white the gun was against the black skin of his hand.

The whole place, everybody and everything in Ruby's, even the sizzle of bacon in the kitchen behind the pickup window, came to a hush. I looked from the sheriff's hand to his face and down the stiff front of his shirt to the badge on his chest.

Whether Ruby had called him or it was just the pace of things, I couldn't be sure. So I stood slowly, pulling out my money just so from my fanny pack, my head cloudy with trying to figure out a tip. I put out ten dollars, just to be sure.

"Ten dollars for a grilled cheese?" Chip said, and I smiled, my lips shaky.

"For yours, too, for showing me a kindness and sharing so many stories," I said, daring to look him in the eye just one last time.

A whistle blew somewhere. I knew it was twelve noon, that men like my daddy and Hogan, men who rose before the sun and worked long honest days, would be taking their lunch breaks or washing their hands and heading for home. The sheriff didn't more than look at me as I walked by him. I dipped my face down, nodding in a way that's known as polite, pulled the sheet over the baby's head, and kept on walking.

As I passed by the men at the front I heard them talking about the chance of rain. One asked Ruby to put on the TV news so they could see the weather report.

# CHAPTER 20

## Annie

A NNIE struggled over the list of battered women one name at a time, each with its own stinging memory. *Dee Pulaski. Rene Stolwyck. Anita Rodriguez. Tiffany White (address unknown). Kate Pantano. Maria Santura.* She closed her eyes to their wounds and wrote down their names and addresses. When she was finished Annie folded the yellow paper in half, pushed it to the middle of the kitchen table, and covered it with her teacup.

"There," she said to the empty room. "I've done it."

She'd give it to the police in a little while. It was nothing to be proud of, but it was something done. Something that might help Dylan, and that made it necessary no matter what the shame.

Outside, Sophie and Nan were sitting at the edge of the wading pool when she found them. Her mother's anxious glance was much like her own, lips hungry and parted, eyes lined with worry.

"Did Dylan come home yet?" Sophie asked, dropping the pink bucket of water into the wading pool and running to stand in the shade of Annie's shadow.

"Not yet, sweetie." Annie bent and put her arms around Sophie. The girl's bathing suit printed a dark wet stain on her denim blouse. "The police are still looking for him."

At that very moment a dozen police officers were searching the boat cabins and portals at the Singing Island marina, poking inside the storage bins of the cruisers, peering into the spaces between the dock pilings, and reading the records of the harbormaster. The Coast Guard was on alert, Mounties on horseback were walking the beaches, the search had spread into the five surrounding counties, and the governor had ordered security tripled in airports and bus terminals throughout Florida.

More than one hundred fifty officers working overtime and double shifts were spread out on foot across Palm Beach County carrying mimeographed copies of Dylan's photo tucked into the breast pockets of their blue uniforms, knocking on doors, stopping pedestrians and commuters, shoppers and strollers.

Even the rookie officer Carlos Molina was back out there on five hours' sleep, the memory of David's wracking sobs still keen on the curve of his arm as he walked the streets north of Singing Island, standing outside the bodegas as they opened, speaking in his native tongue to the people who were starting their day with a cold can of cola or ending a long night with a bottle of OJ.

The rookie, who had a strong heart and a kind disposition, ignored the way the men shifted when he approached them, the way they glanced at his uniform and then looked away.

"Hey, what if it was your baby?" Molina asked, and more than one man said, "That's not my baby, no way," as if he were accusing them of patrimony.

But the girl with the gold tooth and the baby in her belly shifted her weight from one slippered foot to the other and said, "I swear I seen that boy."

Molina wrote everything down in his logbook. He wrote down Crystal Diaz's name, the street corner where they were standing, and number of the apartment building where she lived.

He held his hand out, almost touching her shoulder, and guided her to a stoop in the shade of a scrawny oak tree. Crystal took the picture from Molina's hand.

"Yeah." She nodded. "I think I seen this baby. What do you want to know about him for?"

While Molina told her, she looked him up and down. When he stopped talking, she whistled through her gold tooth. "Well, well. She told me his name's Angel. Said she was going to see her mother. Asked about the bus up to Gainesville. I might be dumb enough to pick the wrong men"—she looked Molina in the eye—"but I never forget a little baby's face. Yeah, that's him. That's the baby I seen yesterday."

When Annie opened the condo door and saw Herrara empty-handed, filling the doorstep, her mouth fell open in a wail. She staggered back into the flat of Joe's palm, watching the lieutenant's mouth moving, struggling to hear his words.

"It's not bad news," the officer said. "It's a good thing. We have a lead."

He held out the sketch: a young woman with dark hair, a long face, troubled eyes.

"A woman?"

Herrara nodded. "Do you recognize her?"

Annie peered at the picture.

"No." She shook her head, feeling the blood spinning. She felt as if any sudden move could push her over the edge, drop her into a place she might never be able to leave.

"Who is she?" Annie reached for the paper, held it between two fists.

"We don't know yet."

"Where are they? Who saw them?"

The questions tumbled out of her in a crush of syllables banging against one another, her own tongue a hindrance for what she really wanted to know, which was when she would hold Dylan again, if she ever would hold him again.

"How did Dylan seem? When were they seen? Is he all right?"

Herrara cleared his throat. He started to answer, but Annie's questions kept on coming.

"Was he crying? Did he look okay?"

Clutching the picture, Annie took in the curve of the woman's lips, the dark circles under her eyes, the hard glint in the set of her gaze.

"How old is she?"

"Young," Herrara said. "Midtwenties, by the witness's estimate."

A shiver ran through Annie, her feet and hands tingled numb with the chill. She pressed a palm against her mouth, gazing at the picture as she moved out of the doorway and let Herrara step up into the porch.

Joe stood over Annie's shoulder, and she held the sketch for him to see.

"What does she want with my baby?" Annie asked, looking from Joe to Herrara and then back again to the picture in her hand, searching for reason in the flat, mimeographed gaze.

She pressed the picture close up to her face, breathing in the scent off the paper—the powdery film of a photocopy, the charcoal stain of ink in her nostrils—as if it might carry the scent of the woman.

"What does she want with him?" she whispered, holding the picture so close that spit from her words sprayed a fine mist onto the paper, spreading a pox of translucent spots across the woman's cheeks. "Where is she taking my baby?"

# CHAPTER 21

## Lynelle

ALONE on Main Street, I walked away from Ruby's fast as I dared, not turning when I heard the door open and shut again nor when I heard the sheriff's car radio buzz with a message striking the air like lightning. I just watched the ground for shadows rising toward me and breathed a low hum into the baby's ear.

I walked by gut instinct, turning this way and that, following the smell of the river and the water in the air seeping into my bones, drawing me closer. The houses were gone fast and I was in the brush, bramble scratching my legs, lizards scurrying out of the way and rattling leaves.

The baby stayed pressed against me, held in one arm while I parted branches with my other hand, moving faster, whispering to him while I watched the ground for sinkholes. I half-expected one to open up and swallow me, take me under and spit the baby back out. The earth can be hungry that way. It's not just cloudy skies that take people but the ground itself, the ocean and rivers. Light danced through a lace of leaf shadows across my face, sun flashed into my eyes and then disappeared over the roof of trees until finally I came to the edge of the brush, finally branches stopped tapping me on the shoulders and the river was there in front of me, black and thick and moving.

I stopped, out of breath, letting the sound of the river wash over me. It was the same. Something at last was the same as I remembered it, dark as a night mirror, quick and deep, smelling like the heart of the earth.

"Every drop of water passes this way only once." Mama's voice came into my head like a bolt, a message of the spirit that found me right there. "It passes this way, and then goes on to another place."

The river was high, and the stones on the side slope were covered. I stood at the edge of the mudbank and held my breath just to hear the echo of Mama's words and the sound of water moving by, the hum of it, the call of it, the song of it. I tried to see the sparkle of one water drop passing by before rising to a cloud and falling somewhere else as rain, but after a while I knew it was impossible. Nothing stayed still long enough to see it. Even my reflection was a broken wave, and I knew the idea that a drop of water matters on its own was something to be believed on faith alone.

"Listen," I said to the baby. He was looking at the sky, his eyes steel gray and shining like the silver side of a trout. "Look."

I turned him around to see the river. We watched a leaf fall into the moving waters, and I thought of those things I'd dropped over the bridge into the fog. I saw my baby girl's face white and stone gone, I saw my mama's face in the coffin with a pink-collared dress and pearl buttons.

Every drop of water passes this way only once.

I looked up at the sky, what I could see of it shaped like the river, a slice of the day uncovered and naked.

"There are worse things than dying," I whispered. I'd come so far to stand alone in a place that felt like the end of the earth, like the end of the world I'd been hoping to find.

"There are worse things, I know"—I was crying—"I know there must be worse things than this, but I don't know what they are, Mama, I don't know what they are."

I pulled the baby to me so hard I was crushing him. He started to squall, his cries mixing with my own.

"I don't know where to go, I don't know what to do."

I'd run away from everything but still had my own self, my own pain inside me bigger than my skin, a pain so big it would take the whole river to drown it, the whole ocean to swallow it. If I could have stepped out of my own skin right then and there I would've done it, like a snake sliding along the riverbank I would have slipped my soul down into the murky black water and left just the shell of myself standing on the shore. An empty body free of pain is what I wanted to be with an ache that went beyond prayer, an ache that had no words, an ache that brought on silent tears that slid from my cheeks and fell into the river, washed away with all the other millions of water drops that would pass this way only once.

I was right there on the banks of the river, choking on my tears, when I heard footsteps behind me, the crack of branches and the bark of a dog. I turned to see the sheriff from Ruby's holding fast to the leash of a tugging hound.

"Lynelle Carter?" he called, more like a command than a question. "Y'all stay right there."

I stepped back and my foot slipped down into the water. Like a baptism, it pulled me in. I cried out but didn't let go of the baby.

"Don't do it," the sheriff shouted. There was a rush of the earth and then a scourge of men pulled Angel away from me, grabbing my arms with thick fingers and tugging me back up while the trees were shrieking, the river was moaning, the sky was wailing, and all of them had my voice, all of them echoed with the long, long cry that rose in my throat and went on and on.

# CHAPTER 22

## Annie

A NNIE opened the front door. At first she didn't see the blue sky behind the lieutenant, or notice the way he bounced on his toes, the way a smile was turning up the edges of his mouth. She saw almost nothing at all except for the picture in the back of her mind of Dylan.

"I think we found him," Herrara said.

"Are you sure?" Something twisted in Annie's stomach, it felt more like a lead pipe of dread than a feather of hope. She pressed a palm against her belly, felt her face flush.

Herrara stepped closer, laid a hand on Annie's shoulders to steady her.

"We can't be sure until you identify him," the lieutenant said, "but I'm pretty sure—"

"And he's okay?" Annie grabbed Herrara's hand, she sought his eyes. "Is he all right?"

"Apparently he seems fine," Herrara hedged.

"But?"

"He's at the hospital now—"

"Hospital?" Annie's knees buckled, she clutched tighter onto Herrara's arms, felt her stomach lurch higher into her throat.

"It's procedure, Annie," Herrara said loudly, to capture her attention and hold it. "It's standard procedure, he's being examined by a pediatrician, but the report is that he seems fine, he's alive and seems to be well."

"You're going to take me to him?"

Herrara took a breath, he nodded. Joe came up behind Annie, shuffling slowly.

"Daddy." Annie turned and hung on to his shoulders. She felt anxiety tumbling away, her heart beating freely, taking every bit of energy that had been keeping her going for the last twenty-seven hours. "They found him. They found Dylan."

"It's over." Joe breathed a sigh, he patted Annie's back but she pushed away, she spun around again to the lieutenant.

"No, it's not over until I'm holding him." Annie's voice rose and fell. "I need to have him with me."

Alerted by a sheriff's messenger, David and Nick drove up in the van and soon added their arms to the embrace on the lawn in front of the condo, their voices to the choir of murmurs and shouts.

David surprised even himself by putting his head on Annie's shoulder and letting a few tears fall onto the fabric of her shirt, but in the midst of it Annie found herself looking at the smear of tears on David's face and wondering what he would say when they were alone.

As he gulped a jagged breath, she patted him on the back in a gesture meant as much to comfort as to say, Let's get on with it, because what she wanted most, at that moment, was to be holding her baby in her arms.

"He's in Arcadia," she said to David, repeating the name the lieutenant had said to her. "We have to take a helicopter to see him."

# CHAPTER 23

## *Lynelle*

ONCE upon a time I knew how fast word travels in a small town, but on the day of my arrest I was shocked to see newspeople tripping over each other on the sidewalk outside the sheriff's office, and at least two dozen regular folks lined up to shout things at me. They leaned over the hot pavement calling me baby stealer and white trash, saying I deserved to die, waving fists in the air with their eyes popping out of their heads.

One blond girl with a little baby on her hip and tears streaming down her face even tried to grab at my arm. "What kind of person are you?" she hissed. I looked at her green eyes, and for a second I thought she might be an old friend of mine, one of those high school girls who liked to tell me her secrets. But it was just a mirage, and her face blended in with the others.

My feet were wet and muddy, they chilled me as three Arcadia deputies pulled me up the stone stairs into the station house, through double glass doors that opened into a cold bright room filled with desks and benches and phones ringing like crazy. There were half a dozen people working, and each one of them stopped right in the middle of talking or typing or sipping tea to stare at me and the deputies as we threaded our way to a tiny room with a table and two chairs nailed to the floor.

There were no windows in there. The walls were light brown and spongy, the kind of wall that no sounds pass through, the kind of wall that would swallow a scream if the deputies cared to close the door and cause me pain. But they left it open, no doubt to show me off like a prize to the folks who were walking by, peering in at me, slapping them on the back with praises.

"Will you lookit this?" The deputy with the big belly took my braid between his hands and rubbed it up and down. "Think she's some kind of half-breed?"

I shook my head, like to shake off a bug, but his hand clamped shut and pulled my head back so I was looking up at the bottom of his chin.

"Easy now," he said in a whispering voice, an evil man whisper. My head was just about pressed into the buckle of his belt. One of the others chuckled. The deputy's hand moved up and down my braid, a horrible, slow, fear-raising motion. I shook my head again and he pushed my face down this time, down into the lap of my breasts.

One of the other deputies leaned over in front of me, his fat fingers spread wide on the table between us. There were long dark hairs sticking out from under his gold wedding ring, and he had bit-up fingernails.

"What were you planning to do with that baby?"

"I didn't mean him no harm," I said, just to set the record right. Then I shut my mouth and listened inside myself for the flow of the Peace River while the deputies took turns barking their questions at me like snapping dogs, whispering and touching at me from behind.

It was the sheriff who broke up their guffawing and jabbering. He stepped into the room and the deputies scampered away, their soft shoes leaving scuff marks on the floor.

The sheriff closed the door and sat himself on the edge of the table. He took his time about it, hitching up the legs of his pants and waiting for perfect stillness. I felt the heat coming off the skin of his bare arms, and I closed my eyes.

"You done a serious crime," the sheriff said. He seemed to suck up the very air and light in the room. "It will be in your best interest if you cooperate with me."

He put a fear in me, a fear far worse than those deputies brought out with their sweaty fingers and liverwurst breath.

"I'm going to read you your rights," he said. "You understand what that means?"

I'd seen enough TV to recognize the words "you got the right to remain silent" and all the rest, but when he was done I just said, "Yes sir," and when he asked if I admitted to taking the child named Dylan Thompson from a stroller in a park in the town of Riviera Beach, I told him yes again.

I nodded my head and said yes sir to everything he asked. I admitted to lifting Dylan out of the stroller, to taking him on a bus and sleeping with him in a motel room. I had no idea about the law, I just kept answering his questions, thinking back over what I'd done and feeling fear and shame mixing with my grief until at last my voice just fell right down the back of my throat.

"You shared a bed with him?"

I shook my head. I could see the baby in that dresser drawer, covered up with a blanket.

"Where did you spend the night?"

I couldn't speak. I looked the sheriff in the face. His eyes were steel gray.

"You admit you touched him improperly?"

"I didn't do that," I whispered, but he kept on asking me horrible things until I was crying just at the idea of what they thought I'd done.

"I think we have enough right here to put you away," the sheriff said. I heard my own weeping and the sounds of doors opening and shutting, saw the slow zigzagging of the hem of my yellow skirt as I was led back through the bright room and down a long hallway to what they called the room of records, where a man with brown teeth fingerprinted and photographed me.

"Next of kin?" the man asked.

I shook my head.

"Unusual medical conditions?"

No, again.

"An attorney or another person you'd like to call?"

No.

When they took off the handcuffs I had to sit with my arms pressed against my chest to keep from trembling, and when at last they were finished I was thankful to be taken to the dank little room they called a holding cell.

"They'll be coming up from Palm Beach to get you," the deputy said, "so don't get too comfortable." He laughed, for the cell was stripped bare to a board for a bed and a door made of metal bars. "You got any questions, you better ask now."

What I most wanted to know was where they'd taken the baby. Back to his rightful mama, I supposed. Back to a lady who would have a lap and a chair and a perfect corner of her life already set out and waiting for his return. Of course I'd never see him again, of course he was as lost and dead to me as everybody else. I'd done wrong to take him, and I was about to pay the price for it. Twenty-three years old and at the end of my life is what I was thinking while I laid down and buried my face against the bare gray wall.

# CHAPTER 24

## *Annie*

A NNIE opened her arms, and the nurse put Dylan into the crook of her elbow.

He smelled of baby powder and rubbing alcohol, his hair dipped in a half-moon over the curve of his forehead. She buried her face in Dylan's neck and pressed her cheek against his.

"I'm sorry, I'm sorry, I'm sorry." Her voice was a jagged whisper as Dylan opened his eyes and stared without moving.

"Oh, Dylan, I'm sorry, I'm sorry, Dylan, Dylan." She said his name over and over, her lips turning the consonants and vowels into a song until his eyes softened, the sea in his eyes smoothed into an aqua tide and he reached his hand out to touch her cheek.

Annie's tears fell onto his face, and all the people on the second-floor pediatric unit of the hospital in Arcadia—nurses and doctors, David and Lieutenant Herrara and Officer Molina, sheriffs who'd never seen Annie or Dylan before—felt their throats tighten, their eyes burn.

"He's a lucky boy, Mrs. Thompson." The doctor's voice came to Annie through the haze of baby lotion and coos. "He was fed and bathed, and seems in fairly robust spirits. All things considered, he's in fine shape."

Annie touched her baby's fingers, counting them as if for the first time. Dylan was wearing a pair of cheap yellow pajamas she'd never seen before, and she wanted to rip them off him, to press her lips against his belly and see for herself that his arms and legs were dimpled and olive-white as always.

"Lucky, yes, we're lucky." Annie turned her eyes onto the doctor's white lab coat, the gloves on her hands and the soft sweep of hair, the sharp brown eyes behind her glasses.

"I'm Dr. Mukarjee." The other woman pulled off a clear plastic glove and touched Annie's hand. "Your son has been well cared for, and unharmed."

"Well cared for," Annie murmured, the idea muddled in her head, yet a relief all the same.

David stepped next to Annie. "We're so grateful." His voice cracked as he wrapped one arm around his wife's shoulder and reached for the doctor with the other, pulling her toward him in an awkward embrace.

"This is him," Annie said, half-laughing, holding Dylan out for Herrara to see. "Now it's over," she said. "Now it's really over. Now he's coming home with me."


They'd arrived by helicopter but drove back to Sparkling Waters in a patrol car with Officer Molina at the wheel, Dylan in the backseat between Annie and David, a motorcade of sheriff's escorts and news camera trucks surrounding them as they rolled onto the highway.

In the back of the police car, with the safety glass shut between themselves and Molina, Annie and David were alone.

"I'm sorry," David said as the road ribboned silently under them. "I'm sorry I said some mean things to you." He meant also that he was sorry for the anger in his heart, sorry for resenting her, sorry he'd been unable to pray. But none of that came out, or even reached the front of his brain where true, confused compassion could be put into words.

Annie looked at Dylan, wanting nothing to destroy the joy she felt at being given another chance to hold him, to take him home, to curl under the blankets and press him against her breast. She couldn't look at her husband.

"Did you hear me, Annie?" David reached across Dylan and moved a piece of hair off her cheek. She glanced at him quickly, one second, the flicker of an eyelash.

"I know it was an accident." He struggled for words, the apology of a man who rarely said he was sorry coming hard across his tongue.

Annie nodded. She kept her eyes on her baby, flickered them out the window to the sunset. It was just beginning to dawn on her, a cold realization on the edges of her fingers and the borders of her heart, the way the impossible happened and could happen again, the way the world could not be predicted, the way people could hurt each other at the exact time when they needed to help each other.

"You hurt me," Annie said at last. "You weren't there for me."

"I'm sorry, Annie, I am. But under the circumstances I think we simply need to move on. Look ahead to getting Dylan home and seeing that woman put in jail."

"I know. I know that's what you think." Annie turned to take in the fine line of his nose, his full lips. "But you blamed me."

He still blamed her, really, she could see it in the flare of his nostrils, the way he looked away from her, out the window.

"I blame myself, too," she said. "I know it was stupid, leaving him with Nick."

"Well then?"

"But I wouldn't have done that to you, David. I never would've added my blame on top of your own. I've never done it, and I don't think I ever would."

David looked at her and remembered that night, before Dylan was born, when she'd talked about aborting. He saw the fragility in her face, the slope of her shoulders, and in spite of himself he felt angry at her. "You don't know what you'd do if the situation were reversed," he said.

Annie ran a finger inside the cup of Dylan's hand. His eyes were closing, the lids darkening with sleep, a rim of purple matching the violet strip of sky on the horizon.

"I'm sorry," David said again, but each time it sounded less sincere to Annie. "I'm sorry, maybe I don't sound nice. But, Annie, we still don't know what happened while he was away from us. We still don't know anything about that woman, why she took him, what she did with him, where she was going."

Annie felt the hollow in her stomach fill with pain. She pulled the sketch from her purse and looked at the woman's face in the flashes of light from streetlamps overhead.

"That's who we have to be angry at," David said. "Not at each other. At her. She's the one who did this."

# CHAPTER 25

## Lynelle

THE police lieutenant Herrara who came for me sounded like my granddad. I went with him mostly because I had no choice but also because it was better than staying in that place, anything was better than what that sheriff and his deputies thought I'd done.

I got a shaky sick feeling riding back to Palm Beach, and felt my breath sucking away when they took me to the dark basement under the Palm Beach courthouse.

The man with soft brown eyes was gone, and a police lady watched me change into starched blue pants and shirt. She patted me all over. I didn't look into her face, and I don't think she looked into mine.

"You'll be arraigned before a judge tomorrow," she told me. "Since you can't afford a lawyer, one will be assigned to represent you."

The place smelled of spit and metal, a kin smell to blood, and it had a long dark hallway marked by black doors. There were people behind those doors, I could hear them breathing and moaning and crying. I could smell them sweating. Even before I went into my cell room I could feel it closing around me like a cage, squeezing my broken heart.

\*    \*    \*

The room was small, with a triangle for a toilet, a cot next to it, and a bare bulb with a small cage around it up in the center of the ceiling. There was a camera up in one corner, a small black eye with a red light, watching me as I laid down.

After a while the light overhead turned off on its own, and I lay on the cot for a long time listening to faraway scratches and voices like whispers. When my eyes got used to the dark I ran my hands along the place in the wall where people had scratched their names and little messages.

I read where it said, *Scream, scream, try to cream*, and next to it somebody wrote, *Use your little finger*. I looked at the shadows on the ceiling and the loose weave of my shirt and wondered if I was breathing the dust of murderers, child beaters, shoplifters, and drunk ladies who'd passed that way before.

Mama's and Grace's faces floated in front of me, and Angel's, the way he looked just before he was carried away. My chest filled up rock hard with milk, and all of it was enough to spin my mind into a panic so that I had to force myself to lay still. I slowed my breath to almost nothing, pulling my tongue so far back in my throat that I thought I might swallow it and choke to death. I thought about being dead, about having my arms and legs quiet and still for all eternity, and after a time I fell into a troubled, halfway sleep and dreamed myself a memory.

I dreamed a memory, for I'd walked and traveled so far that my body was stopped flat and my voice swallowed up but my memory was still moving, like something on the dashboard of a car that keeps on flying through the air even when the car slams to a dead stop.

What I dreamed was my mama's face at last, the way her smile sprang up from a curve on her lips and a lift of her eyebrows. She came into my dream slow, through a day that really happened, my last day of second grade and the day she took ill.

It was hot, of course, hot and dry because the last day of school comes in the middle of June, when the sun is strong and there's no rain. I was sitting in my classroom seat, my fingers busy scratching my name into the wooden lip of the chair in front of me. Some of the other girls had straight pins, and a few of the boys had little pocketknives, but I had to make do with a bobby pin so thin that the letters of my name were just about invisible. I could hear the hum of cars outside the open windows, and the boys behind me carving letters, snapping rubber bands, and chewing gum. It was too late in the year to stop anybody, so Mr. Dominick was settled behind his desk with his feet up and his eyes closed, pretending not to see or hear what was happening.

"Just don't break anything," he said, and we knew it was okay to go wild. Somebody started clapping, and some of the girls stood up on their desks and danced, and the next thing I knew the bell was ringing and I was in the middle of a stampede pushing the school doors open into the sunlight.

Mama stood against the chain-link fence at the edge of the schoolyard with the other mothers, a bright blaze of new lipstick on her mouth and a package in her hand. In my dream her face was clear to me at last, a face I'd been waiting years to see again, a face young and fresh and showing no sign of illness. I ran until I was standing right in front of her, and then I reached up to touch her cheek. Mama kissed the palm of my hand the way she always did, saying, "What a life line you got there, girl. Good and long, the best kind there is." In my dream I looked at her hand as it waved away and saw there were no lines there. I tried to tell her what was coming, but Mama just skipped along the road like she did that day for real, chattering on about all the things we were going to do that summer, not even stopping to take a breath.

"We're going to pick as many berries as we can find and bake as many pies as we can stand to eat," Mama said. "Peach pies, like Granny Pynch used to make, and blueberries, too. And we're going to put your hair into a French braid like they do in the magazines, and I might just get myself frosted blond. What do you think of that, Lynnie?"

The sudden frenzy of her energy I saw as a warning in my dream, too, but I was tongue-tied and silent, in awe of the light behind Mama's head and the promise of so many plans she had in mind for us.

Mama held up the bag she was carrying. "In here I got us some colored chalk. We are going to turn the slate in front of our house into a scene right out of the movie *Mary Poppins*, and then we'll skip rope right over it until the dust from your feet whisks the picture away."

Of course we would be doing some of those things with Aunt Fay and Wilma, I knew, and on slow summer days I would watch the Dobbin brothers squashing bumblebees with their bare feet. By August I'd be bored and itchy, standing on a kitchen chair while Mama measured me for new school jumpers, but all of that was a long way off, and didn't dim my happiness one bit as me and Mama walked along Pebble Road singing songs at the tops of our voices until we were silly and giggling.

That very afternoon I went swimming in a pool the Dobbins filled up in their backyard. Mama sat in the shade drinking iced tea with the other mothers. Two or three times that day I ran over to tell her something and she scolded at me for dripping water on her, but I didn't think she meant it, and in my dream it came out like a soft, sad song.

"Please, Lynnie," she said when I shook my wet braids in her face, slapping the ends against her cheeks and accidentally banging my head into hers.

The bumping of our foreheads startled me, it shook us both. I fell down and Mama jumped up.

"Lynelle, you got to be more careful," she said, rubbing the sore bump rising under my hair. I saw spots, purple and red ones spinning around Mama's head, but I laughed and staggered back to the pool.

That night Mama lay down on the couch and covered her face with a cloth while me and Daddy ate supper from a can.

"My head hurts something fierce," she whispered. I asked if she wanted a glass of water, and she shushed me for shouting.

"Help me into bed," Mama said. She leaned on Daddy's shoulder as they disappeared through the doorway.

I went into my own room. It wasn't even dark yet. Down the street I could hear the Dobbin brothers playing with Marianne and Suzie. They were playing freeze tag, calling out the names of TV shows and screeching when they were tagged.

"Shut up, my mama don't feel good," I called once through the screen in my window, but they didn't hear me.

I rubbed the bump on my head. I didn't doubt for a minute that it was me banging into her that caused Mama's head to ache, and as I'd never seen her sick before I thought it was the very least I could do to put myself to bed.

After a while I heard Daddy washing up the dishes. He tried to do it quiet, running the water real low, moving the soup pan around real slow. When he was done he tiptoed down to my room and looked in. I saw the red glow of his cigarette while I pretended to be asleep. Daddy called my name once, then closed my bedroom door, turning the knob to shut it tight.

Outside it was dark, and the sound of kids playing was gone. I could hear a radio, and the lonely wail of motorcycles, but mostly it was quiet, a deathly quiet so that when my mama cried out I almost peed myself. I got out of bed and laid down on the floor with my head pressed against the crack under the door. Mama was moaning and Daddy was murmuring, running water, murmuring, moaning, floating, flying, and crying through my dream, swirling the way water tugs down the drain, the night turning black and blue and my hands and feet dead cold and me praying to Jesus until I felt the bedroom door pushing against my forehead and Aunt Fay calling my name.

I jumped up. It was morning.

"Where's Mama?"

Aunt Fay didn't even have lipstick on. She looked like a person who didn't feel well herself, like a little bit of a ghost.

"Come sit with me," she said. She tried to take my arm and walk me over to the bed, but I started yelling. Aunt Fay had to shake me and shout into my face. "She's in the hospital, the doctors are going to help her, they're going to make her better."

But she was wrong. Mama was dead of meningitis the next night.

"How did it happen?" I asked my daddy. His face was gray, just as flat and gray as a rock.

"Nobody knows. It comes from a germ that lives in the air and the water," he said. But I knew. I knew my mama was dead of a headache brought on by me banging my wet braids into her head. Even after I was grown and knew in my mind that I hadn't caused Mama to die, I was still haunted by that sadness tumbling inside me, and feared my punishment would be to never see her face lifelike and happy again, until I dreamed her that very night, the night of my arrest.

"I have your baby here with me, and she's a fine, sweet girl," Mama said in my dream. Her face was alive.

"Wait, Mama," I cried. I reached out my hand, I tried to touch her.

"Don't you worry, she's fine with me."

"Wait, Mama." I tried to run but Mama floated away, the glow of her growing dimmer and dimmer in the dark until I was all alone in that jail cell with a far-from-home sadness busting my chest in two.

I woke with my mama's face all pieced together, the thing I'd been wanting above all other things possible, and yet still I wasn't home, still I felt lost and my arms felt empty and my chest heaved for my mama and for my baby and for myself. No place was my home except for the last place I'd laid my head. Flaglerton was no more my home than Frostproof, and that was no more my home than the Ozark Mountains or Elizabeth, New Jersey, which was no home at all to me with my girl's empty cradle shoved in a corner and Hogan walking around waiting for me to wake him from the fog of grieving.

It was still dark in my cell, and I heard only a silence. I felt hot and cold and fell into a feverish shivering as if my mama's illness had at last settled into my bones. There was a storm rising inside me, my breath was hot, my chest a pounding ache, my fingers stiff and holding nothing but air.

# CHAPTER 26

## $\mathcal{A}nnie$

AFTER Nan and Joe shed their tears over Dylan's return, after Nick and Sophie wrapped their bodies around their brother, after Christine was alerted on her cell phone and Sophie held the receiver up to Dylan's mouth so his grandparents in Minnesota could hear him breathing real live breaths, Annie slipped into the bedroom with Dylan and did what she'd been wanting to do for hours: she tore off the cheap yellow pajamas and ran her hands along his arms and belly, inside the dimples of his chubby legs.

"You're okay, yes, you're okay," she said as she held each of his fingers between her own, felt the sinew of small muscles inside his forearms. "Look at you, you're a healthy boy and you're safe now, you're safe."

She took off his diaper and held his penis between her fingers, looking carefully at each piece of skin, under the delicate casing of his scrotum, at the tight pink wrinkles between his buttocks.

"I'm sorry, sweetie, I just have to see for myself," she whispered, running her hands along his bottom, measuring the strength in the kick of his legs.

When she was satisfied she'd felt every inch of his flesh

against her palms, Annie dressed Dylan in his own blue velour pajamas. The slip of his arm into a sleeve, the fit of his foot into the bottom of his clothes were simple movements, but each was miraculous to Annie, each an achievement she watched in slow motion and marveled over as she cooed to him.

When he was dressed she lifted the bottom of her shirt and tugged aside her bra.

"Yes, you're a good boy, you're always such a good boy." She watched Dylan's legs move with anticipation, saw his mouth open as she drew him toward her, cradling his weight in the crook of her arm. "The doctor said we can get back to nursing right away, and I'm glad because I missed you, I missed sitting at night, just the two of us together."

It was true, each time she'd nursed him had been a blessing, one she'd overlooked sometimes in the rush of the day, but one she vowed never to take for granted again.

She wet a finger with a drop of breast milk, rubbed it across Dylan's bottom lip.

"Come on, sweetheart," she coaxed him. "Come on, take a drink for Mommy."

Dylan latched onto her breast, and Annie drew in her breath, the gasp of one body connecting with another.

"Go on," she whispered, "it might taste funny from the medicine, but that will go away soon."

Dylan toyed with the top of her nipple. She adjusted herself in his mouth, waiting for him to start drinking.

"Come on," she urged, tugging the flesh of herself between thumb and forefinger, pulling on it like a teat. Dylan's eyes were midnight blue, his breath a warm puff against her bare skin.

He moved Annie's nipple between his lips the way a child might work a watermelon seed back and forth on his tongue. Then he spit it out.

"Please," Annie begged. She squeezed her breast, and a thin trickle of white liquid slid onto Dylan's mouth. He puckered his lips and grimaced.

"Come on, sweetie. For Mommy."

Annie felt the breath rush from her lungs like a blow to the belly. Could David's prediction be true? Did Dylan have invisible scars that couldn't be seen on the surface of his skin?

Annie forced her finger inside Dylan's mouth, felt the firm red ridge of his gums. The boy puckered and drew back, screwed up his face and twisted away from her hand.

"What is it?" Annie cried. She held him at arm's length and looked at his face, searching for her own eyes in the deep sea blue reflection of his, setting her gaze on the slope of his nose, the soft curl of his ears. This face with eyebrows that arched over his lashes in soft brushstrokes, cheeks that puffed out in a soft moon, lips that curled in a smile like Sophie's.

Where was her history in his face? Where were the hours she'd spent rocking him, where was the soft purse of her own mouth as a child, the poke of David's ears sticking out from under a baseball cap? Where were her father's sweet expressions, where was Nick's grin and the almond shape his eyes softened into when he was tired?

"You belong to me," Annie whispered. She said it in a slow, careful voice, watching Dylan's eyes scan her face, focus on her moving lips.

Whose face was imprinted in his mind now? Who did he see when he looked at her? How much of her life, her love, her history, and her family—the sound of her voice and the yearning of her heart, the red-winged lining of her womb, the deep purple of her birth canal—was already part of him? Etched in a curl of his chromosomes and carved into the folds of his brain?

Annie pressed him against her, wanting to press her skin back under his.

"What happened to you?" she whispered fiercely. "What did she do to you?"

# CHAPTER 27

## Lynelle

THE wind was coming up outside. Even locked away and rattling with fever I could feel a storm coming in the air, I could feel the blood running behind my eyes. In the bend of my fingers I could feel rainwater on its way. I heard footsteps and the soft slide of a lock, my name being spoke by a lady who bent over me with blue eyes ringed with eyeliner smeared at the edges.

"Good morning, Lynelle. I'm Melissa Gordon. I'm an attorney and I've been assigned to represent you."

She held out her hand for me to shake, and when she touched my arm I felt the coolness of her skin. She snatched her hand away and turned to the door.

"She's burning up," Melissa Gordon said in a loud voice that rang down the hall. "She needs to see a doctor."

The big details of that day, the way the hours moved and how I went from the cell room to the hospital infirmary are hard to remember, but I know Melissa Gordon smelled like honeysuckle and lemons and that she held my hand while the ladies in green uniforms put me on a rolling bed and moved me down the hallway into an elevator that opened and shut with keys and levers like it was its own little prison house.

Everything I saw was black and silver and new, and didn't clank but closed with a thick dark shut like forever. Only Melissa, in her pink suit with bright gold buttons, pink fingernails, and a diamond wedding band she kept close to my cheek, brought any hint of life beyond the canyon where my heart found itself.

"Lynelle, I'm here to help you," she said. She said my name in that soft southern way, holding on to each letter like it might hold me together. "You don't need to be afraid."

But I was. I was afraid.


The doctor shined a light in my eyes and put a thermometer in my ear. I saw my girl's face and Dylan's, their blue eyes filled with clouds and the color of heaven.

"Mrs. Carter, I'm a doctor," he said through a mouth of big white teeth. "I'm going to be examining you."

I couldn't see his eyes because of the reflection on his eyeglasses, but his fingers felt cold and sure of themselves on my skin.

"Do you know where you are?"

We were in a small room with a milky glass window high up on one wall. Melissa Gordon was sitting across the room in a brown chair. There was a table with sticks and bandages, and a door with a big silver handle. The light over my head was bright. The air in the room was thick with the smell of invisible medicines. There was a sheriff in a brown gray uniform standing next to the door, his eyes staring straight ahead like a wax figure.

"In a jail hospital?"

"Well, not exactly jail," the doctor said. "You're in the prison infirmary room of the Palm Beach County health center."

It felt like jail to me.

"Can you tell me why you're here?"

"I'm sick."

"That's right. You have a fever. But why did the police bring you here in the first place, Mrs. Carter? Do you understand what's happening?"

"Lynelle?" It was my lawyer. "It would help if you just told us what you can recall, what you know."

"The baby," I said. "I took the baby, I lifted him up. I only meant to hold him a minute."

Melissa nodded. The doctor kept his fingers on my arm, taking my pulse and such.

"Angel," I said, but I heard the names of the dead in my voice, I heard the names Grace and Gracelyn, Granny Page, Grandpa Hubert.

The doctor lifted the front of my shirt. "May I have a look under your blouse?"

I squeezed my eyes shut. He touched my breast, and it was like a blade shooting through me. I cried out.

"Does that hurt?"

Tears squeezed out of my eyes. Another stab of pain.

"That's it," the doctor said. He went over to the sink and ran a towel under the water, came back and pressed it against my chest. It was warm, it made me feel like I was on fire. "You have a breast infection. We're going to take care of it."

The doctor rubbed the inside of my elbow with cold cotton and pressed down to push in a needle. I looked at the needle rather than turn my head, but felt nothing except for the pain shooting in my chest, the ache of loss.

"Mrs. Carter, are you nursing a baby?"

Tears squeezed away from me. I nodded, then shook my head. "I was. But no more."

"Go on, Lynelle." The kindness was back in Melissa's face. "Tell us why you're not nursing anymore."

There are times when a simple answer, a simple word or two, feels all the way on the other side of the world. This is something I learned with grieving, that a voice can be swallowed up and the smallest words are the hardest.

"Lynelle? Please tell us, so we can help you."

"Because she's dead," I whispered, and something changed in the room, the rush of air whooshing through us like the wind. "My baby girl died two days after she was born."

Melissa put a hand on my arm. "Thank you, Lynelle," she said. "That's what Hogan told us, too."

"Hogan?" I pushed up against their hands and pulled away from the dizzy fuzz in my head. "Is Hogan here?"

"He's with the detectives. The police are checking into everything at this very moment."

"I can't see him," I said. Not Hogan with his animal skin vest and his fur ball of sorrow. Not Hogan, who would be wounded by what I'd done.

"You can't see Hogan?"

"I can't see him, I can't." I was holding myself in a half sitting position, elbows bent behind me.

"Has he harmed you?"

"I just can't." I fell back onto the cot. "I can't."

"Okay." Melissa put her hand on my arm and made me see that it was shaking. "Can you tell me why not?"

The doctor's face loomed over me, his eyes magnified by his glasses, his lips moving in a funny way. I closed my eyes. My grieving pain, the pain I'd carried in my chest and tried to rub away with the boy named Dylan, was a pain everybody knew now.

"I need to know, so I can help you," she said. "Go on, honey, tell me."

I looked at Melissa, then covered my face with my hands.

"Why did your husband send you to Florida?" she asked.

"He didn't send me here," I told her. "I wanted to come."

"Why? Why did you want to come?"

"I thought the sound of the sea and the sunshine would help me. I felt like I was going crazy from grief."

I knew right then I'd been running from my pain, running on the banks of its river until I slipped on the mud of my fears and slid right down anyway, slid into the river running through me and rode it because I had no choice. For a while I was scared but then the waters felt calming, the waters were soothing, the waters felt like my milk being drunk up by life itself and the baby Dylan was there to tell me this was true.

But the river always spills to the ocean and the ocean was a storm, the ocean rocked me and carried me and by the time it was done with me every ounce of what I once thought or had was changed. I was tossed and cracked and dropped and shattered like a thousand white shells, and how could I say all that? How could I say I was sorry for what I'd done and yet not sorry, because the boy had saved me from drowning?

"It doesn't matter anymore," I said, for I'd been caught doing wrong and was getting my punishment. "It doesn't matter."

"You're tired," I heard Melissa say through the shadow of my eyelashes, the humming of the storm in my ears. "You take a few minutes to rest."

# CHAPTER 28

## $\mathcal{A}nnie$

ANNIE couldn't have known Hogan Carter flew in with the dawn carrying the smell of an unwashed, sleepless night and the fear of a man who may have lost everything. She couldn't have known but still she woke at sunrise with her heart pounding as Hogan's plane was hitting the ground, as Lynelle Carter's fever was pushing hot blood through her veins.

In the gray morning light Annie knelt by the side of Dylan's crib, watching him sleep. "I always wanted you," she whispered. Dylan's mouth was open, his face turned flat on one cheek. She touched the knuckles of his hand. "I always wanted you."

She took her hand out of the crib before he began to stir, pulled the blanket smooth over his curled spine.

She longed for language, for anything that could tell her where Dylan had been, what he'd seen, the things he'd touched and heard, the smells that were now registered in the smallest memory cells of his brain.

"I want to know what happened," she said. "I need to know everything."

When the Palm Beach district attorney's office called later, asking Annie and David to attend a meeting at ten that morning, her first thought was that maybe she'd learn something. Maybe there would be words for the twenty-seven hours her baby had spent away from home. Maybe she would find out where he'd been, what he'd eaten, why he wouldn't nurse from her.

Slowly, as if in a dream, Annie dressed herself and Dylan. She chose the sleeveless blue shift she'd bought only a week ago at Marshall Field's, a dress she'd paid too much for and had meant to wear for a special occasion.

It was an overcast morning, with a falling barometer that put an unusual pounding in Annie's head. "I guess this is a special occasion," she said as she stood before the mirror in the guest bedroom snapping price tags off the dress.

Annie slipped her head through the cool acetate lining of the dress. For a moment the fabric cloaked her in midnight blue and she was aware of nameless, dark things shifting inside her. Sophie's voice whispered from the doorway and Annie's skin tingled; Dylan's legs kicked at the crib blanket and she shivered with a feverish chill.

Among all the shards and shifts and cracked realities that Annie had discovered in the last two days, the most startling was the realization that once the glass between herself and the world was shattered, what was on the other side was not the freedom she'd expected, but simply the unrelenting possibility of pain and loss and danger.

Yet Annie knew she couldn't afford to be weak or afraid. She needed to walk her own way through the world, to hold on to her children, to be their center. She'd been off balance, and look what had happened. Never again could she make the mistake she'd made that morning at the craft fair. Never again could she let down her guard.

"No one can let you down if you're not counting on them to hold you up," she'd heard Liz say once to a group of battered women. Now Annie understood. She understood that she had to hold herself up. She pushed her head through the dress and saw Sophie's reflection in the mirror. The little girl was standing out in the hallway, watching her.

"Come here, Sophie."

Sophie skipped into the room. She was wearing a Tinkerbell nightgown and a strand of white beads from her grandmother's jewelry box. Her cheeks were pink from the sun.

"Hi, Mommy." Sophie hugged her mother's legs, and Annie ran her fingers through the top of Sophie's soft hair. She sprayed on perfume and let the sweet mist sprinkle over Sophie's arms. She traced on deep red lipstick, then bent down and kissed Sophie's mouth so that a circle of color bloomed on her daughter's lips. Sophie clapped her hands and giggled. "Are we going to a party?"

"No. But it is a special day."

"It's a special day because Dylan's home?"

"That's right, honey."

"And it's a special day because our whole family is together?"

"Yes. And everything's going to be fine now," Annie said, but she had to force herself to smile.

David was standing in the kitchen, tapping his foot and chugging down a cup of coffee, when Annie came into the room carrying Dylan on her shoulder. The baby was wearing a white sailor suit with a red bow tie.

David leaned over, took the baby from Annie. "I think he looks sort of silly in this."

Annie felt stung. She'd spent two hours in the store back home with Dylan on her hip, shopping for something special to bring on this trip. "I like it," she snapped.

"Okay." David put up his hand, a gesture of surrender. But it only annoyed Annie.

"Let's go," she said.

"Don't worry about us." Nan ushered them out the door, putting a piece of toast into Annie's hand. "We'll be right here, and I won't let the kids out of my sight."

The Palm Beach courthouse and civic complex on North Dixie Highway was a long block of pink and sand-colored granite buildings, with wide steps rising from the sidewalk up to dark glass doors. The buildings stood a block from the seawall that held the Atlantic Ocean at the edge of Palm Beach city, and the highest windows held an unblemished view of the ocean stretching to the horizon.

Inside, the ceiling vaulted into an atrium, and a waterfall fell thirty feet over a black marble surface. The long hallways were cinnamon-colored, wide and cool, peopled with secretaries, lawyers, and clerks who took no notice of Annie, Dylan, and David as they approached the metal detectors at the entrance.

Annie put her purse on the X-ray conveyor belt and held on to Dylan's carrier seat while two sheriffs reached under the boy's body with large, ruddy hands, searching for bombs or weapons in the folds of his blanket.

"Sorry, ma'am." One sheriff smiled in apology to Annie.

While she waited for David to empty his pockets, Annie stood with her back to the waterfall, looking out across the lobby and remembering the sound she'd heard through her bedroom window three nights ago. It was the cry that came back to her, the sound of children moaning and then singing. Maybe it had been a premonition, Annie thought. Maybe it had been a warning, urging her to be more tuned in to what was beyond the tangible. Like God on high, looking down over the world, seeing the patterns in things.

When they reached the district attorney's office, Annie paused at the doorway. Behind her, everything was busy and bustling. In front of her, she could hear the hush of a well-insulated room.

The assistant district attorney introduced himself with a gleaming smile. "I'm Mike Tucker. I'll be leading the prosecution of your case." He reached for David's hand and shook it, put an arm on Annie's shoulder and drew her into the room.

"Glad to meet you." Tucker flashed flat white teeth and gestured to a semicircle of deep leather chairs. Lieutenant Herrara was already sitting, and Annie saw that his smile was little more than upturned lips.

"Well"—Tucker rubbed his hands together—"this must be Dylan, the boy at the center of all this."

Annie felt herself shrinking away from him. Instead of listening as Tucker and David reviewed the events of the last two days, she looked out the large office window at the cloudy sky and the Atlantic Ocean, roiling under an approaching storm. Dark pelicans with wings like bats coasted in the wind, circling the water in sets of two and three. What palm trees Annie could see were bent away from the land, their leaves lifting, as if struggling for flight.

"She may try to strike a plea bargain," Tucker said, "but it's my intention to prosecute Lynelle Carter to the full extent of the law."

Annie looked at the water. She could feel her milk coming back, leaking into the nursing pads tucked inside her bra. It hurt her greatly that again that morning Dylan had refused to nurse, filling himself instead with two bottles of formula, and soon, Annie expected, he'd been looking for more.

"Annie?" David's voice was sharp on her left side, but for some reason Annie swung her head right, meeting the strong gaze of Lieutenant Herrara.

"Aren't you listening?" David spoke. "Mike asked you a question."

"Sorry." Annie shook her head, furrowed her brows together. She knew she should be concentrating, but something was pulling her attention away. Something was stirring below the surface of what was being said, and Annie strained to find it.

"I felt a chill." She wrapped her hands around her bare arms. "I always forget about central air-conditioning." She shrugged. "You'd think I'd be used to it by now."

It was Herrara who stood, slipping off his jacket and offering it to Annie. She took it gratefully, with a smile.

"Now if you don't mind," David said.

"Oh, but I do mind," she said suddenly, surprising herself. "I mind how rudely you're speaking to me."

This time Annie looked right at David. Even in his blue blazer he appeared rumpled next to Tucker, irritable compared with Herrara. Seeing him glare at her, struggling to remain composed, Annie felt a new kind of power. "I'm not sure what kind of co-operation you need from us." She turned to the attorney, then looked to the lieutenant. "It seems like a pretty straightforward case to me. What do you think, Lieutenant Herrara?"

"Actually"—Herrara cleared his throat, he opened a folder that had been tucked under his seat—"there is something you need to know now, before you hear it at the news conference later."

"News conference?" Annie felt the words lodge in her throat like a piece of dry toast. "Are we taking part in a news conference?"

"You've attracted national attention." Tucker waved a hand through the air. "You and your son. Now we all get to go in front of the TV cameras to show that Dylan is safe and sound in his parents' arms.

"First the arraignment, then the news conference," he added.

The attorney nodded to Herrara. "Courtesy of the Palm Beach Police Department, of course."

Annie took a breath.

"This puts people at ease," Tucker went on. "Shows we're doing our job, lets everybody who's been praying for Dylan's safe return share your joy."

"And that's what you wanted to tell us?" she asked. "That we're expected to go on television and share our private emotions with the world?"

"Not exactly," Herrara spoke up. "What I have to tell you concerns Lynelle Carter herself."

He pulled some papers from the folder. "It seems Lynelle Carter recently had a baby."

It took a minute for Annie to absorb the lieutenant's words.

"And?" David's voice, impatient, interrupted her thoughts.

"And the infant died two days after she was born."

"You mean she had her own baby?" Annie managed to sputter. "When?"

"And she killed it? Jesus Christ."

"No, no." Herrara looked at David. "She didn't kill her child. The baby died of sudden infant death syndrome at two days old."

Herrara held out copies of the birth and death certificates, faxed to him from Newark Hospital that morning. David snatched the papers from the lieutenant's hands.

"She lives in New Jersey. Her husband saw his wife on CNN last night, flew down on the red-eye, and was in my office at eight this morning," Herrara said.

"When did this happen?" Annie repeated her question. "When did her baby die?"

"This month." Herrara's hands were empty now, spread across his lap. "The child was born February seventh, died February ninth."

"Jesus Christ," David said without looking up from the documents. "How do you know she didn't kill the baby? Was she still in the hospital? How do you know?"

"You have a good point." Tucker jumped in. "Sudden infant death syndrome is an unclear phenomenon, one the medical authorities disagree on. I have a pediatrician who tells me the cause of death for a two-day-old child is often unclear and autopsies inconclusive."

Annie pulled the documents from David's hand, looked at them herself.

Mother's name: Lynelle Page Carter
Child's name: Grace Denver Carter
DOB: 2/7/99 DOD: 2/9/99
Weight at birth: 6 pounds, 8 ounces
Weight at death: 6 pounds, 7 ounces

She'd read once that a body weighs one ounce less the moment after death. One ounce difference.

The weight of a soul: was it gas or light? Was it spirit or energy? Was it anything more or less solid than the sigh that crossed Dylan's lips, or the sound of a song that left a mother's heart when she held her child for the first or last time?

"You're going to use this against her?" She looked at the assistant district attorney, at his fine beige suit, the sharp creases in the legs of his pants.

"It's quite possible," said Tucker, leaning forward, "that the scenario you're imagining, the grieving mother scenario, is a far cry from the truth."

Annie looked down at Dylan. Yesterday he weighed twenty pounds, seven ounces, according to the Arcadia Hospital report folded inside a blue manila envelope in her purse. Today, with formula and the trickle of her squeezed breast milk slipped between his lips, he might weigh two ounces more. If he drank in the love that broke out of her and rained over him, he could gain a pound in a day. Sadness alone could drain away or add five pounds to a woman. Loss of love could suck away half a lung, a piece of the heart, all of a person's reason.

"She lost a baby," Annie said, looking at Dylan, but speaking to something inside of herself.

"Didn't you hear what he said?" David's loud voice startled her. "If anything, this makes things look worse for her. And it doesn't change what she did."

"Doesn't it?"

"No. Absolutely not. She took our son without permission. She terrorized our family, and who knows what she did to Dylan."

Tucker rose now, standing in the center of the ring of chairs. "There's precedent here," the attorney said. "In nineteen seventy-six, a woman in Ohio was convicted of kidnapping and endangering the welfare of a child under similar circumstances. A mother in Pennsylvania was sent to jail for six years for taking another woman's infant from the hospital after hers was stillborn."

"And?" It was Annie's turn to ask a question that hung in the air.

"And what?"

"And what about the woman? What about Dylan? What does this mean for us, and for him?"

"I'm not following you," David said.

Annie picked Dylan up, cradled him against her, keenly aware she was the only woman in the room. The only mother.

Weight at death: six pounds, seven ounces. The weight of a soul, come and gone in two days.

"This puts everything in a new light," she said.

"Not for me," David said. "Except it makes it clear to me she took Dylan because she wanted to keep him. Or maybe because she was jealous, because she wanted to see him dead, too. Did you think of that, Annie? Didn't you hear Mike telling me a minute ago the woman tried to jump into the river with Dylan and drown him?"

"Is that true?" Annie looked to Herrara, who nodded and shook his head in one crooked gesture.

"We know she stepped into the river, she was standing at the edge with Dylan when they found her. But the report isn't clear about her intentions."

"What do you think?" Annie looked at Herrara closely. "You were with her afterward, weren't you?"

The lieutenant nodded.

"And do you think she intended to drown him or smother him or harm him in some way?"

"She did say one thing." Herrara leaned toward Annie and

pulled a notepad from his jacket pocket, turned the pages until he found the scrawl of his own writing.

"'I only meant to hold him,'" Herrara read aloud. "That's what she said. She only meant to hold him for a minute."

Dylan began to squirm. Annie shifted him in her arms, then reached into her purse and pulled out the folded sketch of Lynelle Carter. She unfolded it, smoothed out the wrinkles, and held it side by side with the birth and death certificates.

"You think she wanted to kill him?" Annie murmured, looking from the sketch to Dylan, from the woman's dark eyes to Dylan's gray ones, waiting for feelings of rage and terror and revenge to rise up in her. But what she felt was confusion, what she heard were dozens of questions creating a hum and buzz in her head that shut out everything around her.

"I need to know," Annie said. "I need to know why she did it."

"We can show criminal intent." Tucker was still standing, but his hands were stuffed in his trouser pockets, jingling coins. "First of all, Lynelle Carter was found without any identification, which is certainly an element of suspicion. Second"—he looked right at Annie, waiting until she met his gaze to continue.

"Second, she identified the child as her own. And third"—he held three fingers in the air. "Third, and perhaps most important, one of our investigators this very morning located the manager of a gift shop on Singing Island who swears she saw Lynelle Carter write a postcard to her husband the day before she took your son. And what the postcard said was, 'Save the toys. Don't throw anything away.'"

David spoke up. "Annie, she stole our baby. She was taking him from us. I think that's clear."

"It's not so clear to me, not right now."

Annie looked at Dylan, remembering the pains she'd felt when he refused to nurse, the ache of unwanted milk in her breasts.

"Christ, Annie, what are you thinking?"

"I'm thinking this woman was in pain," she said slowly. "I'm thinking about what it means to be a mother and lose a child. I think I understand that feeling quite well right now."

"Exactly." David pointed a finger at her, he slapped a hand against his chino pants. "My God, Annie, you're defying logic."

"Charges can be filed without you," Tucker said.

"Annie?" David reached over now and grabbed at her arm, but she shook him away.

"She spent two days with my son. She fed him, bathed him, changed his diapers. And now this." Annie waved the documents she was holding. "I want to see her for myself, if nothing else I want to find out what she did with him, I want to know where she took him and what she fed him and I want to know . . . if she—" Annie's voice rose, then dropped.

"Do you think she wanted to kill him, David? Do you think that's why she did it? Because if she did, I want to know that, too."

"The why doesn't matter," Tucker said. "Why doesn't matter in the law."

Annie turned to David. "Is that what you think, too, David? The why doesn't matter?"

David looked at her, a hard cool look. He took a long time to answer. "Listen to these men," he said. "They found our son for us, and I'm going to help them do the rest of their job."

"And what is their job?" Annie looked from David to Herrara. "Justice, or punishment?"

# CHAPTER 29

## Lynelle

I WAS still weak when they took me back to the courthouse, weak and dizzy from the medicine and the infection and from the storm rolling in, the storm I could see in the clouds outside the hospital window, the storm I felt in the air pressing down on me as I walked from the transport van into the courthouse. I was tired and shamed, dressed in green prisoner's clothes and soft cardboard shoes they made me wear. They'd taken my shoes, my clothes, and my rings. The only thing I knew was rightly mine to have was the sand between my toes from my mornings on the beach.

At the courthouse my lawyer left me waiting in a room where I had to sit on a bench with my hands cuffed, my eyes down on the ground. The room was small, with a window that surely was a mirror on the other side.

"We're pleading not guilty," Melissa reminded me one last time before she walked away. She told me again not to say anything besides what we'd said was okay. To follow her cues, is what she said. Then she left me waiting in the room with the sheriff standing guard outside the door.

It wasn't long before that policeman came, the kindly one. He opened the door to the room, and a red light flashed on overhead, a buzzer sounded a loud noise.

My heart was thumping. I thought for sure Hogan would be behind him, and my fingers were already aching to feel Hogan's hand around them and afraid of the way he would look at me, with love and pain and whatever else he could wear under the shelf of his eyelashes.

But the lieutenant was alone. He came all the way in, and the red light turned off. There was only a bench in the room, and so he stood in front of me.

"Mrs. Carter?" He spoke formal and polite. I looked at him because I knew it was bad manners not to, but I'd just as soon have hid my face from the world.

"How are you feeling?"

"Okay, thank you, sir." I pushed myself up so I was sitting up straight, and waited a minute for a woozy feeling to pass. "A little better."

"Your husband's very worried about you."

"Yes, sir," I answered, not trusting myself to say more.

"Lynelle"—he took a deep breath—"Lynelle, did you contact your husband in any way?"

"What do you mean?"

"I mean, while you were in Florida did you call him, write to him, was there any communication between the two of you?"

I looked at my hands, wrapped up in metal handcuffs.

"No, sir. Like I told you before, I lifted that baby up on my own, Hogan had nothing to do with it."

He looked at me like he was trying to puzzle something out.

"What about a postcard? Did you maybe send Hogan a postcard?"

I blanched, then flushed like I'd been caught in a lie.

"I forgot about that." The words came out in wood chips, they stubbed across my tongue.

"Now you remember, though?"

"Yes. Yes, sir, I do."

"So you weren't trying to keep it from me?"

"I just forgot, truly I did."

"Now that you remember, can you recall what you wrote on that postcard?"

I remembered then I wasn't supposed to talk to anybody without my lawyer, and I was scared. What had I wrote on the postcard?

"I think I told him I was all right." I saw in my mind the crib and the clothes and all those toys Hogan made for the baby. "I told him not to throw anything away."

"Anything?"

"The toys, I meant don't throw away the baby toys."

"Why? Why would you write that, Lynelle?"

He leaned over a bit, and he seemed so kind I talked to him even though I knew I shouldn't.

"Hogan made some of those toys with his own hands," I said. "I was afraid he'd throw them out and it would be like throwing away hope itself. Like throwing away memory."

He nodded like he wanted me to keep talking.

"It wasn't what you think," I told him.

"What do I think, Lynelle?"

I looked away. My words came out slow. I wanted him to know I was telling the truth, even if I was going to jail and staying there I wanted him to believe me, more than anything because he seemed like my granddad, both kind and strong.

"You think maybe I planned to steal that baby, but it's not true. Hogan will tell you that, didn't Hogan tell you that?"

Right then I wanted to see Hogan more than anything. The stab of wanting someone familiar, someone who loved me and lived and breathed, was more than I could bear.

"What do you think Hogan told me?"

"The truth. I know Hogan, and Hogan would only tell you the truth."

"What's the truth, Lynelle?"

"The truth is I did it without thinking. I didn't mean that baby any harm. He was alone, and I lifted him up, and then—"

What could I say?

"And then what?"

"And then he was mine. Just like that."

I was ashamed. I felt it flushing from the back of my neck, across my shoulders. I couldn't tell what was fever or what was fear.

"Thank you," he said. "I appreciate your honesty."

Soon after he left it was my turn to go in front of the judge. The sheriff took me by the arm and led me through the door with the red light that buzzed, and we went out into the courtroom. I didn't look neither right nor left, except I heard someone say my name, I looked up and there was Hogan. He was standing in the row behind my lawyer, his hair pressed flat like there was still a cap on it, and he held out his hand like he could touch me.

"You're gonna be okay, Lynnie."

Hearing how hoarse his voice was, looking at his back bent like a question mark, brought tears to me. I could feel how it would be to put my head against his chest, to rest there and pretend nothing had ever happened, not Grace or the boy named Dylan or the way they'd taken away my yellow skirt and stuffed my things into a plastic bag. But of course none of it could be taken back, and I could still feel the hole in my belly Grace had filled, I could still feel those babies drinking my milk, I could still see the river and feel the way it wanted to pull me under when the ground slid away from me.

"I'm sorry, Hogan," I said in a very small voice, like I was talking right into his shoulder.

Melissa stepped up to me, she turned me around by the arm so I was looking at the judge's bench. "Don't say anything, Lynelle," she whispered. "Just look up at the judge."

Look at him in the face for a second and then look back down at the ground is what she'd told me to do, a look of what she'd called honest humility. I did it then, my feet in paper shoes, my hands in front of me, my back to Hogan.

"Lynelle Page Carter." The judge said my name like a tired preacher, the sound washing over me from above. "You've been charged with abduction of a minor and endangering the welfare of a minor." It was short and to the point. "How do you plead?"

Melissa answered for me.

"Not guilty," she said, and when the judge peered at me over the edge of his desk, I said, "Not guilty," also.

If bail was set I'd go free as long as somebody posted it, that's what Melissa'd told me, so I was waiting on the judge, wondering if I was really ready to walk out of that place on my own and where I might go once I did. I could feel eyes staring into the back of my neck, Hogan and his bail money is what I thought, Hogan with his hand on his wallet and his feet ready to run to pay the bailsman, no mind where he would get the money from, no mind to the fact we owned just about nothing and would probably need my daddy there to come up with the cash.

"I'm requesting that bail be set at five hundred dollars, Your Honor," Melissa said. I felt the prickling on the back of my neck again, my breasts heavy with what maybe was fever and maybe was the way the air in the room was changing from the storm outside.

I kept my head hung but turned just enough to see if Daddy was there with Hogan, to see if it was his breathing that I felt like a hot wind on the back of my neck.

I turned just a little bit, and that's when I saw her. The lady in the blue dress staring at me. The lady with the baby in a carry seat next to her, her hands wrapped around the handles like iron fists and her eyes sending heat waves scorching into me.

Dylan and his mama, come to hunt me down. I almost fainted.

"Bail is set." Melissa tugged on my arm again, she pulled me around, I wasn't sure where I was to go or what I was to do. Then I saw the policeman, the lieutenant with the kind voice standing next to the baby and his mama, and I felt for sure God was coming to make me pay for my sins right then and there.

# CHAPTER 30

~⁓⁓

## *A̶nnie*

A NNIE handed a note to Herrara, who reached over and gave
it to Melissa Gordon. She watched the attorney unfold the
note and read it slowly as Lynelle Page Carter was led out of the
courtroom by a sheriff, feet shuffling, long brown braid coiling
down her back.

The attorney in the pink suit approached her. Annie held on
to Dylan's carrier seat, and she felt her heart lurch and thump in
her chest.

"What's the purpose of this, John?" the lawyer said to the lieutenant, holding the note out between them.

"Why don't you ask Mrs. Thompson that question?" Herrara
tipped his head in Annie's direction.

Melissa Gordon looked at Annie. "I just think it would be
helpful," Annie said when she found her voice.

"Helpful for whom? My client has just been charged with two
very significant crimes, and your child is the alleged victim. How
would it be helpful for her to talk to you?"

Annie recoiled: she hadn't expected there would be a need to
explain herself.

"I just want to know why she did it," she stammered. "What

she did with him. And also"—she saw the document in her mind's eye. The one ounce, the weight of a soul. "I saw the documents. The birth and death certificates."

Annie saw the woman's face change, a shift in the shade of her skin tone.

"She's pled not guilty," Melissa said. "I'm not sure that it will benefit her to talk to you."

At this the lieutenant gestured to Melissa. "Can we speak privately, Counsel?"

Watching them talking just outside of her earshot, Annie felt ill. In the long walk through salmon-colored corridors she'd begun to perspire despite the air-conditioning, and now she felt sweat running down her spine into the elastic of her panty hose.

She thought of Lynelle Carter, the way she'd shuffled into the courtroom with her head down, murmured, "I'm sorry," to a man standing near her lawyer. She certainly looked more pitiful than brutal, more frightened than frightening. But what if the district attorney was right, and Annie's instincts were wrong?

The lieutenant and the attorney came back to where she was standing.

"Are you sure you want to do this?" Herrara asked.

Annie took a deep breath. She willed the air to cushion her heart, but there was no fooling the pain in her chest, no escaping the thumping against her ribs.

The weight of a soul.

"Yes," she said. She looked at the attorney, who was sizing her up. "I just need to know some things for myself."


Annie followed Herrara and the attorney through the same door she'd seen Lynelle pass through just moments before. She held Dylan's carrier tightly, adjusting the blanket over his feet, checking to be sure he was strapped in.

"Here we are," Herrara said, stopping in front of a small room, where a sheriff stood outside.

"She's in there?" Annie asked. Herrara nodded. Melissa went in first, a red light over the door lit and buzzed.

"You can change your mind at any time," Herrara said. Annie nodded. "I mean, you can go in there and decide you want to come out without even talking to her. You don't have to stay."

"I'll know when it's time to leave," Annie said as she handed Dylan in his carrier to the lieutenant.

As she opened the door, Annie's mind went blank with fear. She focused not on her racing heartbeat but on the long stainless steel doorknob turning in her hand, the heft of the wooden door against her shoulder, the red light that flared as she entered the room. She was keenly aware of her nervous perspiration, the odor of antiseptic clinging to the corners of the linoleum floors, and, under that, the faint smell of sour milk.

Instinctively Annie glanced down at the small mound of her own chest. She squeezed her arms against her breasts to check for dampness, and in the moment of that distraction she completed her entry into the small room.

Looking not at Lynelle's face but at the green-clothed bend of her knees, Annie stood next to the bench. Melissa Gordon sat between them, her pink suit a bright haze filling the room.

"Well," Annie said. Her voice was faraway. She could walk out now, she could hear Lynelle Carter's story in a courtroom with David next to her and her parents on either side of her and Dylan safe in her arms. She could, by virtue of her intact family, sit straight and glare at this woman, using a court of law to demand some explanation. The idea of such righteous silence led Annie to straighten her spine, her heartbeat to slow itself down.

She looked up, and saw Lynelle Carter. She looked right at her and saw, dotted across the bridge of her nose and around her eyes, the dark, masklike pigmentation that sometimes marks a pregnant woman.

Lynelle's hands were cuffed and in her lap, and she wore a shapeless green prisoner's uniform. Her eyes had purple shadows under them, but still Annie saw how young she was.

She didn't meet Annie's gaze but stared down at the back of her hands, at the iron circling her wrists.

"She'll be out on bail in thirty minutes." Herrara spoke to the sheriff from the doorway. "Couldn't we take the cuffs off for a minute?"

The sheriff moved slowly, as if he wasn't sure how he'd make up his mind, and then he took off the cuffs. Everyone watched as Lynelle moved her wrists in a small circle, bent her thin fingers together, pressed her palms against her face.

"Thank you," she said softly.

Looking at the pigment on Lynelle's face, at the purple shadows under her eyes, Annie wished she had taken some time with Lieutenant Herrara to prepare what she would say at this moment, to at least have a list of questions in front of her. There was so much she wanted to know, and as she tried to bring some words into her throat, as she clasped her hands and pressed the palms together, willing herself to speak or else leave, she watched Lynelle Carter's mouth turn into an open crescent, a wailing half-moon.

It was a long, thin cry at first. High-pitched, single-noted. Sharp. Not a scream but an eerie whirl that comes before a whimper and leads into weeping.

A woman's cry. A child's cry.

Annie squeezed her hands against her temples.

"Stop it." The glass in her mind shattered. She bowed her head, shut her eyes. The wail kept coming.

"Stop it."

"I'm sorry about what I did."

Annie's eyes flew open.

"Is that what you think I came to hear? That you're sorry?"

Lynelle kept her eyes on her hands.

"I don't know, I just know I am sorry." The girl struggled to speak. "I only meant to hold him. It just happened, I'm not even sure how. He was all alone and he looked right at me, his eyes locked me in. He smelled like powder, he felt like my own baby would've felt in my arms and—" Lynelle stopped.

Annie stared hard at her, willing her to look up. She felt angry now, and her voice rushed into the room in a whisper that resonated like a shout. "And you thought it was okay just to pick him up and walk away?"

Lynelle shook her head, her hair snaking across her back. "I didn't think, really."

"You just picked him up?"

Melissa Gordon interrupted. Her voice was soft, but hard at the core. "Lynelle, you don't have to answer."

"He's her baby. If I was her I'd want to know, too."

She lifted her gaze, and when their eyes met, Annie felt a jolt of recognition, as if she knew the woman.

"He's a sweet baby," Lynelle said. She lifted her hands and rubbed her face. "I took good care of him." She began weeping, her lips clamped together.

Annie worked hard at ignoring the tears. "He won't nurse from me," she said. "What did you feed him?"

Lynelle turned her face away. Annie was looking at the side of her head.

"They said you fed him." Annie felt both angry and frightened. "Please tell me, what did you feed him?"

The girl's answer was a whisper. "I fed him myself."

"What? I can't hear you."

"I said I fed him myself."

The attorney put out a hand out as if to protect Lynelle.

"Look, I'm here for answers," Annie said. "I'm asking her a simple question. Did she poison my son or something? Why won't she tell me?"

"I nursed him." Lynelle's head snapped up. Her eyes were deep, frightened puddles of sorrow. "I nursed him myself, I gave him the milk from my own body. I fed him right from here"—she touched her breastbone, "right from the heart."

Annie's breath stopped.

"You did that?"

The girl nodded.

"You really did that?"

Annie stood. She had to get out of the room.

"Wait." Lynelle's hand flew out, she pushed herself up off the bench. "I'm sorry, it was just to feed him, it was just because he was hungry."

Annie stared down at the woman's fingers as they brushed her arm. The nails were clean and smooth, nothing like Annie's own chewed up stubs.

Blackness knocked against Annie's eyes. Anger and pain, demanding to be let in. Everything felt so up close, so right up close and terrifying.

"I'm sorry," the girl said again. She drew her hand away and fell back down on the bench. "He was real hungry. He was real hungry, and my chest was full."

Annie looked at Lynelle. She was biting her bottom lip. She was so close, Annie could have slapped her face.

"Is it true you jumped in the river with him when they found you? You were going to drown him?"

"Oh my God, no. I slipped, I slipped. I'd never hurt him, he's the sweetest thing, he's the sweetest thing, and those eyes, those eyes."

Lynelle put her hands together, a prayer. "I swear I wasn't going to harm him, not ever."

"Then what were you doing there?"

Lynelle looked across the room as if she was looking across a great distance.

"I was going home."

"Don't you live in New Jersey?"

"My first home. The home of my mama."

Annie's heart was racing again. "Where does your mother live?"

Tears slipped down Lynelle's cheeks. "She's passed on, ma'am."

The feeling that Dylan had barely escaped something strange and terrible beat through Annie's chest.

"Your mother's dead?"

"Yes." Lynelle's answer was a whisper. For a moment the sound of the women's breathing swelled, filling the room and emptying it again.

"Then where did you think you were going to see her?"

"I don't know. I wanted to see my home. I wanted to see the place where I grew up. I wanted to feel my mama's spirit looking down on me."

Annie covered her mouth with her hand. She felt the hair on the backs of her arms rise up. It was just like the first time she'd counseled a battered woman: she was close to the core of Lynelle, and she knew it. She let herself slip down and sit on the bench. Melissa slid out of the way. Annie and Lynelle were face to face.

"Is that what you did with your daughter?" she asked quietly. "Did you try to take her home to see your mother?"

Lynelle looked at the wooden floor, she shuffled her feet together.

"What do you mean?" she asked at last.

"I think you know what I mean," Annie said.

The lawyer stepped closer.

"This isn't appropriate questioning." She looked at Lieutenant Herrara. "Do you hear me, Lieutenant?"

"What does she mean?" Lynelle's voice was small and frightened, the voice of a seven-year-old girl.

"That's what they're saying," Annie said quietly. She looked at Lynelle's thin arms and wanted to touch one, touch the delicate wristbones that were turning and twisting around each other.

"What are they saying?"

"Enough," Melissa said. "I won't let this go on anymore."

"They're saying maybe you meant to do my son harm." Annie needed to have it said, she needed to hear it in the room, needed to see what it changed in the air between them. "Maybe it would have been like sudden infant death syndrome for him, too."

Lynelle's hands flew to her cheeks.

"Oh no," she cried, the wail again threatening to come up and fill the room. "Oh no, you can't think that, nobody can think that."

She grabbed Annie's arm, and Annie felt the pulse of sorrow passing through her fingers. Lynelle pulled on her hair, it came out of the braid and pieces stuck to her wet cheeks, forming a dark net across her face.

"That's not true," the girl wailed. "That's not true, that's not true."

Annie felt Lynelle's pain swimming with her own, she recognized the face of grief.

"My baby girl was the best thing I ever did," Lynelle cried, covering her face with her hands. "She was my hope, she was what I'd been waiting for all my life without even knowing it."

She grabbed again at Annie's arm. "You have to believe me."

She looked up at Melissa. "Nobody thinks that, do they? Nobody thinks I killed my baby?"

Annie saw fear seeping across the woman's face. She watched Lynelle curl herself into a ball, moaning softly, holding herself together with the lonely embrace of her own arms.

"I believe you," Annie said. She put a hand out and touched the woman's arm. It was a thin wrist, she felt the bone when she touched her. "I believe you."

# CHAPTER 31

## $\mathcal{L}ynelle$

"I'M sorry about your baby," she said to me, and ten thousand sorrowful heartbeats rose in my chest, salt tears of the sea swelled up and stopped just behind my heart.

"It was a waste for my girl to die," I told her, "a waste of a beautiful life. A waste of fine blue eyes that won't ever see the sky. She'll never smell a flower or walk on the grass, never taste a cookie or ride a bike."

I talked and talked, I couldn't stop what was pouring out of me, it was one more thing that seemed right even though it sounds strange now.

My lawyer tried to stop me, but I was opened up, I was a sea without a dam. I couldn't stop, and each question Dylan's mother asked me I answered until there was nothing left to say.

I told her everything: how I carried her baby in a sheet wrapped around me, how he slept in a drawer while I watched to make sure he was breathing. I told her how his eyes changed color, and she nodded right at me like she was glad I knew it, too.

I cried and she cried along with me, both of us crying for ourselves and for our babies, I guess, knowing the same pain split in half, standing as we were on either side of motherhood, each of us looking at the horror of an empty cradle.

When finally there were no more questions she could think of, we held hands and I looked her full in the face.

"I know it was wrong. I know he belongs with you," I said. That was all. That was all of it.


When she left the room I fell back against the bench, bathed in sweat and tears, the ends of my hair full of knots where I'd worked them between my fingers.

Something had happened. Mama in my dream held out a hand, Melissa Gordon gave me help, and then Dylan's mother. She touched my arm like she was giving me something, and after she was gone I knew I didn't want to be alone in the dark hole of my own sorrow anymore. I wanted to start climbing out. If there was any hope for me, I wanted to be with the living.

# CHAPTER 32

## *Annie*

"**Y**OU don't think she killed her baby, do you?" Annie asked Herrara. She was leaning up against the marble wall of the courthouse, outside the elevator bank.

"She's suffered enough," Annie looked at the lieutenant. "She's suffered more than enough. If jail is about suffering for your crimes, I don't think we need to put a lock and key around her."

Herrara's answer was tentative. "You can't be the one to decide something like that," he said. "You're too emotionally involved."

"But it's clear to me she's a grieving mother. I don't think we can punish someone for that. There's a place in the world for compassion, isn't there? There's a time in life to take responsibility for what happens to somebody else."

Annie felt the lump her words made in her own throat. "Why else did you take me there? Why else did you let me see her if you didn't think her story mattered?"

"Her story matters," he said. "I agree with you there."

"If there was no intent, what's the crime?"

Annie stared at Herrara, but she couldn't read his eyes.

The lieutenant looked down at his watch. "It's after noon," he said. "Tucker scheduled the press conference for twelve-thirty."

Annie stood. "I should be there. I have to be there."

Herrara took her elbow. "The quickest way is outside, along Dixie Highway." He turned her in the direction of the nearest doors.

Outside, a wet wind was whipping over the Atlantic Ocean, throwing itself against the granite walls of the courthouse and the federal building.

"Forget it." Herrara pulled Annie back from the open door.

"No." Annie pushed her way out. She felt the fresh air and rain pelt against her. She stretched the blanket so it covered Dylan from head to toe, and bent her head into the storm.

"What's going on?" she had to shout above the wind. "This feels like a hurricane."

"These storms blow out of nowhere." Herrara put his arm around Annie and pulled her closer in toward the shelter of the building as they rounded the corner. "It'll pass."

Up ahead were news trucks lining North Dixie Highway, sheriffs and police officers patrolling the street, and a throng of people standing outside the federal building with their umbrellas open.

Annie and the lieutenant pushed through the commotion to the front steps, turned through a set of revolving doors. Inside the vaulted lobby of the federal building, Mike Tucker stood at a podium on a small stage surrounded by news cameras, reporters, and photographers with their bulbs flashing. David stood between the district attorney and the police commissioner.

Annie strained to hear, but even before she could make out what Tucker was saying, a circle had opened around her and a reporter was standing at her shoulder.

"Aren't you Annie Thompson?"

She nodded. Herrara put an arm out to keep the reporter away, but there was another one on her left, and a camera flashing in front of her. Annie stretched the blanket firmly across Dylan's carrier and held him up, against her chest.

"Why aren't you up there with your husband?"

"What do you make of the woman's story?"

Annie shielded her eyes from the glare of the flash, but soon a circle opened around them, news cameras and lights swung through the room and shone down on them.

"In light of Lynelle Carter's unusual story, what do you think of the charges that will be brought against her?" It was a woman at Annie's shoulder, a reporter whose question pierced through the confusion.

"I just met Lynelle Carter for myself," Annie turned to tell her. She spoke as if she were addressing only one woman.

"I honestly believe Lynelle Carter had no intention of harming Dylan. I don't think she ever meant to keep him."

Annie bit her lip, aware that she'd just spoken words that couldn't be taken back, any more than Lynelle Carter's actions could be undone.

She felt a noise in her head, but around her the whole room was hushed. She sought out the reporter's eyes but could see little beyond the glare of lights on her face. It was the protective glass, solidified in her life. Annie knew how to cut through it: she kept on talking, as if it wasn't there.

"I don't think Lynelle Carter had evil intentions, and I don't feel like we're her victims," Annie said. "I think this has been a terrible ordeal for everyone, and we'd all simply like to put it behind us now."

"Are you suggesting that the charges should be dropped?" A man's voice came through the lights, a microphone was thrust under Annie's chin. She felt heat from the spotlights flush her cheeks and warm her damp clothes.

"Yes, I guess so," Annie said. "I don't think there's anything to be gained by sending this woman to jail."


At the condo, Nick was watching his mother on TV. He saw how small she looked next to the reporters, how she was pressing her lips together the way she did whenever her mind was made up. And he saw something else: pale rainbows over her shoulders, a halo of shimmering vapor and light around her head, as if there was a spirit rising right out of her.

"Look," Nick whispered, afraid he was the only one who saw it. But then his grandmother gasped and reached for Joe's hand. "Will you look at that," Nan whispered, never taking her eyes off the screen.

"I see," Joe said. Of course he knew it was only vapor rising. In his years as a tailor Joe had stood in front of enough steam presses to recognize instantly the bend of light, the quiver of heat and water in the air, so delicate it would have been imperceptible if not for the spotlights.

Joe squeezed his wife's hand, he patted Nick on the shoulder. "Your mom's really something," he said.

While they were watching, the front door opened and Christine strode in, briefcase in hand, blue blazer wrinkled from a long flight, hair wet from the rain. Everyone looked up at once as the warm wet air followed her into the condo.

"Christine, my God, you're soaked," Nan said, rising from her seat to take her daughter's coat and bag.

"Aunt Chris, Mom's on TV." Sophie raced over to her aunt and grabbed her hand. Chris hugged her father and Nick in greeting, but they were mesmerized by the scene unfolding on the television screen. Sinking onto the couch next to her niece, Christine listened to a newscaster's summary of the day's events.

"I'll be damned." She slapped her hand over her mouth, gave a sidelong glance at Sophie. "Oops, don't listen to me, honey."

"What do you think of our Annie?" Joe said.

"I think she's got a lot of guts," Christine said.

"Do you think she's right?" Nan's voice didn't shriek, it simply carried across the room.

Christine looked at the television. She saw the screen flash the sketch of Lynelle Carter, and a close-up shot of the birth and death documents of Grace Carter. She rubbed a hand across the back of Sophie's neck, pulled the little girl close to her.

"Maybe," Chris said. "Maybe she's right."

It was David whom Annie had to contend with after the press conference. David and Tucker.

"How the hell could you do that, Annie?" David's face was bright red. "We're up there announcing that Dylan's safe and the criminal is apprehended, and you're down there saying she should go free?"

Annie clamped her teeth together. "I think you're both wrong," she said, looking from David to Tucker. "I talked to her, and I don't think she meant to harm Dylan, I don't think she hurt her own baby. I'm sure of it."

"What the hell is the matter with you?" David was shouting now, he was exhausted and angry and felt he hardly knew the woman who was sitting in Tucker's office, holding their son in her lap.

Herrara came to the door, then moved to stand at Annie's side. "Your sister's here," he whispered.

Annie jumped out of her seat. Christine swept into the room. She always swept into a room.

"Annie." She pressed her cheek against Annie's, grabbed Dylan and crushed him against her. Then she turned to Tucker.

"Don't do it," Christine said sharply. "If my sister doesn't want to press the charges, I don't think you should press the charges."

"Look, miss—"

"Christine Verducci. Boston attorney."

"Ah." Tucker nodded, but he wasn't impressed.

"I know you can press the charges without her, but what for?"

"Because a crime's been committed."

"I don't think it was a crime," Annie cried. "I think it was an act of grief. A horrible, desperate cry for help."

Christine held a palm out in Annie's direction. "Look." She

spoke to Tucker. "If you think you're going to advance your career by prosecuting a visible case with a mediagenic victim, think again. It won't look very good for you if my sister testifies on behalf of the defendant, will it?"

"So that's what we're looking at?" Tucker smiled, but it was a smirk. "I'll have to give that some careful thought."

It was almost three o'clock by the time they left the courthouse, Annie carrying Dylan in her arms, Christine walking beside her with the empty baby carrier, David up ahead, his back straight, shoulders stiff.

"I'm exhausted," Annie said to her sister. The courthouse was quiet, the waterfall by the front entrance cast a sonorous peace over the lobby.

"Sit here for a minute." Christine gestured to a bench next to the falling water. "I want to see Dylan, anyway."

Annie sank onto the bench, she felt her knees nearly give out under her.

"I'm hungry," she said. "Dylan must be starving." She reached into her diaper bag for a formula bottle, but as she did, the rush of water around her, the way her baby brushed against her breast, let her milk down.

"Maybe," she said quietly. She took the blanket and draped it across her shoulder, unbuttoned the front of her dress. She didn't look right or left, she just looked down at her baby, his lips curling in anticipation.

"Come on, sweetie," she said. Then she closed her eyes, and put Dylan against her. And he drank.

# CHAPTER 33

## $\mathcal{L}ynelle$

I<small>T'S</small> strange, what sticks with you and what gets lost. Whole people leave and take away all memory except the way their eyes look just before they cry or smile. My mama, she just about disappeared until I used all my will to call her back. Others, like the baby Dylan and my girl, they stay whole forever, the talc smell of them, the sway and weight of their bodies.

Annie Thompson, her face is with me. Sometimes it haunts me, but sometimes I see her kind forgiveness.

It was with me the rest of that day when I got my things back, changed into my yellow skirt, and slipped my wedding ring and diamond back onto my hands. It was with me when I was called back into the judge's chambers, which my lawyer said was rushed and due to the unusual nature of things. I thought for sure they were going to say I couldn't go free, like maybe Hogan hadn't paid the bail or his check had bounced already. But it was just to tell me the charges were being dropped. The lawyers had changed their minds.

"Mrs. Carter, your attorney informs me that you admit to taking the child in question, but that you were not fully aware of your actions or the ramification of your actions," the judge said.

"The district attorney has agreed to drop the charges due to un-unusual personal trauma and lack of criminal intent. What do you have to say for yourself?"

The words came, they poured out like the rain mixed with wind that was howling and dying and moaning outside.

"It's clear in my mind that the baby Dylan isn't my child, but on that day when I saw him alone in the stroller, I thought he was left for me. I thought he was a sign, I thought he was sent to help my grief."

"And now?"

I don't recall whether I stood still or rocked back and forth, but I know that I finished by saying I was sorry, that I'd told Annie Thompson I was sorry and that I meant it, that I truly had only intended to press that child against me for a minute.

They brought me back into the courtroom then, and Hogan was there with my daddy and Aunt Fay. Hogan's tongue was working the ends of his teeth like mad. Aunt Fay was wearing a hat, and Daddy had a shirt buttoned all the way to his neck for once. I could feel them all looking at me, I could feel them calling me back to the living. I felt my own soul rising up, get-ting lighter, looking for a place to land, and all of them waiting with their arms open to catch me, to hold me, to soothe and comfort me.

The judge said I was released under the custody of my hus-band, and Hogan had to promise to get some kind of counseling for me. Court-ordered psychological evaluation and support, they called it. He made Hogan stand in front of him, to make sure he understood.

"Yes, sir," Hogan said, running his tongue against his chipped tooth.

"And finally, Lynelle Carter, you're to have no contact, nor make any effort to have contact with, the family of Dylan Thompson, nor with the child himself," the judge said, and so they, too, were gone to me except in memory.

\*     \*     \*

We walked out the front door of the courthouse. Me, Hogan, Daddy, Aunt Fay, and my lawyer Melissa. There were tears in Hogan's eyes and he didn't do anything to hide them, so soon we were all crying and hugging and I was saying I was sorry for causing so much trouble for everybody.

"You're okay now, Lynnie," Hogan kept saying, his arm wrapped around me like he needed to hold me up, which maybe he did.

The sun was out, the storm was gone without me ever seeing it, leaving only puddles on the brown steps. Melissa shook my hand and wished me good luck. Reporters crushed around us, taking my picture and asking how I felt.

"We're tired, and we're ready to go home," Hogan said.

Home. Well, I guess I knew by then that home is where Hogan is, but maybe it's where my daddy is, too, or maybe it's close to where my girl is buried, to where her body lies at rest.

I put my arm around Hogan. I looked at Daddy, who was chewing on his unlit cigar, and at Aunt Fay, who was putting on lipstick and staring out in the direction of the ocean.

"I never made it to Mama's grave," I said in Hogan's ear. "That's where I was going, and I still want to go there."


We all went together in Daddy's car, down the back roads, past low white houses and dogs tied to trees, past shopping malls and gas stations and McDonald's restaurants, until at last the houses thinned and I could smell the Peace River coming through the window, the smell of mud and water.

We circled around the outside of town, up past the New Covenant Baptist Church standing like a painted white ghost on top of the hill. The road was skinny and the pavement broken, our tires bumpity-bumping in a hundred little holes, and the branches of overgrown cypress trees scraping the car roof, dropping their leaves through the open window onto my lap.

Nobody said anything. Even Aunt Fay was quiet. Daddy's

cigar turned round and round in his mouth, and Hogan kept his hand holding mine tight.

It was early evening when we got there. The cemetery was inside a small picket fence. I tried to tell Hogan to wait by the car, but he'd have none of it. "I got a responsibility to stick to you like glue," he said, but at least he let go of my hand and let me walk ahead of him to where I knew the grave was, at the corner of the cemetery.

*Gracelyn Pynch Carter.* Not dusty or old, not overgrown or forgotten. The gravestone looked so new it could have been yesterday.

I knelt down on the grass. All kinds of pictures came up in my head but I pushed them away in favor of the one I wanted, the one of my mama holding a baby in her arms. My baby girl.

In my pocket were the little things I'd found on my walks those first days in Florida, things I'd taken when we went to get the rest of my things from the Hideaway.

I touched the pieces of shell, the yellow baby's barrette, the stones. One by one I lined them up along her gravestone. They spoke to me, and they shared my secret, a secret I didn't tell anyone, a secret more solemn than not recalling my mama's face, more secret than any prayer or Bible page.

My secret is this: I'm sorry, but I don't regret what I did. I needed to do it, and I believe that baby Dylan knew he was the spirit that found me, that I was looking for my mama when under the circumstances and in light of all my losses the best thing I could've hoped for, that baby named Dylan, was already in my arms.

He's the one person I lost and still can think upon without sadness, who I can think about and know he's alive on this earth, laughing and growing. He doesn't have my blood, but he took my milk, it's in his bones, part of me is stuck to him on the inside.

It was grief that put me in touch with the spirit world, a world of wombs and wings and clouds and fog. I know I was crazy with grief, I know what I did was a dumbstruck crazy thing to do.

That's all fine, that's right, to know I crossed over, fell into the river of my sadness, ran from it so hard it knocked me down.

Maybe I went over the edge taking Dylan, but maybe I'd have gone twice as far if I hadn't been able to hold him in my arms.

I don't know. That's why I say it's hard to understand unless there's been a baby in your belly, unless there's been a sorrow in your heart so deep it tears you in two.


I felt around the base of Mama's gravestone and found a pebble, black and smooth. Round. It fit right into my hand, it was cool under my thumb. I slipped it into my pocket. Then I stood to go. I turned, and Hogan was there, his back half-turned away, his head tipped to the sky, looking up.

Thank God he was there. Hogan. Thank God he was there.

"Okay?" He put his arm around me. I slipped my arm around his waist.

"Okay."

Back at the car my daddy was crying. I put my head on his shoulder and told him it was all right.

"You got Tina now," I said. "You have what you need. And I have what I need."


After that there was nothing to do but go home. Daddy took us to the airport, where him and Aunt Fay tried to say the right things, but there was nothing more important than having them there, and we all knew it.

"I love you," everybody said, all of us standing around saying it for the first time together, all of us teary-eyed.


When we left Florida the sky was dark, the world glittering underneath us like a land full of stars.

Hogan had his John Deere cap on his head. It was snowing

like blazes in New Jersey, but all he had was a cap, that's how much of a hurry he'd been in to reach me.

Sometimes I wonder what would have happened if Hogan hadn't come, and when I think of it like that, I think it was Hogan who saved me. Hogan, with his pieces of whittled wood, with his breath sometimes smelling like beer in the morning. Hogan, who knows the names of all the flowers that grow in the valleys and hills of the Smoky Mountains.

"Tell me the names of the flowers," I asked him when the plane was coming in to land. I had the stone from my mama's grave slipped into my pocket. Hogan was holding my hand, our fingers laced one between the other. He held up our hands and started counting off the fingers, one for each flower.

"Sky blossom, black-eyed Susan, jack-in-the-pulpit, hollyhock, opal eyes," he said, and he kept going, but I got stuck on opal eyes. Opal eyes. If I ever have another baby I think I'll name her Opal. I didn't say it to Hogan, though, I just laid my head down on his shoulder and let him keep on talking. I like the sound of his voice. It keeps me on this earth, it keeps me from hearing the howl inside me.

When I was running I thought the center of me was a wail and a howl, I thought the center of me was grief, but it's not. The center of me is life, the center of me is a woman whole and to myself.

I've got life inside me, that's what I found. With the help of the living I pulled myself back to me, pulled up those million shell shards and found myself.

And I am loved. Thank God for that. I was forgiven, and I am loved.

# EPILOGUE

⌇⌇

*F*OUR *years passed before Annie and David brought their family back to Singing Island. They came in early spring, with Nick's voice cracking from hormones, Sophie sporting newly pierced ears, and Dylan just past his fourth birthday, brave enough to chase waves as they slapped and teased on the edge of the shore.*

*Annie was finished with her master's degree and working three full days a week at the women's shelter. She'd seen more broken arms and shattered hearts than she'd ever expected to see in one lifetime. But no life, she always told the women, was ever beyond hope.*

*Their marriage was changed, David would be the first to say that as he watched his wife holding Dylan's hand, running along the beach with her shoulders back and her face lifted toward the sun.*

*There was something new in Annie's eyes, a bold defiance she'd discovered those few days in February four years ago. He admired her grit, but he didn't agree with what she'd done. He'd never agree.*

*They rarely talked about what had happened, not after the first year of counseling and therapy and the long nights each had spent sleeping alone on the couch or sitting in front of a lighted desk, working through insomnia.*

*But the smell of the salt air made it all seem like yesterday, and with* the sound of tides came the familiar ripple of fear. Only Dylan's foot-prints in the sand and his voice, testing out sentences the way a new piano player plucks out a tune, kept them in the present.

"It worked out," Annie said to David at the end of their trip. She meant everything—this visit, her dad's health, their marriage, and Dylan's sure-footed strutting into the tides. But David heard something else in her words.

"We were violated," he said. "I might feel bad for that woman, I might even feel sad for her, but it didn't give her the right to destroy our lives." He was lit from behind, the living room lamp illuminating him in silhouette.

"Are our lives destroyed?"

"No. But they could have been." His voice came to her from a shadow. "They almost were."

"But they weren't," she said.

And her face wasn't pressed up against the glass anymore, either. It was her life, full of pain and noisy fear, thick with disappointment and bold courage, permanently marked by a woman named Lynelle Page Carter, who'd picked up Dylan and carried him to a small cor-ner of the earth and tucked him under her breast and fed him a piece of her own nightmares. A violation, an outrageous violation. But not the end.

"My life isn't destroyed," Annie said. "And Dylan's isn't destroyed, either."

Behind her, in the room where the kids were sleeping, she heard small footsteps. Annie turned to see Dylan in his yellow pajamas, moving toward the open window.

"I hear something," he said. "I hear music outside."

She scooped him off the floor and pressed him to her, listening to the beating of his heart in his chest, to the whirling of blood through his temples.

Annie carried Dylan to the window and lifted the shade high. Dark-ness had descended, the Florida night was still. Breathing in the cool air, Annie heard the sound in the distance, the same sound she'd heard four years before. Only on this night it didn't sound like children cry-ing, it sounded like a song.

"It sounds like a lady singing," Dylan said.

Annie shivered. No one had told him yet what had happened to him in Florida, and Annie had come to believe nothing in that time had caused him permanent harm. She believed it, because she had to.

Dylan took his hands and pressed them against the screen. Annie saw Lynelle Carter's face, and she kept the image there until she could picture the woman surrounded by children, one a toddler, one in the cradle, and another in her belly, turning and turning like the earth itself, tumbling its way toward life.

Somehow, Annie knew that image was true.

"It's just the ocean, sweetie," she said. "It's just the ocean washing across the shells."

She felt the milk of the other woman's body passing through him, she felt the sea inside of him and the dome of the sky, the pulse of things to come, the pulse of a life with her and a life beyond what she would know. A life filled with love and pain, with loss and discovery.

A long life, as big as the ocean, as clear and wide as the open sky.

# ACKNOWLEDGMENTS

THIS work could not have been completed without the love, guidance, and counsel of friends, family, and peers. Thank you to the people in Chicago who were there at the beginning, especially Corinne Peterson, Laurie Martin, writing comrades Jennifer Sheridan and Melinda Rooney Florsheim, and Cindy Zallick, who always believed in me.

Thanks to my father, Larry Lico, who gave us a place to live and space to work; to my cousin Darline Duffy and my sister Donna Lico, for that long, important weekend.

My mother-in-law, Rosemarie Albanese Helm, was my saving grace and a helpful editor as well. Thanks and hugs to my sister Linda Lico for talking to me any time, day or night. Laura Morowitz, a brilliant and loving friend, was vitally important to me during the rewrite period.

Angela Miller, my agent, is clearly a karmic gift in my life. Her partner, Coleen O'Shea, helped me reimagine important parts of the book. Jennifer Moore, my editor, buoyed my confidence with unflagging enthusiasm and extremely thoughtful editing. Thanks also to the New Jersey State Council on the Arts, which supported my efforts.

My Montclair writing group—Nicole Bokat, Alice Elliot Dark, Ed Levy, Deirdre Day McCloud, and Naomi Rand—gave good and thoughtful criticism and encouragement as the work progressed. The attorneys Michael Jay and Jeff Kampf answered legal questions patiently and thoughtfully.

Thanks to Melissa, a splendidly creative young woman, and to John, a little person who is a bright light in my life. And thank you, Frank, for reading everything twice, and listening to everything three times.